THE DOCTORS CAT

By
Richard C. Weisenberg

For Faye

1

Jack Keaton's presentation had been a disaster. It may not have crushed his scientific reputation forever, but it had done nothing to advance it. In a few hours he had gone from the flush of excitement (Complete with fantasies about "little-known scientist revolutionizes research on aging."), to anxiety (Did he miss something?), to despair (At least he could still teach.). He should have expected as much. Scientists, like most people, tend to respond unfavorably when their established beliefs are challenged. To be fair, Jack would probably have reacted the same way to the meager data he had to show. Glazed eyes and wry smiles were to be expected, but it still hurt.

Part of the problem was that he had submitted his application after the official deadline for the annual meeting of the American Society for Cell Biology. As a consequence he was not included in the scheduled session on the biology of aging. Normally, researchers studying the same topic would have their posters together in one section of the cavernous convention hall. This area would become a mini-meeting for researchers of similar interests. Jack was presenting in a session reserved for discoveries that occurred after the deadline, but were supposedly so exiting they deserved their own special showing. Everybody knew, however, that this so-called "hot topics" session consisted mostly of routine results that happened to be submitted late, and the special session was always poorly attended.

So it was no surprise to Jack that only a few people paused in front of his poster. A handful actually looked seriously at the data, and they all had the same question. "How could satellite DNA, which had no known genetic function, control aging?" In response Jack could only sigh, as he had no good answer. The day wore on, and the hall began to empty. With nobody interested in his presentation, Jack took the opportunity to chat with the young postdoc at the adjoining poster. The work was nothing unusual — the discovery of yet another protein that regulated cell growth — but Jack listened politely as the experiments were avidly explained.

Thus engaged, he did not notice the group that had gathered in front of his own poster.

"Unbelievable!" The grunted comment got Jack's attention. He recognized the voice immediately. George Potts was a frequent speaker at meetings such as this. These invited talks identified Potts as one of the "stars" of aging research, although in Jack's opinion he had little scientific talent. Nevertheless, Potts ran a large group at Thomas Jefferson University that published several papers a year. These were mostly pedestrian reports that filled in some minor gap in existing data, but occasionally, among all the dross a significant result came from his lab, adding to his reputation as a leader in the field.

What Jack remembered most vividly about Potts was an incident from a conference a few years ago. Potts had given his typical lecture, characterized by glossy graphics and grandiose claims. At its conclusion, the audience was invited to ask questions. The first to rise was a young man who had not a question, but a comment: "The data in your first slide was incorrectly labeled," he said. "The treatment group was represented by the red line, and the control the blue one." This brought a collective gasp from the audience, as this would change the entire thrust of the experiments. Somebody in the audience shouted out, "How can you be sure?" To this the young man replied: "I'm a postdoc in Dr. Potts' lab. The experiments shown in that slide were done by me." Surprisingly, the incident seemed to have little impact on Potts' career, although the postdoc was never heard from again.

Potts stood in front of Jack's poster, surrounded by a half dozen young men and women. These were no doubt his current crop of students and postdocs. He waved the back of his hand dismissively toward Jack's work. "Any fool who pays his dues can submit a poster for the annual meeting," he informed his entourage. "Even if the results are nonsense, like this." Potts removed a note pad from his pocket and scribbled something on it. "At the Executive Board meeting tomorrow I'm going to recommend we start to apply more quality control to what can be presented by members." Potts left, trailed by his lab group.

"What an idiot." Jack mumbled, referring not to Potts but to himself. His experiments, he realized, were not yet ready for public display, and he had set himself up for the humiliation he now felt. He began to pull out the pins that he had used to impale his figures to the poster board.

"Oh, please. I want to look your data." The young Chinese women who spoke these words wore a name tag that said Meiling Liu, Thomas Jefferson University. She was, he guessed, one of Potts' postdocs. Apparently not all of them had dutifully followed him to their next destination. Foreign scientists like her came to America by the thousands from countries, such as China, with excellent schools, but with poor job prospects. The booming economy of China may have provided plenty of menial jobs for children, but highly trained scientists still flocked to the U.S. for the opportunity to do research. American science would grind to a halt without these poorly paid, hardworking immigrants.

Jack sighed and considered lying that he had a meeting to attend, but she seemed sincerely interested, and it was not in his nature to push inquisitive minds away. He did his best to run through his data as quickly as possible.

"This DNA gel, very interest, you do more?"

"Yes, we've repeated this result several times" She asked several more routine questions, which Jack tried his best to understand and answer.

"Sorry, my English no so good yet."

"It's fine. Much better than my Chinese I'm sure. How long have you been in the U.S.?"

"Three month." She said.

"Who are you working with?" Jack asked, although he already knew the answer.

"George Potts, at Jefferson University, here in Philadelphia. You know?"

"Yes, of course. I work just a few miles away, at Drexel."

"You very kind to answer my questions."

"It's nice to have someone show an interest," he said. Then came the question he had dreaded all day.

"How you think satellite DNA works?"

"I really don't have a clue, but the correlation is very strong."

"Yes, I see. Perhaps we know not enough to understand yet." She pointed to one of his DNA gels. "Very nice result. Someday you find explanation. You think?"

"I hope so. I plan to keep working on it till I do."

"Not be discouraged. In China we use acupuncture many centuries. Westerners laugh. Only soon we know how it works."

"I just hope it doesn't take me many centuries!" She smiled at this and her smile made him feel good for the first time all day. Then she said something that he would always remember.

"You are very brave."

As the Chinese postdoc hurried away to rejoin Potts' group, Jack returned to disassembling his poster. When he was done, he considered what to do next. He had turned down several invitations to dinner, which was probably a mistake. Much of the value of scientific conferences took place outside of the formal program, when investigators with similar interests assembled over drink and food to compare results and gossip about those not at the table. Tonight they would probably be having a good laugh at his expense.

"What the hell happened to Keaton?" someone would ask. "He used to be levelheaded. The next thing you know, he'll be selling redwood DNA as an anti-aging elixir at your local health food store!" This would be followed by much laughter. Jack had a lot to think about, and he decided to return to his office at Drexel and make notes about today's fiasco.

Back at his office he found Snuffles curled up on the desk.

"Shoo, I'm busy," Jack said, and brushed the cat away from the computer. Snuffles took a swipe at the mouse, and stalked away to look for something else of interest. On another day Jack might have taken a break to play with the cat, but he needed to focus on saving what remained of his career. First on the agenda was deciding if he should even continue to work on the possible function of satellite DNA on aging. The correlation he had discovered, that long-lived plants and animals had a unique satellite DNA sequence, was strong, but well outside the mainstream. He needed stronger data, something more than a correlation. What he needed was a direct experimental test of the ability of satellite DNA to control the rate of aging.

His thoughts were interrupted by a noise. On the other side of the desk Snuffles had discovered a ballpoint pen to attack. She batted at it with her paws, cautious and alert, as if the inanimate object might suddenly turn on her.

The cat probably violated one or more government regulations. Jack suspected that a rule, buried in small print in one of his several licenses and permits, must forbid a cat's presence in the laboratory. He believed this even though a search of the relevant documents had uncovered nothing that remotely dealt with a pet animal in a research facility. Once, to satisfy his curiosity, he had phoned the Director of Laboratory Animal Welfare at the National Institutes of Health to get the official view.

"Is the cat being used for experimental purposes?" the Director had asked.

"No, it's just a pet."

The Director had been silent for quite a while and then finally responded. "Our office only deals with research animals. Perhaps you should check with the animal control people of your local municipality."

The Animal Control officer for the City of Philadelphia, not surprisingly, had no interest in an animal that was not running wild on the streets or keeping neighbors up at night. "This sounds like an issue for the University to decide," he said. "I am sure they have rules about pets in dormitories and classrooms. These probably cover labs too." However, neither the Vice President for Student Housing nor the head of the University's Office of Health and Environmental Safety could find anything in their rules that would apply to a laboratory pet.

"Do you have any other animals in your lab?" asked the Assistant Provost for Health and Environmental Safety. Jack admitted that he maintained a colony of research mice. "I think you should check with the committee that regulates the use of laboratory animals." So Jack contacted the head of Drexel University's Research Animal Care and Utilization Committee, who suggested that Jack fill out the stack of forms that are required to experiment on animals. Jack explained that he could not complete a form that asked, among other things, how the animal would be euthanized. This produced in response the suggestion that Jack contact the Director of Laboratory Animal Welfare at the National Institutes of Health. Only the chairman of the Biology Department, undeterred by the vagueness of the legal situation, had taken a position on the issue.

"I think it's a bad idea to keep a pet in your laboratory," he said.

The chairman, like most of the university administrators Jack knew, hated to give a direct order. Whether the chairman's behavior reflected his lack of meaningful power over tenured professors, or that he was by nature weak-willed, Jack never figured out. In any case, Jack ignored the chairman's hint, as he often did, and the cat, legal or not, had stayed.

His laboratory mice, by comparison, were certifiably legal. The mice lived in government-approved cages and ate government-approved chow. A veterinarian, hired by the university, inspected his animals twice a year to certify their well-being. Each week Jack replenished their bedding of wood chips and cleaned and sterilized their cages. Most of a file cabinet, and a large fraction of his computer's hard drive, was filled with the records of each animal – when it was born, its weight for each month, and the results of its periodic health exam.

The cat had no records, and had simply appeared, still a kitten, at the back door of his house one morning. Her plaintive cries had awakened Jack from a sound sleep and he had opened the door with the expectation of chasing the annoying creature away.

He was about to sweep the cat from the porch with a broom when his wife, also awakened by the kitten's cries, had appeared.

"What are you doing?" Mary said, in that all too familiar tone that told him that this was not a question, but an order to cease and desist. At the urging of his wife, Jack agreed to keep the cat until a "proper" home could be found – which turned out, of course, to be theirs. They named the kitten Snuffles because of a wheezing noise that she made with each breath. The noise disappeared with a shot of antibiotics, but the name and the cat stuck.

That was almost fifteen years ago. Jack was really a dog person, and at that time his three-year-old mutt Tippy (whose name reflected its tendency as a puppy to stumble over its own feet) was less than thrilled to discover a cat within his territory. After an initial tense stand-off, Tippy had accepted Snuffles into his domain, eventually allowing the cat to curl up with him as he slept and tolerating the occasional surprise pounce on the tip of his tail. They became, as much as dogs and cats could be, the best of friends.

His dog had died several years ago at the impressive age, for a dog, of fourteen. Jack had watched Tippy get old before his eyes. In just months, it seemed, he went from an energetic dog, full of play and enthusiasm, to a blind creaking invalid. The decision, when it eventually came, to make the final trip to the vet had been difficult, even though it had also been the right one. It had been painful to watch Tippy go so compliantly, but with head down and tail dragging, one last time through the familiar door that led to the veterinarian's examination room.

Snuffles had been distressed by the sudden and mysterious disappearance of her longtime companion. Restless, she paced the house as if searching for the dog's hiding place and had mewed plaintively for hours on end. In the ensuing days the cat's distress had not eased, but changed in its expression to a kind of anger, and she began to take vengeance on the house. After a week of shredded furniture and drenched carpets, Jack had surrendered. One morning he forced an unwilling Snuffles into her crate and carried her the few blocks to the lab. He was uncertain how she would respond, and planned to lock the cat inside his office if necessary. His worries were needless. Snuffles was immediately at home in the new environment, and the trips to the lab soon became routine.

At the lab she would sit for hours on the edge of a bench opposite the animal cages – watching the mice with saucer eyes, tail twitching nervously, alert and patient as only a cat can be. She never tried to get into the clear plastic boxes that held the animals, but seemed to know instinctively that she would never succeed, and that to even try might get her banned permanently from the lab. When she tired of watching the mice she would curl up in a quiet spot and sleep until it was time to go home.

In recent months Snuffles had begun to sleep for ever longer periods, a clear sign of her advanced age. Jack's research specialty was the biology of aging. In his lab he explored the reasons why animals got old and died at predictable rates – why every species had a genetically predetermined life-span. Cats, for example, usually lived longer than dogs. To most people this fact might seem unremarkable, but it violated one of the most revered "principles" of aging – that smaller animals, all other things being equal, had shorter natural life-spans.

His interest in this field had, oddly, been started by one of the worst of his college teachers. Dr. Rinehart would walk into the classroom with his eyes on the floor, as if he had dropped something, and they generally stayed there throughout the fifty minutes of agony that passed for teaching. It was during a particularly boring presentation on biochemistry that Dr. Rinehart had noted that animals with high metabolic rates tended to be short-lived.

"Animals are only able to process a certain amount of energy," he had explained, "and the sooner they use up their allotment of energy, the sooner they get old and die." This immediately struck Jack as a strange statement and he had taken the unusual step of interrupting the drone of the lecture.

"What about parrots?" he had asked. "They have very high metabolic rates, yet they can live for thirty or forty years."

Dr. Rinehart had raised his eyes from his yellowing lecture notes and glared at Jack. "Parrots probably have more efficient DNA repair mechanisms," he said, and returned to the exact spot in his lecture where he had been interrupted.

Jack found the answer unsatisfactory. Was longevity dependent on metabolic rate or DNA repair? He didn't dare interrupt Dr. Rinehart again, but after class he had gone online and looked up articles on aging. Parrots, he discovered, could live well beyond forty years. Indeed, there were well documented cases of birds living into their eighties. The oldest parrot on record was thought to be more than one hundred years old, and had once been owned by Winston Churchill (who had taught it to speak anti-Nazi curses). His readings convinced him that the processes and mechanisms of aging were as great a mystery as any other subject in biology. A few years later, when it became time to choose a research topic for his PhD doctoral thesis, he had selected a project on the mechanisms of aging.

At the start of Jack's career several competing theories of aging were under investigation, and it had seemed then that research would soon sort out which was correct. But decades of work by hundreds of investigators, and his own experiments, had yielded few clues to the process. Researchers argued over whether aging was caused by the accumulation of DNA mutations, or the damage caused by chemical poisons such as free radicals, or the gradual destruction of the fragile ends of chromosomes, or the loss of certain hormones, or possibly by a process not yet discovered. But in the end, when all of the arguments were over, the question that Jack had asked Dr. Rinehart, and which had led Jack into the field many years ago, was still unanswered. Parrots could easily live ten times longer than a rat, an animal of similar metabolic rate and size, and no one had a clue why this was so. At least that was the situation a year ago when he had begun the experiments whose results now suggested the existence of a universal DNA clock that controlled the rate of aging.

The clink of metal against concrete interrupted Jack's thoughts. Snuffles had managed to roll the ballpoint pen off of the desk. Jack retrieved the pen, and then used it to write on a yellow note pad:

NO FURTHER PUBLIC DISCUSSION OF SATELLITE DNA THEORY UNTIL DATA IS FIRM!

This would at least avoid further embarrassment. He attached the note to the wall, next to the door where he couldn't miss it.

2

Meiling Liu returned from the Cell Biology Meeting excited by the new ideas she had been exposed to and by the people that she had met. Dr. Potts had scheduled a seminar the day after the meeting for his graduate students and postdoctoral staff to share what they had learned. Liu arrived early for what would be her first formal meeting with all the members of Dr. Potts' staff, and found the room empty. She hesitated to enter. The room, like much of what she had seen in America, seemed designed to intimidate. A long wooden table with a gleaming polish and an extravagant grain dominated the center. Around the table, plush leather chairs were arranged in precise order. The walls, paneled with darkly varnished wood that matched the table, were hung with paintings of distinguished looking men (there were no women) who Liu guessed were famous professors of the school. Brass light fixtures, as rich and shimmering as gold, hung from the ceiling.

She had no idea where she should sit and decided to wait outside for a while. Dr. Potts staff consisted of a senior research associate (Dr. Zachary Campbell, who had worked for Potts for twelve years), four postdoctoral fellows (including Liu, who was the most recent addition to the staff), two graduate students and three laboratory technicians. They entered the conference room as a group, chatting with each other and largely ignoring Liu. Finally Dr. Potts entered, and took a seat at the head of the table, next to the window. Liu slipped in as unobtrusively as she could and grabbed a chair at the far end of the room.

Liu had read all of Potts' research papers when she was in China, but did not meet him until she arrived in Philadelphia. She had been disturbed from the beginning by his physical appearance, and had never quite gotten used to it. His angular face was divided by deep crevices that ran through his cheeks and under his eyes. As a child he must have had acne or some other disease, because his skin, dark and rough as leather, was sprinkled with pockmarks. Potts' face reminded her, more than anything else, of the desiccated ducks that hung by the thousands in the markets of Beijing. It was his nose, though, that disturbed Liu the most. Narrow, impossibly large and hooked like an eagle's beak, it dominated his face, and whenever she talked to Potts she had to force herself not to stare at his nose.

"Let's get started," Potts said. "We'll go around the room and each of you that attended the meeting should tell us what you found most interesting." The discussion began with Dr. Campbell, who described the work of a University of Wisconsin researcher who was looking at genes in flatworms that, when mutated, caused accelerated aging.

"I thought this was potentially a major breakthrough. They have developed a genetic strain of flatworms that seem to undergo senescence in just a few days. This could make our own work go much quicker."

"Did you talk to him about getting a sample of this strain?" Potts interjected.

"No. I really didn't have a good opportunity to meet with him." Campbell said.

Potts seemed displeased with this answer. "You know, I'm sure, that making personal contact is one of the main reasons I spend the money to send all of you to these meetings. It is much easier to obtain information or materials from people when you deal with them face-to-face." He turned to talk Campbell directly. "You will, I assume, call Wisconsin this afternoon and see what you can do about getting this new strain of worm."

"Yes, of course." Campbell responded. "As soon as the meeting is over." The presentations continued, working down the table toward Liu. The seminar was scheduled to last an hour and Liu glanced regularly at the ornate wall clock that showed the time in X's, V's and I's, hoping faintly that her turn would never come.

"Now we'll have our final presentation, by the newest member of our group, Meiling Liu" Potts said.

The trouble with being last, Liu realized, was that all of the major discoveries that had been announced at the conference had already been discussed. Of the various presentations at the meeting that Liu found significant only the unusual discovery by Jack Keaton had not been mentioned. She knew that Potts thought little of Keaton's work, but she could think of no other report from the meeting that had as much potential significance. As briefly as she could, painfully aware of the inadequacies of her English, she described Keaton's analysis of the satellite DNA of redwood trees, and the correlation he had reported between longevity and satellite DNA structures.

"I think this be important discovery," she concluded. After each of the earlier presentations there had been a period of questions and discussion, but now only a deathly silence filled the room. After what seemed like several minutes to Liu, but was in reality only a few seconds, one of the graduate students broke the silence.

"Did Keaton explain how satellite DNA might alter the process of aging?"

Liu shook her head. "No," she said, "but I thought Dr. Keaton have strong datas."

"Thank you Liu." Potts said. "That was very interesting. In the future, however, you might want to concentrate on presentations from reputable labs. I think you will find that they will give you more than enough data, real data, to satisfy you, and to justify the expense of your trip." Potts adjourned the meeting and everyone but Liu quickly left. She remained in her seat for several more minutes, fighting back her anger and her tears.

3

Potts left the conference room in a foul mood. The meeting with his staff had not gone well. Zachary, who had been around long enough to know better, should have approached the Wisconsin group immediately about obtaining their mutant flatworm. Most of the presentations had been poor and offered little that was truly novel or of practical value. The new Chinese girl, Liu, had ended the discussion on a low note with her discussion of the absurd satellite DNA analysis. She was bright and quite talented in her way, but she needed to learn to keep her eye on the ball (an Americanism that would be lost on her). At every major conference there were always plenty of wild claims and reports of impossible to believe experimental results. One needed to learn to ignore the peripheral side show that took place around the main events. He went back to his office and called his technician, Mindy Tobin, in.

"Did you do the experiment yet?" he asked. She nodded and handed him a folder. The folder contained a set of computer-generated graphs. It took just a second for Potts to see that the results were what he had expected. His lab had been working on a difficult problem for most of a year, but had made very little progress. An enzymatic reaction that was critical to DNA repair (and presumably to aging) would not work as expected. They had tried everything, or so they thought, but without success.

In an effort to gain some new ideas he had sought out William Bellamy at the Cell Biology meeting. Bellamy was a bright young investigator from the University of Chicago who was working on the same problem as Potts. They had met in the hotel bar for drinks after the last session of the evening. Potts had not expected anything of value. After all, Bellamy was a virtual unknown and had little funding. But Bellamy had surprised him. After a couple of drinks, and lots of pointless small talk, Potts had mentioned the difficulty he had experienced in obtaining the needed enzyme activity. Bellamy proudly announced that he just discovered, only days before coming to Philadelphia, that the key to activity for this enzyme was . . . manganese! The result was a surprise to Potts, who was unaware that this minor metallic element might be important in regulating cellular processes.

"That's very interesting" Potts had admitted. "Have you submitted the results for publication yet?"

Bellamy informed him that he expected to finish writing up the data as soon as he returned to Chicago. Potts asked that he be sent a preprint of the paper as soon as it was available, and Bellamy had assured him that he would do so.

Later the evening Potts logged onto the Internet through his laptop computer. A search of the biology and medicine databases revealed that manganese was a known regulator of a number of important enzymes. Potts had not hesitated. He had phoned Mindy at her home, not the least bit concerned that it was the middle of the night, and given her instructions for an experiment that she was to do as soon as possible.

Once one had the idea of testing manganese, the actual experiments were straight forward, and Mindy had completed their analysis that morning. The data, which was in the folder she had just given him, fully confirmed Bellamy's claim. The gaps in their DNA polymerase data had been filled, and Potts was now confident he could get his results published in a major journal.

It was Potts' custom to begin writing research papers even before the final results were in. In the competitive, fast-moving world of biological research it was important not to lose any time getting discoveries into print. Entire careers had been ruined by excessive concern over minor details. Research was not ballet, it was a hundred-yard dash, and crossing the finish line first was all that mattered. Much of a research paper, such as the introduction and the description of the methods, was minimally dependent upon the actual data obtained, and could be written well in advance. His manuscript on DNA repair enzymes was already nearly done, and it took Potts just a couple of hours to enter the newly obtained data on the effects of manganese and to finish writing the other missing parts.

Only one issue gave him some concern: How to introduce the rationale behind the manganese experiment? He knew that he should acknowledge Bellamy for giving him the idea, and in the Acknowledgment section at the end of the manuscript he added the words: "The author thanks William Bellamy for suggesting the manganese experiments." Potts read the sentence a few times and then deleted it.

One problem with the sentence was that it was not strictly true. Bellamy had not suggested the manganese experiments, but had simply informed Potts of the results from his own laboratory. More importantly, it gave too much credit to Bellamy and left the impression that Potts would not have thought of testing manganese on his own. One thing Potts was sure of, eventually he would have uncovered the effects of manganese himself. It may have just taken a little longer without the information from Bellamy.

Potts wrote a new sentence. "The author thanks William Bellamy for allowing access to his manuscript prior to publication." Like the deleted sentence, this statement was also not strictly true. Potts had not seen Bellamy's manuscript, which had not even been completed, but had only been told about data that it would contain. Nevertheless, it was close enough to the truth to meet the loosely defined ethical standards of science. Bellamy might complain about the specifics of the acknowledgment, but the fact was that his assistance would be recognized in Potts' paper. As far as Potts was concerned, there was no ethical requirement to even cite a source of information when it was given freely and without conditions by another researcher. He was doing Bellamy a favor by citing him at all. It was likely, of course, that many people would assume that Potts had come up with the manganese experiments on his own. This was not something that Potts would lose any sleep over.

He called Mindy back into his office and gave her the computer disk with the completed manuscript. "I want you to drop everything else, and to work on getting this article ready for submission right away." Mindy would take care of the routine work of editing the paper to meet the publisher's guidelines, creating all of the figures and printing out the necessary number of copies.

"What journal do you want to send it to?" She asked.

Potts considered this question. A full paper in a prestigious journal like Cell would get the most attention of his colleagues, but these were notoriously slow and it could take months to have his work reviewed and actually in press. Furthermore, Potts was in the process of negotiating a grant from BiTech Pharmaceuticals, and Robert Hopkins, the CEO there, needed evidence of productivity. The sooner the paper was in press the better.

"Send it as a rapid communication to PNAS," He told Mindy. Potts had several friends who were members of the prestigious National Academy of Sciences, and they would ensure that the manuscript would be accepted and published as quickly as possible. With luck, Potts' paper would be out before Ballamy's.

"I'll take care of it right away," Mindy responded. "Is there anything else you need me to do? I have to order supplies soon, so let me know if you want something other than the routine replacements"

"Now that you mention it, there is something I have been thinking about. Check the catalogs of the major molecular biology supply companies and see if any of them stock DNA from trees, particular redwoods."

4

In the weeks following the Cell Biology meeting Jack continued to fixate on the problems raised by his research. The meeting had made Jack sure of only one thing – there was no point in attempting to publish his results yet. "It is only a correlation," his colleagues would argue. "It does not prove cause and effect." Technically they would be right, but deep down Jack knew the correlation was too strong to be a result of pure chance. A direct link of causation must exist between satellite DNA and the rate of aging. Causation could be hard to prove, however. He needed to alter satellite DNA in some way and determine if there was a resulting change in the process of aging. Without such evidence to even attempt to publish his data would probably be futile, and just result in more unanswerable questions and personal ridicule. Not everyone would be as open minded as that Chinese postdoc.

In truth, the original experiments had been done on a whim – with a little help from Snuffles. The cat had settled down on the padded seat of the spare office chair, and appeared to be asleep. As he watched the cat, he remembered the night, just over a year ago, when the idea of looking at redwood DNA occurred to him...

It was the evening after Tippy's death and Snuffles was nervously pacing the house. Jack fully understood the cat's distress at the death of the dog. Barely six months before Tippy's last trip to the vet, Jack had driven Mary on her final ride to the hospital. It was cervical cancer, not old age, that had taken his wife. The cancer had consumed her for over a year, causing her to deteriorate in a way that mirrored the toll of age on Tippy, but greatly accelerated. Near the end, she and the dog seemed to be linked in their illness. If Mary vomited or had diarrhea it seemed that Tippy would soon suffer in the same way, while a restless, painful night for the dog seemed to always promise one for his wife.

"Maybe you should take us both to the vet," she would say, without a hint of humor, when the pain became unbearable.

After the cancer had finally taken Mary from him Jack had, like the cat, wandered the house himself. He always had a reason for his excursions. A missing book. A futile attempt to straighten up the ever growing disorder. In each room she seemed to be lurking, just out of view. Each shadow glimpsed out of the corner of an eye was HER ... but it never was.

The night after Tippy's last trip to the vet, Jack found himself unable to concentrate on the book he had been reading, or to find any relaxation in the mindless programs on television. He went to bed early, but was unable to sleep. Snuffles, finally exhausted from her futile search of the house, briefly settled on his chest as a substitute for the warmth of the dog. She purred mournfully and kneaded his chest with her soft paws for a few minutes before curling up in a tight ball to sleep. Unlike the cat, who was blessed with an ignorance of death, Jack was unable to find any rest. Images of his wife and dog, both gone forever from his life, filled his mind.

Jack tossed restlessly, and his unease eventually awoke Snuffles from her sleep of innocence. The cat stretched and jumped from his chest and onto the bedside table. In the process she brushed against a framed photograph that Jack had recently placed there. The photograph toppled over onto its face. Snuffles, like most cats, was usually very careful in her movements, and her apparent clumsiness, Jack assumed, reflected the short time that the picture had been on the table. Jack picked up the photograph.

It was a picture of Mary, taken just months before her death. She was standing alongside a redwood tree, supporting herself against the withered bark with an extended hand. The trip to Yosemite occurred shortly after the doctors had given them the unbearable news. Mary had wanted to see the redwoods for years, but they had never been able to fit it into their tight schedules. Facing death, they had easily found the time.

He returned the photograph to the table, and a thought burst into his head as if from nowhere.

That redwood tree was thousands of years old. Each season, new leaves formed from ancestral cells that were present before the birth of Christ. As far as anyone knew, within the living tissue of the tree were cells that had been alive, and functioning, for thousands of years. The same cosmic rays, the main cause of genetic mutations, blasted through the redwood tree as they did through every other living organism. Within the nucleus of each cell were DNA molecules that controlled all of the functions essential to life, and the DNA of a redwood tree differed from that of humans only in its details. Like all DNA molecules it was composed of the same four building blocks, the As, Ts, Gs and Cs taught in every elementary biology course. The precise arrangement of these building blocks differed from species to species, and even from person to person, but DNA was the same chemical everywhere, from the lowest bacterium to man.

As Jack thought about the issues that night, it occurred to him that aging must be like everything else in life – there were only two possibilities: Things either happened <u>because</u> of what you did. Or things happened <u>in spite</u> of what you did. Most researchers in aging subscribed to the theory that getting old was something that happened to you, not something you did to yourself. Old age was viewed as a natural process that organisms, with different degrees of success, could delay but not avoid.

The alternative view was that aging was an active process that organisms did to themselves. If they did nothing, they would never get old. In a flash of insight it occurred to Jack that this explanation was the only one that could explain the near immortality of a simple tree.

That night, he had sat on the bed for hours, staring at the photograph of Mary and her redwood. Where would one logically look for evidence of the mechanisms of aging? Why not in the oldest living thing? Unless fire or disease attacked it, a redwood could probably live forever. These living cells of these trees lacked either a factor that would cause them to age, or they produced a powerful inhibitor of aging. Either way it was there, in the forest, that he should look.

Viewed this way, the idea of studying redwood trees struck Jack as obvious. On the other hand he knew the idea was so far out of the mainstream of research that it would be considered bizarre by his colleagues. Nobody, as far as Jack was aware, studied the aging process in plants. They all used animals for their experiments, particularly those, such as flatworms and fruit flies, that had very short life spans. A scientist investigating the processes of aging would have to be crazy, or at least unconcerned about research grants and tenure, to work with an organism that lived for hundreds of years. He tried to put the redwood idea aside, and for several days it floated in his mind, vaguely present, but rarely in his conscious thoughts.

In truth he thought of little but his own misery.

About two weeks later he had gone out to lunch with his friend Tom Winston. Jack first met Winston when they were both newly hired professors at the University of Pennsylvania (where Jack had worked before his wife's illness resulted indirectly in his move to nearby Drexel University). Unlike Jack, who was struggling to establish a research career and obtain tenure, Winston seemed to have more interest in non-academic pursuits. Playing the violin, painting portraits, firing ceramic pots, performing magic tricks, almost any activity that did not involve academics, or excessive physical exertion, was fair game. Then one day while in the middle of a lecture in an introductory Psychology class he realized, as he later explained, that he was actually just pretending to teach to students who were pretending to learn -- so why bother. He had walked out of that class and had never returned. Fortunately Winston was a computer wiz, and he now made a good income working out of his home.

In appearance Winston could easily have been mistaken for one of the homeless men that hung around Penn's campus, begging for quarters from its upper-crust, Ivy League students. Today, as an accommodation to Jack's more conservative style, he had tied his long, unruly hair into a ponytail and put on relatively clean jeans.

His gray beard, which was often decorated with crumbs from the Oreo cookies that sustained him during long stretches at the computer, was freshly shampooed, causing each kinky hair to jut out as if repelled by the presence of its neighbors.

Winston's idea of a good restaurant was one that put more sausage than cheese on its pizza. Wine was not even an issue, but a restaurant better have four or five quality beers on tap to be even considered as worthy of a quick lunch. Jack ordered a Caesar salad and a bottle of water while Winston went for a sausage pizza (with extra sausage) and a mug of beer.

"You're going to kill yourself eating like that" Jack said as their meals were placed on the table.

"Maybe, but I will die happy," Winston responded, taking a cautious bite from the hot pizza. "In any case I am counting on you and your ilk to figure out how to keep people like me alive forever."

"That's not our goal. We just want to understand how organisms age."

Winston made a disparaging grunt. "Then I am wasting my tax dollars. I thought the whole point of spending all that money on medical research was so people would never need to die."

"Not exactly," Jack said. He picked at the soggy lettuce in his salad. "The goal of medical research is to cure specific illnesses, like cancer and heart disease."

Winston pointed a finger at Jack, and then swept his hand up in a large arc toward the ceiling. "Extrapolate Jack. Extrapolate. Picture a child born today, then jump ahead, say seventy or eighty years, close to what today is a typical life span. What do you think medical science is going to look like seventy-five years from now?"

"I have no idea."

"Well I do," Winston said. "At the rate research going, we will have probably discovered cures for cancer." Winston took a large bite from his pizza, unaware or unconcerned about the tomato sauce that dribbled down his beard. "I take back what I just said. It's not probable we will have cured cancer in seventy-five years, it is as certain as death and taxes . . . as least as certain as taxes."

"What? You don't think death is certain?"

Winston shrugged. "Nothing is for sure any more. Didn't the Red Sox win the World Series? In a few decades I am sure that scientists will have perfected artificial hearts and other organs to replace the ones that go bad. I even read somewhere that scientists think that they will soon be able to grow human organs in animals."

"That's true," Jack said. "In theory, all we need to do is replace a few of the animal's genes, the ones that control the structure of a cell's exterior, with human genes. Your immune system would treat such cells as if they were of human origin, even if their insides contain nothing but goat proteins. We know, in principle, how to do that today."

Winston scratched his beard and contemplated this information. "Interesting," he said. "I can picture the day when the hardest decision parents will have to make is whether to grow their child's future organ transplants inside a cow or a pig. That ought to give the religious fanatics something to cogitate." Winston finished his beer and gave a satisfied burp. "So just what do you think the child born today will die of when the time comes?"

"Old age," Jack responded. Jack finished his salad. He was still hungry, and found himself hoping that Winston would not eat his last slice of his pizza. "People will still get old and die, like they always have."

Winston stared at Jack as if he was seeing him for the first time. "You're telling me that you are planning to fail. That despite years of experimentation by brilliant researchers like yourself, and millions of dollars of tax money from hard-working shmucks like me, we will not eventually understand, and be able to control, the process of aging. Hell, a lousy Galapagos turtle can live more than two hundred years, and a redwood tree for thousands of years, why not humans?" Winston picked up his last slice of pizza.

Jack laughed. "It's amazing how an idea can come out of nowhere, and once it shows up, keeps reappearing like a bad zit." Jack told Winston how the idea of studying redwood trees had come to him recently. "I know it's a nutty idea," Jack said, "but I can't get it out of my head."

"I'm no biologist," Winston said, "but it sounds like a logical argument to me. So are you going to pursue it?" Winston put down the last slice of pizza without taking a bite. "I'm full, would you like to finish this? Keep in mind that it might take seconds off of your life."

"I'll take the risk." Jack ate the slice of pizza while he pondered Winston's question. "It's unlikely I will actually do the redwood experiments. Dozens of others must have considered the same facts, and come up with the same idea."

Winston sipped quietly on his beer for a while. "Let me ask you something," he said when the glass was empty. "Where do squirrels shit?"

"What?"

"You heard me. Where do squirrels shit? I know you have lunch outside on nice days, and I have seen you feeding the squirrels. Have you ever seen one defecate? For that matter, have you ever seen squirrel droppings anywhere?"

Jack admitted that he had never seen either the act or the consequences of squirrel defecation. "I confess I can't answer your question, but I don't quite see the relationship between where a squirrel does its business and the scientific study of aging."

"My point is that the world is full of mysteries, but most people don't even know something is a mystery because they never ask the right questions. Until you ask, you can't get an answer. I suspect most of your brilliant colleagues have never even wondered why redwood trees live so long."

"You must be wrong. It's an obvious question."

Winston laughed. "Excuse me Dr. Einstein, but how many years have you been doing research in aging? I have known you for over six years, so it has taken you at least that long to come up with something you think should be obvious."

"OK, I admit I am slow. I never wondered where squirrels defecate, or until recently why redwood trees can live for thousands of years. Still, others quicker than me must have considered this issue."

"Maybe they did, and maybe they didn't, but if they did they probably stopped there, and wound up doing the same thing you are doing, which is nothing." Winston waved to the waiter for another beer.

"I've thought a lot about it, but to drop what I am doing and chase a fantasy seems unwise."

"I thought you had a license to steal."

"What?"

"Tenure. Didn't we recently have a party celebrating your elevation to tenured professor at Drexel?" Jack admitted this was so. "Do you want to piss away the rest of your life filling journals with articles that hardly anybody will read, and that will have little impact on those who do?"

"That's a bit harsh," Jack said. "I try to be the best scientist I can. But I can't do everything."

"You didn't ask, but I am going to give you my philosophy about decision making." The waitress came with his fresh beer and Winston paused until she was gone. Jack sighed and sat back. Winston was known for his philosophical musings. They were always profound, and usually impractical.

"As a scientist, would you say you can predict the future of your life? Can you tell me, with any certainty where you will be ten years from now, what you will be doing and even if you will be alive?"

"Of course not, not with any certainty, but I can make reasonable guesses."

"Fine, but the bottom line is that you cannot predict the future with any certainty. Nor do you know if the redwood theory is right or wrong." Jack admitted that this was true. "Do you know what fuzzy logic is?"

"It was what my high school gym teacher used. He apparently thought that I could become an athlete. All he had to do was embarrass me often enough."

Winston ignored Jack's joke. "Fuzzy logic is actually a computer program that makes decisions based upon incomplete information. In this sense, it attempts to emulate the way people actually think. People don't normally make decisions by running a series of numbers through their heads. So many points for costs, so many for benefits. People tend to act intuitively."

"People act intuitively because they do not know how to think logically," Jack countered.

Winston shook his head. "I thought you were a biologist. Survival of the fittest is the foundation of biology. People make decisions intuitively because that was what worked in the days when our dim-witted ancestors first began to think. Imagine a caveman with a computer made of stone chips and bits of bone. It would have been of little use in deciding if that strange movement in the grass was a saber tooth tiger or a puff of wind. Intuition is simply the neurological program that integrates a lifetime of experience. Your brain has done what evolution designed it to do, which is to make the best decision possible based upon the limited facts on hand."

"So what you are saying is that the redwood theory is my brain making a guess, and a guess is better than a logical analysis?"

"My point, for what it's worth, is that intuition is often better than logic. The real world is not a multiple choice exam. Sometimes more than one answer is right and sometimes all of the choices are wrong, but you have to act nonetheless."

"So it doesn't matter what I do, as long as I do something?"

"You are not listening!" Winston said with irritation. "Your idea, any idea, is the brain attempting to make sense of incomplete and inaccurate information. A computer faced with the same lousy database would simply crash. Your brain does not. I can't tell you if your redwood idea is nutty or brilliant, but it is what your intuition has come up with. I would say trust your instincts."

Jack paid the bill, and thanked Winston for his help. "By the way," he asked as they walked to the parking lot, "Where do squirrels shit?"

"I have no idea," Winston said. "You're the biologist, you figure it out," he added as he got into his car and closed the door behind him.

Winston's encouragement had been enough, and Jack decided to pursue the redwood tree project. The first task was to obtain the necessary funding, which meant writing a grant proposal. All of Jack's colleagues despised writing proposals. At conferences, during chance meetings in hotel lobbies or around a pitcher of beer at a local pub, the common theme was the hated chore of preparing grant proposals.

Jack, however, loved writing grants. He never admitted this to any of his colleagues, as he knew it would make him even more of an outsider than he already was. Grants were the nearest thing in his profession to creative writing, and it was the creative aspect of science that had attracted Jack to the field in the first place. Sometimes he wondered if he shouldn't have been a novelist instead.

The weeks that followed could be described with little exaggeration as manic-depressive. During the manic phases, his fingers flew over the keyboard, barely keeping up with the ideas that cluttered his mind. Inevitably, this was followed by the realization that the previous splurge of creativity was banal and incoherent. The resulting depression led to creative paralysis, during which he would do little but play computer solitaire. Then, while doing something as mundane as placing a black queen on a red king, a spark of an idea would ignite a new manic phase.

Several weeks later the grant was nearly ready, which was followed by the hard part. This was followed by several more days of meetings with university budget officials, and the filling in of assorted forms (He was studying trees, but the Research Subject Protection Declaration was still required). It was with relief that he clicked the "Submit" button that sent the proposal from his computer to the one at the National Science Foundation. Several weeks later the reviews came back:

> Dr. Keaton's proposal is excessively speculative
> and completely lacking in preliminary data. Aging, as
> is well known, is confined to animals. Furthermore,
> he has not said which genes he plans to study. In
> essence, Dr. Keaton proposes a fishing expedition,

with no bait, in a pond with no fish! While this proposal is well written, and Dr. Keaton seems to have the necessary training and experience, the prospects for success are not good and we cannot recommend funding.

Jack was not surprised that his grant had been rejected, which after all was the fate of ninety percent of the proposals sent to the major government funding agencies, but it hurt nonetheless. The reviewers had not even shown the decency of letting him down gently. He showed the rejection letter to Winston. "I knew I shouldn't have listened to you. You talk about trusting your instincts, and lord knows that's what you do, but look where that got you."

Winston ignored Jack's insult. "You expected a Nobel prize and a kiss on the butt, just for coming up with an idea?"

"No, but I didn't expect, or enjoy, being treated like I was an idiot."

"If you want to be a scientist, Jack, I suggest that you check your ego at the laboratory door."

Winston was right, of course, and Jack swallowed his pride and resubmitted the proposal to the Institute of Aging at NIH -- with similar results, although with a different metaphor:

"This proposal reminds me of the joke about the drunk searching under the street lamp for his lost keys on the wrong side of the street, because the light is better there. The missing key (to aging in this case) is certainly not hidden in the DNA of a tree, no matter how long it might live."

Attempts to obtain funds from private sources produced similar results, although the rejections were more polite. They took the form of "This is an exciting and innovative proposal, unfortunately it does not meet our current program goals ..." Months passed, and Jack's interest in the redwood tree project waned, but never disappeared. He was like a pre-med student with straight B's, fully aware that success was unlikely, but keeping hope, even if it was enveloped with an aura of fantasy. Perhaps his critics were right, he told himself, and his proposal was simply a bad idea. Perhaps the classroom was his proper place.

Then chance led him to Mrs. Stromberg. Eva Stromberg was a recent widow when he was introduced to her at a reception for the new classroom building at Drexel. Her late husband had established the KopyKat chain of copy centers, and she had inherited a great deal of money, a large chunk of which would go to the school he had attended in his youth. It was apparent that Eva had done what she could to could to ward off the ravages of age, at least as it altered the face. Modern technology had provided her with wrinkle-free cheeks, but could do little about the bone-thin hands and their mottled, papery skin. He guessed she was in her mid-eighties.

Jack had perhaps downed a few too many glasses of cheap wine and found himself telling this nice elderly woman all of his troubles. She had been quite tolerant of his drunken blathering and had even asked some cogent questions. By the next morning he would have been hard pressed to remember having ever met her. Thus it was a considerable shock when the call came from the director of the University fund-raising office.

"Dr. Keaton, I understand you do research on aging." Jack admitted this was true. "Do you know a Mrs. Eva Stromberg?"

"The name sounds familiar, but I couldn't tell you why."

"She passed away recently, and in her will has had donated 4 million dollars to the University. Half to go into the general fund, and a quarter toward a scholarship fund. The remaining million is designated exclusively to support research on aging by a university professor. You seem to be the only one on staff doing that kind of work."

The University officials were not happy with this arrangement, but there was little reason to challenge the will, and they wanted the money. Jack was in science heaven. Spread out over a few years he had enough money to pursue his ideas, and no need to write grant proposals or even annual reports. As a tenured professor he would even have the luxury of waiting until he had definitive results before publishing his work. Except for six hours a week of teaching and occasional committee work Jack could devote himself to his new research program.

5

Jack's experiments began with a trip to Yosemite National Park and to Mary's tree. He could probably have purchased redwood DNA from one of the many genome "libraries" that serviced the molecular biology industry, which would have been much cheaper than the business class air fare for a brief trip to California. For Jack it was not even a hard decision – the redwood DNA had to be from Mary's tree. Jack knew that he was acting irrationally, but like the primitive hunter who honors his prey by decorating his body with their fur and bones, Jack had to honor the spirit of Mary.

Jack flew into Sacramento. After an overnight stay he rented a car and drove to the park. Mary's tree was less than half a mile from the Visitor's Center, but Jack chose to take a five-mile hike along a trail that would loop around and bring him to the tree at the end of the day. Walking through a redwood forest has often been compared to being in a cathedral. Jack understood the comparison – the sense of space and light was similar – but he found it inappropriate. A church is designed to inspire awe and fear among the faithful. He had been to some of the great cathedrals of Europe and what had struck him were the sounds, the hollow echoes that seemed to repeat forever. One could almost hear in the reverberations the accusing voice of God, damning you to eternal hell for your sins. It was no accident that movie makers often placed dramatic scenes in a church, or in an acoustically similar factory or parking garage. The reverberating echoes of these spaces provided a naturally scary sound track.

The redwood forest produced the opposite effect. Among the towering trees, sounds disappeared without a trace, absorbed by the endless expanse of leaves and by the soft shaggy bark – the perfect acoustical tile. Even footsteps were made inaudible by the centuries-old carpet of discarded needles. As Jack glided through the redwood forest, it was not awe or fear of eternal damnation that he felt, but a sense of belonging, of being in the right place, as if he had returned to his ancestral home.

Jack stood for long time in front of Mary's tree. Before her death the cancer had spread to her bones and she had been in nearly constant agony. Yet she had refused to take morphine, relying on less potent medications, which took the edge off of the pain but did not eliminate it. Jack had begged her to accept the morphine. When he asked her why she refused she had, at first, just shaken her head and said "I don't know." Later she tried to explain, struggling to make sense of what she herself admitted seemed inexplicable.

"Think about the people who climb mountains," she said. "They don't take pills to make the trip pain-free. The struggle itself, to go on in spite of the pain, is one reason they are there. Perhaps dying is my mountain."

Only near the end she had finally relented and taken the morphine, although Jack had always felt she had done so mostly to relieve the pain of those who loved her and who could not bear to watch her dying in agony. In his misery he had become upset with her. "Do you realize how hard it is for me, and all of your friends, to watch you suffer needlessly? For God's sake, take the morphine, if not for you then for us."

Mary had actually smiled at his outburst. "Someday it is possible you may be thankful for how I have chosen to die," she had said.

This inexplicable statement had astounded Jack – how could he ever be thankful that she had to die in pain. It was not until the funeral that it came to him what she meant. After the eulogies and the ancient evocations of her religion, came the lowering of the casket into the ground. The harsh mechanics of the process had grated on Jack. The rusty steel winch used to lower the casket creaked in its own agony as it was operated by the grave diggers, who were clad in blue uniforms more appropriate for valet parking lot attendants. Jack had been angry at the harsh disruption of the muted voices and colors that characterized the ceremony itself. It was good, he thought, that Mary could not see how crudely her body was being treated. She had suffered enough …

That, of course, was her point. When the end finally came she had welcomed it and, in his own way, so had Jack. His sorrow at losing Mary had been tempered by his relief that the misery was finally over for both of them. If she had died pain-free he might have forever wondered if he should have fought to keep her alive longer. But more radiation and ever more toxic doses of chemotherapy could have extended her life, such as it was, for at most a few weeks or months. Weeks or months of additional misery that would have led to the same inevitable end.

Jack stood in front of Mary's tree until the forest, shadow-grey even on the brightest of days, began to darken with the approaching night. A ranger appeared to inform the handful of lingerers that the park was closing. Jack wiped the wetness from his cheeks and then took from his pocket the sharpened tube he had brought with him. It was normally used in the laboratory for cutting holes in corks, but it would do for his purposes. While the ranger was distracted by some unruly children, Jack pushed the tube as deep as he could into the soft bark. Satisfied that he had gone far enough to reach the live tissue underneath, he pocketed his sample. Minutes later it was in a cooler packed with dry ice.

Back in the lab he began the process of extracting the DNA from the redwood tree and the analysis of its genes. While technically sophisticated, the actual work was tedious, and mostly involved transferring solutions from one container to another. The first job was to increase the amount of DNA he had to work with. The small quantity of DNA in the sample of tissue could be copied to make as much as needed by use of the Polymerase Chain Reaction. This involved raising the temperature high enough to blast apart the two strands of the double helix. Each of the separated strands could then be copied, using the enzyme DNA polymerase, to make a new matching strand. In this way one DNA molecule became two, and then two became four, and four became eight, and so on. Jack began the experiments by placing the DNA in a thermal-cycler, which would raise and lower the temperature as needed to produce the required amount redwood DNA.

While Jack was waiting for the PCR reaction to produce enough DNA the door swung open and Winston barged into the lab. "Up for a beer?" he said. "I just finished a job for the Provost, and need to wash my mouth out."

"I don't see the connection."

"He wanted me to construct a data base for evaluating professor productivity. Number of students taught, papers published, citations, that sort of crap. I asked him if he wanted to factor in creativity, and he looked at me like I had used a four letter word." Winston peered at the small plastic tubes waiting their turn in the thermal-cycler. He bent over to read the microscopic labels. "RW? Does that stand for what I think it does?"

"Yes, I'm analyzing redwood DNA."

Winston picked a tube out of an ice bucket. "TAQ?"

Jack smiled and shook his head. "Who would have ever thought . . ." he muttered.

"What's so funny?"

"Not funny, just odd. The enzymes that I use to copy DNA from the Yosemite redwood tree, they originated in Yellowstone National Park." Jack explained that the enzymes came from bacteria whose normal habitat was the volcanic hot springs of Yellowstone. These bacteria had adapted to the near boiling temperatures of the springs and their enzymes, including those essential for the reproduction of DNA, were the most stable known to science. This stability had made them key components in the field of genetic engineering, and no molecular biology lab or police forensics facility could function without these Yellowstone enzymes.

"So no beer tonight."

"No, I have to babysit my experiment."

Winston took a moment to pet Snuffles, who was rubbing her head against his leg. "Let me know if anything interesting comes from your national park expedition."

"Will do."

In just a few days he had made enough redwood DNA, but the truth was Jack had no idea what he should look for. He had an assortment of DNA for purposes of comparison, but the redwood had thousands of genes, not to mention thousands of regulatory sequences and control elements. If you were going to look for a needle in a haystack, you should have some idea which stack the needle might be in. Jack assumed that if there was a common aging system it should reside in genes that would be found in the DNA of all organisms that underwent senescence. This restriction still eliminated a surprisingly small number of genes. A mouse and a redwood tree differed in thousands of genes, but they also shared thousands of genes, including those responsible for cellular reproduction, for protein synthesis, for basic metabolic processes and for the construction of common subcellular structures.

Keaton started by making a list of known genes that would be most likely to control the processes of aging. The accumulation of genetic errors was widely viewed by most researchers to be a primary cause of aging. So Jack's first entries on his list were the names of the various genes that help prevent or repair damage to DNA and thus reduce the rate of mutation.

Many believed that aging was accelerated by the action of damaging chemical toxins such as free radicals. These were mostly formed as a natural result of metabolic processes, but a diet rich in antioxidants could reduce their level (which was one reason that different cultures often had different life expectancies). Jack added to his list the names of genes that were known to help remove or neutralize free radicals and other chemical poisons.

Other researchers were pushing the idea that aging is caused, in part at least, by the gradual loss of DNA from the fragile ends of chromosomes. With each round of cell division a bit of each chromosome tip, called a telomere, was lost, and when enough of this DNA was gone the cell died. A special enzyme, telomerase, could repair the lost DNA and allow cells to divide indefinitely. An increase in telomerase activity was one of the hallmarks of cancer cells. Jack added the telomerase gene to his list.

Another hot area of research was the phenomenon of programed cell death, also known by the term "apoptosis." Programed cell death helped shape the growing embryo (the death of cells between the bones of the fingers turns the fin of a fetus into a hand), but many researchers believed that apoptosis was also important in aging. Apoptosis was a complex phenomenon, forcing Jack to add several more genes to his list.

Pared down to a minimum, and including only known genes, Jack's list contained the names of hundreds of genes that he might need to study. This was still too many. He needed help. Briefly he considered calling some of his research colleagues for suggestions, but Jack knew that the redwood project could lead nowhere, and the last thing he wanted was the "I told you so" scorn of his colleagues.

Tom Winston had encouraged him to do this project and although he was no biologist he had an uncanny ability to perceive the essential elements of a problem. Winston agreed to meet him for dinner.

At Jack's insistence, Winston met him at an expensive seafood restaurant in center-city. The restaurant was in a building that had once been a bank, with marble walls and pillars that shouted wealth and security. Unfortunately they also created echoes that made conversation in the crowded restaurant a challenge.

"Do they serve pizza here?" Winston asked.

"No, but if you ask nicely they might put cheese and tomato sauce on a flounder fillet for you." Winston passed on the suggestion and they both ordered grilled sea bass, the specialty of the restaurant. Winston listened silently as Jack described his dilemma.

"I hate to tell you this," Winston said when Jack had finished his explanation, "but I didn't understand a word you just said. Can you give me a summary in English?"

Jack sighed. He needed to be more aware that words like apoptosis and telomere were not in everyone's vocabulary. "The basic problem is one of too many choices, and no obvious reason to pick one or the other."

Their dinners came. Winston said little as he slowly and methodically picked the flesh from the bones of his sea bass. Jack, who had accepted the waiter's offer to debone his fish, finished his dinner quickly, and sat quietly while Winston completed his dissection.

"Well," Jack said after a while. "What do you think?"

"Not bad, but it would be improved with a bit of melted mozzarella and some tomato sauce."

"I was referring to my dilemma."

Winston put down his fork. "I have a proposition for you," he said. "There is an empty building across the street. Why don't you and I pool our resources and open a nice restaurant?"

"And why would we want to do that?"

"I really love good fish. We could open a quality seafood restaurant."

"But we are eating in a good seafood restaurant now. Why would we want to open another one across the street?"

"Because seafood restaurants are so popular."

It finally occurred to Jack that Winston was not talking about the restaurant business. "I think I get your drift. Repair enzymes, free radicals, programmed cell death and the like have already had their share of attention."

"From all you have said, it looks that way to me. If you are going to do this weird redwood project you might as well go all the way. Use an organism no one else has studied, and focus on a gene that other researchers have ignored."

"And what might that be?"

Winston shrugged his shoulders. "How the hell would I know?"

In the following days, Jack considered his options. Winston had made a good point, but Jack still had to pick which genes to focus his research on. The selected genes should be common to all higher organisms and have a central role to play in the functioning of cells -- and no one else considered them likely to control aging. This still left a very large list. There had to be some way to cut the possibilities down to manageable size.

The solution came to him, as new ideas often did, when he was not consciously thinking about the problem. Jack normally watched very little television. Sitcoms, with their insulting canned laughter, he found repellent more often than entertaining. Nature shows were sometimes interesting, but even the cute lion cub at play became boring after you had seen it for the tenth time. More than anything else Jack watched the do-it-yourself shows to be found on PBS and on various cable channels devoted to such programing. Programs such as "This Old House" and "Furniture on the Mend" were the staples of his television watching.

Mary used to make fun of him. "What is the point of watching Norm Abrams make a colonial style chair from scratch using a hundred-thousand dollars' worth of power tools? You don't even own a saw." But he enjoyed watching skilled people do those things they were good at. The only do-it-yourself programs that he actually made use of were the cooking shows. He was particularly fond of Good Eats with Alton Brown, which combined cooking and science in ways that were often amusing.

It was during a commercial that the insight came to him. Although the TV Food Network was a cable channel devoted, in its programing, to the joys of eating, much of its advertising came from companies that made "lite" foods. A particularly skinny model was pushing a low calorie cheese. "She will probably live to a ripe old age" he thought.

The idea made him sit up. Scientists had found exactly one thing that could reliably extend the life span of an animal – an extremely low calorie diet. Mice that were fed just enough to keep them from starving to death could live a third longer than mice fed a normal diet. Not only did they live longer, they looked and acted as if they were much younger than they actually were.

There was an ongoing debate as to how a low calorie diet increased longevity, with most researchers leaning toward an explanation based upon a reduction in free radical concentration. Jack didn't care who was right, what struck him about the low calorie data was that it was so rare. Why should it be so difficult to increase life span? Researchers in aging had found many mutations that could speed up the onset of senescence, but where were the mutations that resulted in animals living longer lives?

New mutations that shortened life span were constantly being found, usually accompanied by a press release which claimed that the discovery would provide important clues to the secrets of aging. The believers in the accumulated-error theory of senescence had found a host of mutations that screwed up the functioning of DNA repair enzymes, and which led to a premature death. The believers in the free-radical theory had a similar collection of mutations. It sometimes appeared as if there was a contest to see who could make a mouse or fruit-fly drop dead first.

Equivalent mutations that increased life span were, by comparison, extremely rare. It was true that a mutant gene had been found in fruit-flies which extended their lives by almost thirty percent, but the excitement that this discovery had generated was what Jack now found interesting. Just about the only "evidence" that Jack could think of for a mutation that increased life span in humans was the biblical story of Methuselah. It was just a little late for a genetic study of him! By comparison a mutation that caused premature aging in humans was so common it had a name -- "Werner's syndrome." But if the rate of aging depended upon the activity of a single gene, or even several genes, mutations that increased longevity ought to be more common.

A model formed in Jack's mind. A living organism could be viewed as a kind of machine, like a car. How far a car could travel under ideal conditions was limited by the amount of gas in the tank, but hundreds of things could go wrong, from a flat tire to a blown gasket, that could bring a car to a premature stop. Tuning up the carburetor or adjusting a spark plug added, at best, just a few miles to the distance you could go on a gallon of gas. It occurred to Jack at that moment that there was no point in looking at specific genes to determine how long an organism could live. That would be like checking the antifreeze level to see how far a car could travel before it was consigned to a junk yard. Rather than focusing on individual genes, he needed to look at the overall structure of the DNA to find the key to aging.

The fact was that in higher organisms, including humans, only a small fraction of DNA was genetically functional. Over ninety percent of DNA, according to current knowledge, appeared to be useless. When discovered, these nonfunctional sequences were at first referred to as "junk DNA." Clearer heads pointed out that these stretches of apparently unused DNA may have an as yet undiscovered biological purpose, and "junk DNA" was not a wise term (and could well wind up on some congressman's hit list of worthless research grants).

Several types of DNA with no apparent function had eventually been identified, but the most common type was called "satellite" DNA (the term was based upon an experimental anomaly and had no functional significance). There were different types of satellites, but they all shared a common feature – they contained multiple copies of a repeating base sequence. A satellite DNA could be constructed from a string of a few bases, such as AGGTC , or of much longer stretches in a large satellite. Whatever the sequence of bases, it would be repeated hundreds of times in tandem, like beads on a string, to form the complete satellite.

Perhaps he, and every other researcher, had been fishing in the wrong place, and it was time to cast some bait into a different pond. The analysis of satellite DNA was relatively simple and while it seemed to Jack extraordinarily unlikely that anything of value would be found, it was at least a place to start looking.

The name came from the fact that satellite DNA formed distinct bands surrounding the main DNA band after separation in a high speed centrifuge. This was a classic technique, often taught in undergraduate laboratory classes. The procedure, involving the fractionation of the redwood DNA and its analysis by electrophoresis, took most of a week. For comparison he used DNA taken from humans and a variety of laboratory animals. The end product was a photograph that displayed sequences of satellite DNA sorted by size. At first glance no obvious difference stood out, but as Jack glanced back and forth, between the redwood sample and the various controls he noticed a pattern. One band was particularly dark in the fruit fly DNA, was less prominent in the mouse sample, even less so in the human DNA. The differences were subtle, and he would have missed it if not for one striking fact. That particular bit of DNA was absent altogether in the redwood sample.

Jack could not take his eyes off of the photograph. The rows of dark bands seemed to shimmer. Again and again he compared the redwood sample with the controls, half expecting the difference to disappear. It did not.

Over the next few months he worked late into the night, and through the weekends, gathering and analyzing DNA from various organisms. Animals, such as parrots and turtles, that had long life spans also had less of the DNA satellite. The differences between various animals were not as dramatic as the mouse-redwood comparison, but then most animals had very similar, and very short, life spans when compared to the nearly immortal redwood tree. Anybody could have seen this correlation years ago, if they had a reason to look. But they hadn't, and now one of the biggest discoveries in decades appeared to be in Jack's hands.

At night Jack couldn't sleep. Every time he closed his eyes he would see the dark bands of the DNA, lined up like the rungs of a surrealistic ladder. He thought about the responses of his peers. They would be skeptical. His was a small lab, in a universe run by large and powerful groups. Some would not take kindly to losing out on this discovery, one that they could have easily made themselves. Jack knew that he would need to firm up the observations and do some more controls before he submitted the results for publication. However, the data were already sufficient for presentation at a meeting. Professional meetings were the place where preliminary results would often get presented for the first time, and the comments and reactions of his peers could prove useful.

Early the next morning Jack logged onto the American society for Cell Biology web site. The deadline for regular submissions for the annual meeting had passed, but they would still accept late submissions of exciting new results. His discovery would certainly qualify. He wrote up a short paragraph describing his results and sent it off as an e-mail attachment.

The next order of business was unrelated to the scientific issues. He had enough grant money to hire a part time research assistant, and had posted an ad on the department bulletin board. A couple of students had applied and been interviewed, but neither struck Jack as likely candidates. The third applicant appeared at his door without notice or an appointment.

First impressions were less than favorable. He was thin and lanky, like a sprouting adolescent, and wore torn jeans and a T-shirt decorated with an airbrushed painting of what appeared to be a rock musician in the midst of an orgasm with his guitar. The casual dress had not bothered Jack (it was typical student garb), but he did not care for the three silver rings that hung from his right earlobe. Jack could not understand why anyone, particularly a male, would undergo personal injury for the sake of fashion. The last thing he needed in the lab was a street punk.

"Hi," he said casually. "My name is Peter Cooke, I'm here about the research position," he said, waving the notice which Jack had posted and which would now have to be replaced.

"I'm kind of busy right now," Jack replied. "Leave your name and I will get back to you."

"Sure, doc. I understand." Peter paused, but gave no sign that he was about to leave. "Could I ask you a question?"

"Sure."

"I tried to read one of your papers, the one about aging in cancer cells. You say cancer cells are immortal, and don't always die when the person dies. How can that be?"

Jack was surprised that Peter had taken the time to read his article. "Normally that's true, but scientists can sometimes remove cells from the tumor and grow them as long as they want in the lab. This was first accomplished using tumor cells from a woman called Henrietta Lacks. These HeLa cells, as they are called, have been used in labs around the world ever since."

"So she's dead, but her cells still live."

"Yes."

"Awesome! How old was she when she died?"

Jack had to admit that he did not have this particular detail in his memory, but a few minutes on the Internet provided the answer. "She died at thirty-one."

"So she would only be over a hundred today. That's old, but not unheard of. Why do scientists' think that her cells are immortal?"

Jack paused to think about Peter's question. It was a matter of faith among biologists that given a constant supply of nutrients and essential growth factors transformed cells, such as those from the tumor of Henrieta Lacks, could live and grow forever. "They seem to be immortal, compared to noncancerous cells, but I guess we will know for sure in a few more years."

"What kind of cancer did she have?"

"Cervical."

"Are you ok, Dr. Keaton?"

Jack was not ok, but he forced himself to respond. "I'm fine," he said, pushing back the memories that had flashed into his mind. "So you think you might like to work in my lab?" After a few more minutes of conversation Jack realized that considerable intelligence and curiosity hid behind the orgasmic T-shirt and dangling earing, and he hired Peter as his research assistant.

6

Jack was in lab, discussing his plans with Peter. "The best way to prove causation would be to alter the satellite DNA, and see if aging is affected. But that seems impossible with current technology."

"I thought that it was possible to change an organism's DNA," Peter said. "Isn't that the whole basis for genetic engineering?"

"Yes," Jack admitted. "We can introduce foreign DNA into cells, and get them to produce proteins they ordinarily would not make. A cow, for example, can be genetically engineered to produce human insulin in its milk."

"How do they get the human DNA into the cells of the cow?"

"There are different approaches, each with benefits and drawbacks. You can actually buy a kind of gun that shoots microscopic pellets of DNA into cells. Or you can use a virus to introduce foreign genes into a cell. Many viruses cause an infection by inserting its DNA into the DNA of a host organism. If you add the desired gene to the virus DNA, it gets inserted into the host along with the virus genes."

Peter seemed puzzled. "Wouldn't that make the host animal sick?"

"Not necessarily. A virus can sit inside a cell for years, totally harmless, until some signal causes the DNA to start reproducing. Many people carry dormant viruses. Cold sores, which are caused by a benign herpes virus, are not new infections, they are sleeping viruses awakened. The most popular virus for genetic manipulation is a modified cold virus called AAV, for adeno-associated virus. It has a high rate of infection and has almost no effect on the health of the infected cells."

"So why don't we make use of this AAV virus?"

Jack shook his head and explained the situation to Peter. "Our problem is that we are not attempting to add a new gene to replace a dysfunctional one. The satellite DNA is functioning just as it's supposed to, and we would need to remove it from the DNA to prove its role in aging. Biologists can add DNA to cells, but we don't have any way to reliably get rid of parts of a DNA molecule."

Peter had a suggestion. "What if we try to alter the functionality of the satellite DNA sequence, instead of getting rid of it?"

Jack shook his head "Satellite DNA, as far as we know, does not have a function. It doesn't code for proteins. It is not a regulatory element. It does nothing."

"Except control aging."

"Apparently. But how it does so is a complete mystery."

"It has to be in the sequence," Peter said. "DNA can only function through its sequence of bases."

Jack had to admit that Peter was correct. In fact one of the first things he had done was to look for some pattern in the base sequence of the satellite DNA. For weeks he and Peter pondered the problem. They printed out hundreds of satellite DNA sequences and burned their eyes looking for patterns. Each night strings of As, Ts, Gs, and Cs floated in his mind before he fell into a restless sleep, but no pattern, not even in his dreams, could be found.

"Perhaps there is no pattern," Jack said to Peter. "The gene jockeys might just be right. Satellite DNA consists of random, meaningless sequences."

"Doc, didn't you tell me time and again not to trust the experts. You have always argued that wrong results are worse than no results at all."

"True Peter, but every now and then even the experts are right."

Peter thought about this for a while. "I'm just an undergrad Doc, and I don't know much, but the correlation we found between satellite DNA and aging looks real to me."

"Your point is ..."

"The satellite DNA has to work somehow. There must be a mechanism that links the satellite DNA sequences to aging. This implies a common feature in their structure. We already know that satellite DNA doesn't code for proteins, so looking at the sequence traditionally isn't going to work."

"You may be right, but our computer programs should pick up a pattern if it is there."

"The software was written by biologists," Peter said. "Maybe we need a fresh approach."

Jack called Tom Winston and described the experiment that Peter had done, and their failed attempt to find any pattern in the satellite DNA sequence. "It may sound crazy, but I want someone who has no knowledge of molecular biology to look at the data."

Winston laughed. "So my ignorance of science has finally found a use," he said. "Anyway, your request doesn't seem crazy at all. It sounds like a problem that might interest me. I happen to be unemployed at the moment, and I will be glad to give it a stab. Come on over."

Winston lived in a converted barn on Willow Lane, a narrow private road that bordered the forested Wissahickon Valley section of Fairmount Park. Jack drove carefully since the road was regularly bisected by speed bumps that were almost indistinguishable from the asphalt. As far as Jack knew this was the only residential street anywhere in the city with speed bumps. At night the unlit road was pitch black and it was all too easy to pop off a hubcap or bust an axle. He could easily imagine the surprise of first-time visitors, their attention focused on finding a house number, when they flew off of the first bump. The speed bumps were indicative of the "leave-me-alone" attitude of many of the road's residents, including Tom Winston.

Winston's home office was in a back room, lined with glass on the side that looked out over the woods. The sun was just setting behind the trees, casting flickering shadows across the floor. Jack handed Winston a CD. "Here are the nucleotide sequences of what is called satellite DNA. They are from a variety of animals, and plants, with different life spans."

"Including redwood trees?"

"Good question. It seems that the redwood has a unique satellite DNA. That leads me to think that satellite DNA is somehow related to the process of aging, but it is a mystery how it might work. Satellite DNA has no known function."

Winston placed the disk in a computer and called up one of the files. A bewildering string of A's, T's, G's and C's filled the screen. He shook his head. "Good grief Jack, what am I supposed to do with this! It's nothing but gibberish."

"Actually it's not quite gibberish. The letters represent the molecular building blocks of DNA. An oddity of satellite DNA is that it consists of repetitive sequences. What is on your screen is a sequence that is repeated hundreds of times throughout the cell's DNA. The sequence is highly conserved, which means it is the same, for example, in all humans. The total number of repeats in any satellite can vary, but the repeat sequence itself is fixed."

"And somehow these letters are supposed to tell us how long an organism can live."

"That's what the correlation suggests, but I don't have a clue how it happens. That is not important to your job, however. I just want to know if there is any pattern to these sequences."

Winston stared at the incomprehensible string of letters. "I think I am getting a headache already, but I'll see what I can come up with."

The call from Winston came a week later. "This was a tough nut to crack, but I think I found something. Come on over." Jack was at Winston's house within fifteen minutes.

"So what did you find?"

"A very interesting pattern," Winston said with a self-satisfied grin.

"But we looked for a pattern in the repeating sequences. Our computer analysis found nothing."

"I am not surprised. Most computer programs would identify Beethoven's 'dum-de-da-dum' as just noise. Computers are lousy at picking out long-range order, a skill that the human brain excels at. Let me show you what I found." Jack was surprised when Winston led him to a stereo system instead of a computer. "I put this on tape so you can have a copy. Play it at night, it might help you sleep." He inserted the tape and hit play. A strange but yet appealing warbling sound emerged. There was a pause, followed by another "tune" that was similar, but different in a subtle way from the first. This was followed by several other sounds of similar musical quality.

"Very nice, I didn't know you were a composer along with all of your other talents."

"The composition was written by nature, not by me. I was surfing the Internet looking for ideas when I came upon a discussion of "Genetic Music" and how scientists had used the sequence of bases in DNA to compose a kind of music. They assign a note to each base in the DNA to turn genes into musical compositions."

Jack interrupted. "Every molecular biologist has heard these tunes. Before sophisticated computer programs they were one way of identifying repeating patterns in a gene. But the music you just played doesn't sound anything like the DNA tunes I have ever heard." The genetic music that Jack was familiar with was very simple, consisting of just four notes representing the four bases in DNA. Winston's tunes were much more complex than that. "Your tunes sound almost like jazz."

"Very perceptive of you," Winston said. "When I tried the standard rules for genetic music to the satellite sequences, all I got was an awful noise. So I started playing around. I did not like being limited to just four notes, so I assigned a different note to each pair of bases. This gave me eight possible notes, but the music was still unbearable noise. Then I did some more research and learned that the four bases consist of just two kinds."

"The pyrimidines and purines."

"That is what you call them, but I refer to them as the big one and the little one. What struck me was a simple diagram that I found on a Web page for introductory biology." Winston went to his computer and made a few mouse clicks. A familiar diagram, similar to one found in dozens of biology textbooks, appeared on the screen. The two purines, A and G, were illustrated by large red and orange bars, while the pyrimidines, T and C, were illustrated by smaller blue and green bars. Jack could see how the bars, arranged in a line to represent a strand of DNA, could remind one of a musical score.

"I started by assigning one note to the big bases and a different note to the small ones. This only gave me two notes and some very ugly noises. The same thing happened when I tried using two, three and four bases per note. The miracle occurred when I used five bases, which gave me some very interesting music. The reason it sounds like jazz to you is that jazz uses a pentatonic scale. I have no idea why five should be the magic number."

Jack thought about this. Three bases at a time were used to encode amino acids according to the rules of the genetic code, but there was nothing related to the number five that he could remember. He looked at the diagram again. It showed a simplified "ladder" model of DNA structure, not the more realistic and complicated double helix structure …

"Of, course!" Jack blurted. "In the DNA molecule there are ten bases per turn of the double helix, which actually means that two DNA strands crossover at every fifth base unit. So the pattern you are hearing in the music is based upon the actual shape of the DNA molecule." Winston laughed. "That's good to know. I was concerned that I was just playing a computer game that had nothing to do with reality."

"So what is the pattern? I can't publish a musical score in a scientific journal. They kind of prefer something more … concrete."

Winston responded by walking to a table that was piled with assorted magazines and books. He pulled a book from the middle of the pile and opened it, flipped through the pages for a moment and then handed the book to Jack. "Read the third paragraph."

Jack glanced at the cover of the book. It was "Godel, Escher, Bach" by Douglas Hofstadter. He found the paragraph that Winston wanted him to read:

Music is not a mere linear sequence of notes. Our minds perceive pieces of music on a level far higher than that. We chunk notes into phrases, phrases into melodies, melodies into movements, and movements into full pieces ...

He understood Winston's point. Jack would never be able to explain in words the nature of the "music" that could be produced from the satellite DNA sequences. Even more problematic would be to explain how such DNA music might somehow be related to the process of aging. Explaining that connection was going to be like describing the relationship between the printed score of Beethoven's Ninth Symphony and the emotions that the music produced in the listener. Tremendous challenges, Jack realized, would have to be overcome before the music of satellite DNA would be viewed as anything but a meaningless novelty.

Jack was disturbed, by Winston's discovery. There was, as Peter had correctly argued, a pattern to the base sequence of the DNA, but Jack knew of no way to link the pattern to the functions of a living organism. That a musical theme could be extracted from the DNA structure was fascinating, but living cells were not concert halls. They were chemical machines that worked according to well-established principles.

Once again Jack felt his inadequacies as a scientist. Jack, like every modern scientist, was a specialist in a narrow field. This was a necessary evil. The successes of science, and the explosion of information that had resulted, made it impossible for any one person to know more than a minute fraction of the world's scientific knowledge. He needed to talk to somebody who was more familiar than he was with basic chemistry and physics.

He found Harrison Jones in his cramped office, barely visible between the stacks of reprints and books. Harrison was probably the smartest man that Jack knew, and one of the most difficult to get along with. He was already a full Professor in the department when Jack came to Drexel, and seemed old and crotchety even then. To Jack's amazement, he was still going strong and was as ornery as ever. The students and most of the faculty in the department were afraid of Harrison, and for good reason. Once, during a departmental seminar, he brought a colleague nearly to tears. The speaker clearly did not have a full grasp of his own subject area. Most people would have let this go out of a sense of politeness or decorum, or at most would have asked one or two questions to reveal the speaker's weaknesses. Harrison took him on like a pit bull after a poodle, each succeeding question revealing deeper layers of his colleague's ignorance, until his inadequacies as a scientist were clear to all.

Jack was one of the few people in the department that regularly talked to Harrison. From the beginning Jack had stood up to Harrison's assaults, and had earned his respect. Jack also discovered that Harrison's gruffness was because he cared about truth and integrity — and he had little patience for people whom he felt compromised on these. Now that Jack had become confident of his results he could risk bringing them to Harrison.

"This is pretty amazing stuff." Harrison said after carefully examining all of the information Jack had brought to him. "Are you sure the data is real?"

"Completely sure. We have repeated the experiments many times, and carried out every control we can think of." Jack had brought a copy of his Cell Biology abstract with him, which he gave to Harrison. "The problem is what to do next." He directed Harrison's attention to the last sentence in the abstract. He had written: "The mechanism by which satellite DNA could influence the processes of aging is unclear, and will be a subject for further investigation."

"Ahh, the old 'please send more money' conclusion. I have been known to use it myself, but I don't think anyone ever read to the end of any of my papers."

"I am not so much concerned about grants. It seems to me that I should offer at least some kind of plausible mechanism. DNA is supposed to operate through its genes, and genes code for proteins that do the actual work. Satellite DNA, as far as we know, doesn't do anything."

"Have you been able to identify any pattern in the base sequence?"

Jack described the "music" in the sequence that Winston had discovered. "Although there seems to be a long range pattern, it doesn't suggest a mechanism."

Harrison sipped a cup of coffee that was always nearby. One difference between Harrison and most people was that he felt no obligation to carry on his end of a conversation. If you asked him a question, and it took him five minutes to formulate an answer you just had to tolerate five minutes of silence. This time the silence lasted about thirty seconds.

"Do you recall some experiments done in France, by Jacques Benveniste, in the eighties on the response of certain cells to antibodies? Benveniste reported that you could dilute the antibodies to the point that not a single molecule remained, and yet living cells would continue to respond as if the antibody was still present."

"I vaguely remember those experiments," Jack said. "Before that work Benveniste was a well-respected immunologist. He got his results published in Nature, but it ruined his career when they were proven false."

"You are right that it ruined his career. The French government even ordered his lab closed down. You are wrong about the results being proved false. That never happened."

"Are you saying they were real?"

"I am saying that the work was carefully done and well documented. That was why Nature published the paper in the first place, although they never really accepted the results. They even had a professional magician called the Amazing Randy go to the lab to see if some kind of slight-of-hand was involved. He found nothing."

"Were Benveniste's results ever repeated?" Jack asked. "I don't remember any follow up to the original work." Replication of a result by others, as Jack always told his students, was the key to establishing scientific credibility.

"Seeing what happened to Benveniste, who in his right mind would attempt to repeat such experiments, and if someone did repeat them what reputable journal would publish the results? As it was, the editor of Nature got reamed out by the scientific community for even considering Benveniste's paper."

"I can understand why people might be upset," Jack said. "After all, Benveniste claimed that a molecule could have a measurable effect, even after it had been diluted to the point where nothing of it was left. If his results were true, it would require a complete reworking of modern science. No law of physics could explain such a phenomenon."

"No known law. But an Italian physicist came up with a perfectly plausible quantum mechanical explanation." Harrison sipped more coffee as he searched for an explanation Jack might understand. "Imagine plucking a guitar string in outer space. Without air resistance the string could vibrate for hours. With proper design it might vibrate for years."

"But no one would hear it in the vacuum of outer space."

"Exactly my point. You would need to do a test that would reveal the vibration of the string. Benveniste's experiment, according to this theory, revealed quantum vibrations that had been set going in the water by the initial treatments."

"You think something similar might be happening with satellite DNA and aging?" Jack shook his head in confusion. "But DNA does not, as far as we know, make waves or vibrate, so how can Benveniste's hypothetical water vibrations be significant?"

Once again Harrison was quiet for several seconds as he thought about a response. "You presumably know about the paradox of the double slit experiment?" He asked when he had finally completed his thinking.

Jack was familiar with the basic idea of the double slit experiment, every first year physics class covers it, but he shook his head and Harrison continued.

"The double slit experiment is used to demonstrate that light is a wave. This is shown by the interference pattern that forms when a beam of light passes simultaneously though two side-by-side slits." Harrison went to the blackboard that covered one wall of his office, and drew a crude sketch. "Imagine you are in a bath tub and you wiggle your finger in the water."

The sketch, which looked meaningless a moment ago, resolved itself into a stick figure of a man sitting in water. "He is making waves," Jack said.

"Right. And the waves spread out from his finger across the bathtub and eventually strike his big toes which, as you can clearly see in the diagram, are sticking out of the water."

"So those are toes? I assume that in your metaphor the toes represent the double slit."

"Correct. And the critical fact is that the wave front strikes both toes at the same time. The wave is distorted by the toes and bends around them and as a result you now have two wave fronts instead of one. On the other side of the toes these two new waves bump into each other and interact. The result is an interference pattern." Harrison went to the blackboard and made some alterations in his sketch. "The man is now holding a gun in his hand. Think of him as a deranged teacher of pre-meds, and he has decided to end his misery by blowing his big toes off, both of them. But he has only one bullet."

"So he will only be able to hit one toe."

"In the word of classical physics, that's correct, but in the quantum world one particle can indeed be in two places simultaneously. If our disgruntled professor has a quantum gun he could blast both toes off at once, or to return to our more realistic experiment, a particle can pass through both slits at the same time. In that sense particles can act like a wave."

"That would require that the particle is in two places at the same time. That's impossible."

"Not according to quantum theory. Most physicists would tell you that light sometimes acts like a wave, sometimes like a particle, a so-called wavicle. But this response is an intellectual copout. Light is what it is, neither particle nor wave."

Jack was getting lost. He attempted to bring Harrison back to the issue at hand. "I don't quite see what photons and double slits have to do with satellite DNA and aging."

Harrison sighed in frustration. "Jack, at the atomic level a particle, and its associated quantum wave, can be simultaneously in two places at the same time. In truth, the quantum wave that comes with the particle is simultaneously everywhere in space and time. Similarly, a quantum wave associated with satellite DNA is present not just in the DNA, but everywhere. And not just everywhere in the cell. It is everywhere in the organism, and in principle, everywhere in the universe."

Jack shook his head. "Excuse my ignorance, but that sounds impossible."

"Apparently you never listened to the radio, or watched the local news on television."

Jack got the point. Every square foot of the atmosphere was filled, to a greater of lesser degree, with electromagnetic information broadcast by all of the radio and television stations on earth. "What you are saying, if I can put this in my own words, is that satellite DNA may alter some kind of quantum level vibration that extends throughout the organism."

"You are finally paying attention." Harrison grunted. "Consider the vibrating string again. Think about the difference between a Stradivarius violin and the one you learned on in school. A small crack, a microscopic defect, in the wood of a violin can turn a beautiful instrument into a piece of junk. What is important in the violin is its overall pattern of resonance. Perhaps aging is the crack in the violin."

7

Jack took Harrison's ideas seriously. But Harrison was wrong in an important detail. He thought of the satellite DNA sequence as a negative agent, rather than as a positive effector of aging. The satellite DNA was not the crack in the violin, it was the tune itself. What Jack needed to do was to find a way of disrupting the tune -- to create a crack in the DNA violin. But even if Benveniste's experiments and the quantum mechanic explanation were valid, they did not suggest any way of altering the functioning of the satellite DNA. This project was testing his abilities, and once again he was not passing the exam.

One of the things that Jack had learned as a teacher was that one of the best ways to learn was to attempt to explain a concept to someone else. Once again he called on his friend Winston. An offer of beer and pizza at his favorite spot was enough to entice him. Jack explained to Winston, as best he could, Harrison's ideas. Winston had little training in the natural sciences and Jack's attempt to explain double slit experiments, quantum fields and interference patterns left Winston lost.

Winston interrupted Jack's explanation during a particularly complex explanation. "I am feeling deja vu all over again." He moaned. "You are making me relive the tortures of my youth."

"What?" Jack responded in puzzlement. "I am just attempting to explain my theory of how DNA could control aging."

"You are lecturing. I hate lectures."

"You were a college professor yourself once." Jack pointed out. "No doubt you gave your share of lectures."

"Yes, and that's one reason I quit. I hated giving lectures even more that I did listening to them."

"Why was that?"

"Giving lectures made me feel like a whore."

"A whore?"

"A woman that sells her sexual favors for money. A prostitute. The world's second oldest profession," Winston explained.

"I know what a whore is," Jack said in irritation. They were supposed to be discussing DNA and aging. "But I thought that prostitution was the world's oldest profession."

"A common misconception. Teaching is clearly older."

"I can accept that, but what does prostitution have to do with teaching?"

"Consider this fact," Winston said. "A lecturer and a prostitute both provide a service that can easily be had for free by those that choose to make the effort. A typical lecturer provides information that is readily available in textbooks or on the Internet. You don't need a talking head to learn, for example, the basics of biology, nor do you need to hire a professional to have sex."

"But students won't usually do the work of finding knowledge themselves." Jack replied. "That's why they need teachers."

"Of course. And the prostitute's clients don't want to put in the effort of finding true love. They want instant gratification – sex without the commitment or struggles of a real relationship. What is sad is that many students have no meaningful experience with true learning. They think that what they get in class is the real thing. But a teacher can no more give them real learning than a whore can give them true love."

"You sound bitter. You shouldn't blame the students."

"I don't. It's the institutions that promote this situation. College administrators are usually more interested in numbers such as 'contact hours generated per full time faculty equivalent' than in any measure of true learning. If the typical college president was a pimp he would no doubt evaluate the success of his stable of hookers by "orgasms generated per contact hour.""

Jack had to laugh at that image. "Ok, I won't lecture to you anymore. But how can I help you understand what I am getting at?"

"If you keep talking gobbledygook to me, I will never understand a word. You have got to put this in terms I can relate to."

Among Winston's many talents was the ability to play the piano, which he did informally as part of a semi-professional jazz band. Jack described the "crack in the violin" metaphor. Winston immediately perked up.

"Now that I can understand!" He said with relief. "You know, I have often thought my own life was like an out-of-tune piano. No matter what key I hit, all I seem to get is an ugly noise, and the more I strive for harmony, the more I seem to get dissonance." Winston promised to think about Jack's problem. "But don't expect miracles. A scientist I am definitely not."

Winston called back a few days later. "I think I might have a perspective on your problem that could be of value to you, or at least will amuse you. Come to my place tonight"

Jack knew that the more modest Winston was about something, the more interesting it was likely to be, and he drove quickly to his house. It was a moonless evening and one of Willow Lane's unmarked speed bumps almost sent Jack's car careening into the woods. Winston answered the door with a half-eaten Oreo cookie in his hand.

"I'm sorry to interrupt your dinner," Jack said. I would have been here sooner, but one of your damn speed bumps almost took me out."

"Well, they do help keep the riffraff away." Winston finished his cookie, and lead Jack to his office. He sat at a computer, and made a few keystrokes. A familiar sound came from the speakers. "Recognize this?"

"Sure" Jack had listened to the tape of the satellite DNA music over and over again. He could hum it if asked. "That's the satellite DNA sequence converted to music."

Winston made a few more key strokes. A new sound, little more than a pleasant hum came from the speakers. "How about this?"

"I can barely hear it."

"That's the point," Winston said. "That was the satellite DNA tune along with another tune that is out of sync and dissonant with it. I generated a new tone that was of equal intensity but out of phase with the original. When the two sounds are played simultaneously, the ear hears only the average of the two tones."

"I am impressed," Jack said, trying to hide his disappointment. He had hoped for something more than a musical trick. "But I don't see how this can be of use to me."

"You said, if I remember correctly, that you needed to interfere with the activity of the DNA sequences."

"Yes, but as far as I know DNA does not produce music." Even as Jack said this, he realized that this was perhaps not strictly true.

Harrison had argued that some type of quantum wave could be generated by DNA. Waves in any form behaved in much the same way. The same equations describe the undulations of ocean waves, the movement of sound through the air, and the interference of light in the double slit experiment. If the satellite DNA did generate quantum waves, they would behave in some respects just like the sound waves that Winston had generated from their base sequence. Just as two musical tunes could be combined to produce a meaningless noise, in theory so could the quantum waves from the DNA.

Jack's disappointment turned into excitement. "Tom, you just might have stumbled onto something useful after all."

That evening Jack reviewed the ideas that he had obtained from Winston and Harrison. If Harrison was correct, what he was looking at was not only a possible revolution in scientific understanding of the processes of aging, but a revolution in the laws of physics. It seemed, in a word, impossible. Yet this was the logical consequence of the facts in hand.

Jack remembered the reaction of those who had viewed his poster cell biology meeting. With the exception of the young Chinese postdoc, they had all shown through their words or their body language that they found his conclusions preposterous. The lack of a viable mechanism was the killer. If he proposed a mechanism based upon a controversial principle of physics he would be lucky to ever publish a paper again (if one didn't count getting written up in supermarket tabloids), and he would no doubt join Benveniste as a scientific outcast.

Jack wondered what had become of Benveniste. He did a search of the Internet and quickly uncovered that he had died in 2004, after a career marked by controversy. His research went well beyond the high dilution experiments that had been so controversial. In the most striking experiment, he reported that chemical waves could be recorded by a computer, then sent over a telephone line and cause the same physiological activity as the original solution! Jack's first reaction was to discard the whole idea as nonsense (were drug treatments going to be phoned in?!), but he nevertheless took the time to read the reports. He was surprised to find that they contained a substantial amount of actual data, including measurements of the frequency of the (hypothetical) chemical waves.

Benveniste's professional career had been destroyed by his claiming to have results that were inconsistent with accepted theories. The same thing, Jack realized, could happen to him if he was not careful. Only if he could directly modify the process of aging by altering the activity of the satellite DNA would he be taken seriously. The demonstration would need to be convincing and well documented, and preferably involve increasing life-span, not just creating yet another drop-dead gene. How he might accomplish these goals was the big question.

The trick that Winston had played with his DNA music was the only thing that came close to providing a way of interfering with satellite DNA. A DNA molecule that was the inverse, according to Winston's musical scheme, of the structure of the satellite DNA might conceivably cancel its activity. It was a long shot, a very long shot, but it was the only one that Jack had. Procedures for making DNA of a predetermined sequence, and introducing it into the cells of an organism, were well established. A common approach was to modify the DNA of a virus, which was then used to infect a host. The DNA of the virus would become incorporated into the cells of the host, along with the modified genes. A handful of such experiments had even succeeded in altering the DNA of human subjects. Unfortunately, the side effects, if you could call cancer and death side effects, had brought such experiments to a near halt. All of these efforts had been directed at a single goal – the replacing of a mutated gene with a functional one. Jack's task was actually easier, as he did not need the DNA to be genetically active, only to be present. It was worth a try.

Jack had worked for years with senescence-accelerated mice, so it was natural to choose them as experimental subjects. These SAM mice carried mutations that caused them get old and die in under a year. Even so, it was going to take a few years for definitive results to be obtained. This would be on top of the several months of steady work needed to construct a virus that had the desired properties. The virus was itself harmless, and could not reproduce on its own, but it would reliably find and insert into many locations within the host DNA. Since its DNA contained no active genes the virus had no effect on the normal processes of life, but it would, he hoped, interfere with the hypothesized quantum waves.

The first group of a dozen mice was injected with the virus along with an equal number of control animals injected with an unmodified virus. "What now Doc?" Peter asked.

"We wait."

Peter graduated a few months after the first batch of mice had been injected, and moved to Baltimore to start medical school. The initial excitement that Jack had felt from his possible discovery was replaced by the dull routine of scientific research. Each day he examined the animals in the experimental and control populations. They were weighed weekly and photographed monthly. At random intervals they were subjected to a battery of behavioral and learning tasks. Between these routine chores and his teaching duties the next four years passed quickly...

8

Jack finished writing the paper that would announce his results to the world on the first Monday of September. Since the death of his wife, holidays such as Labor Day had no significance to him, and the still deserted campus allowed him uninterrupted time for writing. Tomorrow the university would be transformed, as if by magic, from a peaceful village to a swarming city. Hundreds of students would clog the biology building, many with problems and questions that would require his attention.

He printed out a copy of the paper and read it through one last time for errors and ambiguities. The title, "Indefinite Extension of the Life-span of the Mouse with a Genetically Modified Virus," was not great, but conveyed the essential facts. It would have to do. No matter what the title, the article would get his colleagues' and the world's attention. The clink of metal against concrete interrupted Jack's thoughts. Snuffles had managed to roll the ballpoint pen off of the desk. Snuffles strutted across the desk and brushed against the sleeve of Jack's lab coat, hoping to be petted.

Even to him the results seemed too good to be true, and he looked once again at the mice as they scurried around in their cages, to reassure himself of the reality behind the words he had written. His hope, when he began the redwood tree project, had been only to uncover a hint as to the secret of their longevity. A minor paper, reporting on some interesting anomaly in the biology of the trees, would have been more than enough, but what he had discovered went well beyond that.

Now, four years after the first batch of mice had been injected with the modified virus, Jack was sure of the results. The control animals, injected with an inactive virus, had all died over a year ago. Before their deaths they had gone through the classical stages of senescence. Their hair had turned grey and brittle.

Cataracts had clouded their eyes. They would sleep for most of the day and get up only to nibble on food or to take water. In the end, each animal got old and died, just like every other mouse before it.

By comparison, the animals injected with the active virus remained young and healthy. Only one animal from the first group of treated mice had died, and that was from a simple infection. The others were still alive. They were better than alive. They were downright frisky. A single injection of the concentrated virus appeared to be sufficient to prevent aging. No other treatments were required.

There would be a firestorm of interest when his paper came out. Anyone with the proper knowledge, a well-equipped lab, and a modicum of skill, could construct an anti-aging virus as Jack had done. It was essential that Jack's results be released to everybody at the same time. Normally a paper submitted to a scientific journal would first be logged in by a secretary who would then distribute it to a managing editor. The editor in turn would select two or three reviewers who would make recommendations on publication. The process, even for a weekly journal, could take months. In that time rumors could spread and unethical use made of information that was supposed to remain confidential.

In the years since the humiliating experience at the cell biology conference he had been careful to maintain secrecy. At first he did this to protect himself from further ridicule, but as the results had come in he had maintained secrecy for its own sake, and he had told no one about the experiments. Truth was, after Mary's death his social life had become almost nonexistent, and there were few people he talked to regularly. Even his colleagues in the Biology Department did not know what he was doing with the mice in his lab, and when asked he gave only the vague response "aging research."

Continued secrecy was essential until the formal publication of his results, but this could not be accomplished under the standard procedures for submitting and reviewing manuscripts. He picked up the phone and called the offices of the American Association for the Advancement of Science, the publishers of the prestigious journal Science. After the usual voice-mail runaround he was finally connected to Jean Goldman, the senior biology editor. He tried to explain his dilemma to her, but she cut him off.

"I get these requests more often than you might think. You would be surprised how many scientists think their data will be misused by someone here or during the process of review. Send the manuscript directly to me, marked personal. Include a cover letter explaining the need for secrecy. All I will promise is that I will give it careful consideration."

Jack returned to his computer to make some critical last minute changes in the manuscript and to write the necessary cover letter. Finally, more than five years after Snuffles had first brushed against the photograph of Mary and her tree, it was time to take the next step – to announce to the world that aging was unnecessary. That in theory man could live, if he wanted, as long as the redwood.

A single copy of his paper, announcing his discovery, was sent later that afternoon directly to Jean Goldman by overnight mail.

9

Meiling Liu awoke to the grey, early morning light of the city. Above her one of the several water stains in the ceiling took on the appearance of a grinning face. The stain changed from day to day, depending upon the lighting and her mood. Today the stain mocked her. She dragged herself out of bed and began to prepare for another day. The cold rice in the refrigerator could have been converted, with a little fresh ginger and an egg, into a satisfying breakfast, but she did not have the energy for even that effort. She ate the tasteless starch cold, making it palatable with a cup of hot tea.

She collected the morning newspaper from the lobby of her apartment building, glad to find that no one had yet stolen it, as often happened. The newspaper was one of her few extravagances, and one of her few links to the world outside of her work. Today, according to the paper, was an American holiday. Labor Day it was called. Liu remembered that it was Labor Day, five years ago, when she had first arrived in Philadelphia, dazed and disoriented from the twelve-hour flight from Beijing.

Liu rarely had a holiday, or even a day off. Her job in Dr. Potts laboratory demanded her presence almost every day. Scientific research, particularly in an active field like the biology of aging, was highly competitive and it required a constant effort to stay on top. George Potts was one of the leaders in the field, and people like Liu kept him there. Working is such a high pressure job gave her little time for any kind of social life. Once a week, just for the exercise, she worked out at a Karate school, and now and then she would treat herself to a movie or a concert. The few men she had contact with showed little interest in a skinny, thirty-two year old Chinese woman. Nor were they of much interest to her.

Liu had come to the U.S. five years ago determined to establish a scientific career for herself. China had given her an outstanding education, but offered few opportunities for independent research, and she had been thrilled when Potts offered her a position in his laboratory. He had smoothed over the difficulties of obtaining the necessary visa, and she had arrived in Philadelphia full of enthusiasm and hope. Today, Labor Day, she would have done almost anything to avoid another day of dreary work at her bench.

Before her were hours of transferring solutions from one vial to another, of inserting and removing tubes from the centrifuge, of entering numbers and notes into the computer and of listening to Dr. Potts' instructions for tomorrow. What was not before her was any real hope of creative or meaningful intellectual activity. But she needed the money, much of which went back to China to help support her elderly parents, and she continued to harbor hopes that a better job would come along soon, one that would allow her to make better use of her creative abilities. Such a job, Liu knew, would require a positive recommendation from Dr. Potts. In the meantime she would continue to do the best she could in his lab.

It was a warm day, suitable for walking the several blocks down Market Street to Jefferson, and she dressed in shorts and a light weight blouse. She preferred walking to work, which gave her some much-needed exercise and allowed her ancient Toyota to stay in its precious parking space for another day. In America, Liu had discovered, it was essential to own a car. Although she rarely drove anywhere she would have felt trapped in the city without it. The automobile allowed her to run into Chinatown for her shopping and too more easily visit the few friends that she had in various parts of the city.

The elderly black woman that Liu knew only as Jogi was sitting at her usual sidewalk spot on the corner of Market and 12th Street. Liu reached into her pocket and removed the two quarters she had purposely brought with her.

"How are you feeling today, Jogi?" She asked politely and dropped the coins into the battered felt hat that sat on the concrete in front of her.

"Bless you dear. I am wonderful, wonderful … wonderful …" Her voice, weak to begin with, faded into the sounds of the city.

"That's nice." Liu responded and turned to walk on. Their conversation was the same every morning.

"And how are you today dear?" Jogi asked, in a voice that was suddenly strong and brisk.

"I'm fine." Liu lied, and walked on.

10

George Potts was not happy. The latest issue of Nature had an article on the stimulation of P53 activity in aging cells. This was supposed to be Potts' discovery. P53 was a protein that was critical to the repair of damaged DNA, and thus to the processes of aging. Potts was convinced that if he could find a way to stimulate the activity of P53 he could reduce or delay the ravages of old age. The idea had already proven of value, since it was the basis of a large research grant from BiTech Pharmaceuticals, but success would move him into the very top ranking of scientists in the world.

Through years of effort Potts had positioned himself as the leading proponent of the theory that aging was a consequence of damage to DNA. His lab had worked on the P53 project for more than six months. Meiling Liu, one of his three Chinese postdocs, would be particularly upset by the report in Nature. She had been putting in twelve to fourteen hour days, often seven days a week on this project, and was close to completing the crucial series of experiments.

Liu came into his office and he handed the issue of Nature to her. "Bad news I'm afraid." He watched as she read the brief article. She was wearing shorts under her lab coat, which was unbuttoned, and he could not help admiring the smooth skin on the inside of her thighs. The Chinese girls always seemed to have perfect skin.

Liu brought him out of his reverie. "This is nice work," she said. "It complements very well what we are finding. We should try to establish a collaboration with them."

This was not what Potts wanted to hear. "That is not possible. Remember, your work is supported by a grant from BiTech, and they would not want us sharing results with other labs." He did not need to elaborate. Liu understood that her results could have potential commercial value and that they were to be kept confidential until the lawyers at BiTech had cleared them for public release. Even the other members of Potts' staff did not know the details of her experiments. "For now I need you to get all of your notes together, with your analysis. We need to get a paper ready for submission immediately."

"There are still some experiments that need to be done."

"There are always more experiments that need to be done," He said forcefully. "I need to get something in print before it becomes irrelevant." Liu stood up and buttoned her lab coat. (Could she read his mind?)

"I will see what I can do," she said coldly

"Do that, and remember the grant from BiTech, the one that pays your salary, is up for renewal. We need results."

11

Robert Hopkins was concerned. The computer on his desk showed nothing but bad news. Earnings for BiTech Pharmaceuticals were down significantly for the last quarter. This was not good for BiTech or for Hopkins. His contract was scheduled to be renegotiated at the next board meeting, and a new five-year appointment as CEO with a large salary increase would normally be automatic. Also automatic would be the bonus of a large number of shares of BiTech stock, but when the results of the last quarter came out he knew that its value would collapse, making his bonus nearly worthless.

Investors were concerned because of the end of BiTech's patent on Trilaxx. For years Trilaxx had been a popular drug for constipation. The name Trilaxx had an interesting origin. One of the chemists on the research team had commented that the new drug he was working on "was trivial to make." From this fact, Hopkins came up with the name Trivex. Marketing was less than thrilled with his idea, however, and the name was eventually changed to Trilaxx. Although trivial to make, Trilaxx had a nontrivial impact on the earnings of BiTech. But with the patent running out every drug company with excess manufacturing capacity would soon be making Trilaxx and selling it for a lot less than BiTech had been getting for it.

Spread out on Hopkins' desk was the latest reports from each of his research teams. For the upcoming board meeting he needed to present a plan for the next Trilaxx. He had spent the night reading the reports, but all he had gotten for his efforts was a splitting headache. Lately his body had been betraying him. While he had always been healthy and active, the stress of his job, and the accumulation of years, had begun to take their toll. In his youth he had climbed mountains (literally and figuratively), sailed his own boat single handedly from Philadelphia to Bermuda and played a wicked game of squash. Now it was all he could do to get himself to the health club twice a week for a quick workout.

He wished the reports on his desk would simply disappear. Nothing in the world seemed more unpleasant at this moment than reading one of them again. Yet a decision had to be made. BiTech could not survive on its history, and a constant flow of new drugs into the market was essential if the company was to survive and prosper. He had prayed that at least one of his research teams would have developed something of value. Even a treatment for a minor illness could rake in millions of dollars in its monopoly stage.

The files on his desk made it unpleasantly clear that no substitute for Trilaxx was on the horizon. His reputation as a manager was going to take a severe hit, as would his net income. Even his job was potentially at stake. Hopkins locked the files in the office safe (his own spies had on occasion found critical information sitting open on a competitor's desk). It was getting late and he had some other serious business to take care of.

His chauffeur dropped him off at his home just after six o'clock. Quickly he got out of his expensive silk "power" suit and into casual slacks and a sports jacket. Attached to the house was a four-car garage which held a Mercedes, a Ford Explorer SUV, a Dodge Dakota pickup truck and a lowly Subaru. The Mercedes was his favorite car, but tonight's meeting required an unobtrusive vehicle, so it was out. He considered using the Explorer, which he also enjoyed driving, but the Explorer was out for today's task, however, as was the pickup truck. What he needed tonight was to be inconspicuous. The Subaru, with its reliability and a styling that made it look like every other Japanese econobox, was what he needed tonight. As an extra precaution he attached a fake license over the real one, as he routinely did before a sensitive meeting.

The fake was made from a printout of a digital photograph on high quality paper. Hopkins had discovered that a warm soldering iron could be used to raise the letters so that they resembled the embossed ones of the real thing. His handiwork would withstand all but close scrutiny. He knew this for a fact from the parking ticket he had gotten once. Briefly, he had considered not paying it. The poor shmuck whose license plate Hopkins had photographed would have a hard time explaining how his Subaru (of the same color and model as Hopkins') had been ticketed when it was probably still in his driveway.

He drove slowly to the restaurant in south Philly, occasionally checking his rear-view mirror, and stopping unnecessarily for gas. Convinced that he was not being followed, he turned down Passyunk Avenue and found a parking spot a block from the restaurant. Homer's Bar and Grill was the kind of place that you might expect to be a Mafia hangout, although Hopkins doubted they never ate there since it had some of the worst spaghetti in a city filled with outstanding Italian restaurants. The last thing that Hopkins needed was to be inadvertently mixed up in a mob investigation. At the restaurant he was shown, at his request, to a table facing the entrance.

Mikhail Rostov walked in, as scheduled, thirty minutes later, just as Hopkins was finishing his soup. Misha, as he liked to be called, sat down at a corner table and placed an order with the waitress. No one would have paid attention to the casual way Misha surveyed the room or would have noticed the brief eye contact that passed between them. Ten minutes later Hopkins got up slowly, folded his napkin and placed it on the table. He walked casually to the men's room at the back of the restaurant. Misha joined him a few minutes later, stepping sideways through the bathroom door to allow clearance for his broad shoulders. "Built like a tank" was a trite expression, but one that could be applied to Misha without too much exaggeration. It was a mystery to Hopkins why Misha's bulging muscles did not rip right through the cheap fabric of his Russian-made sport coat. Misha's friends had even tagged him with the nickname "Muscular." Apparently when Misha arrived in the city someone had tried to describe him, and "He is muscular" was interpreted by his fellow immigrants as providing a name rather than an adjective.

Hopkins had met Misha during a business trip to Moscow. BiTech was attempting to get Trilaxx approved as an over-the-counter medicine in Russia. This could never happen in the US, with its many layers of regulation and its strict enforcement of bribery laws, but in post-Soviet Russia anything was possible – with the right connections and an appropriate distribution of US dollars. Hopkins made the necessary contacts and payments and was certain that he had a deal, but then a key bureaucrat had demanded more money. Hopkins could have easily afforded the extra cash (what seemed like a fortune to the Russians was pocket change to Hopkins) but did not want word to get out that he could be shaken down like a mere pimp. He made some enquiries and was introduced to Misha.

In the USSR Misha had been a rising star in the KGB, but had quickly discovered that his talents and training were of greater value in the frontier atmosphere of capitalist Russia. Misha "disposed" of Hopkins' problem so efficiently and professionally that Hopkins had offered him similar work in the US. At first Misha had declined the offer, but quickly came to realize that his career, and probably his life, would not last long if he stayed in Russia. Most of his work nowadays was for mobsters and drug dealers, but he still did occasional jobs for Hopkins.

Misha closed the bathroom door behind him and locked it. "Why do we have to meet face-to-face like this?" he said angrily. "I don't like it. My other clients, they leave me messages in drop-offs. They don't even know what I look like."

"You know I won't put anything in writing." Hopkins was proud of the security arrangements he had put into place. A phone could be tapped, and a written note might fall into the wrong hands, or be used for blackmail. When he needed Misha's "special" services he placed an ad in the help wanted section of the newspaper. The ad told Misha, in a simple code, where and when to meet him. It was never the same place twice, but it was always a restaurant that had a men's room with at least two stalls.

"How do you know I am not wired?"

Hopkins laughed at this threat. "The authorities would be very interested in the cause of the 'accident' that killed my wife." Hopkins felt a momentary pang of sadness at the thought of Joan. She had not been a bad woman, but her threatened divorce would have brought lawyers into his financial affairs. This was something he could not have allowed. Misha had done several jobs since Joan's death, and all had been done professionally. He was well worth the hundreds of thousands of dollars that he had been paid.

"Let's skip the empty threats and get to business." Hopkins took a thick envelope from his jacket. "Ten thousand now, ten after completion."

Misha took the envelope and placed it in his pocket without looking inside. "What's the job?" he said.

Hopkins gave the details that Misha needed to know. A factory in St. Louis had become a financial burden. The building was old, as was the equipment inside. Changing demographics had driven out the best workers and created a security nightmare. The building was fully ensured for replacement value, and if it should happen to be destroyed by fire a new facility, with modern automated machines, could be built to replace it.

Hopkins did not write the rules of the insurance industry, and could see no reason why he shouldn't take advantage of its practices. Destroying the factory would allow him to instantly layoff hundreds of workers, and to rebuild a modern facility in a more favorable location. If the insurance system made any real sense it would pay to rebuild the factory and to retrain its workers – without the need to first burn it down. Hopkins guessed, based upon experience, that Misha would start a fire that would look convincingly like an accident. The fire would be blamed on faulty wiring or on kids playing with matches, but would not be traceable to Hopkins or BiTech.

After giving Misha his instructions for the St. Louis job, Hopkins returned to his seat and finished his meal. A few minutes later Misha did the same, but neither of them even glanced in the other's direction.

12

Sulli was happy. He and Rocky had spent the day begging for quarters around St Louis's remodeled Union Station, and Sulli had done better than usual. Like many train stations around the country the one in St. Louis, originally built as a monument to the power and wealth of the railroad barons, and had become a monument to the power and wealth of the American consumer. It was now an upscale shopping mall that was designed to attract suburbanites, and their money, into the city. Most city dwellers had long since learned to ignore the pleas of bums like Sulli and Rocky, who were now referred to as "the homeless." Fortunately for Sulli and Rocky enough people could be enticed to part with their loose change to maintain their simple life style.

Sulli checked the money in his cup. It held a few dollar bills and a fist-full of coins, mostly quarters. He made a quick estimate and figured that there was already enough for a jug of cheap wine. A well-dressed woman was heading his way. Her deep tan and coiffured hair spoke money and Sulli eagerly held out his cup.

"I am sure hungry lady. Fifty cents more and I could get a burger." The lady stopped and opened her purse. She placed a dollar bill in his cup.

"You poor man!" She said.

Sulli's day was ruined. He fumed as the woman walked away with mincing steps, her ridiculous spiked heels clicking on the concrete, and her ass fighting to escape the clinging silk of her dress. "Poor man" indeed! Sulli had never felt richer, or happier. What did she know? Sulli had been "rich" once, and it had been misery. Two years ago Sulli (people called him Mr. Sullivan then) had a profitable law practice that specialized in medical malpractice cases. They provided a steady stream of income that enabled Sulli to live a comfortable, if not extravagant, life style.

Then one day a young woman came to his office. She had been having back pains and her doctor had suggested that she have some misaligned vertebra fused with stainless steel pedicle screws. The result had been a disaster. A minor back problem had become a debilitating illness. As a result of the surgery the woman was in constant pain and was unable to work or even stand upright for more than a few minutes at a time.

The doctor, whose only training with the pedicle screws had been a two-hour seminar held at a resort in Hawaii, had botched the job. He had installed the screws incorrectly and, more importantly, had done so on a patient who was not even a proper candidate for them. To Sulli, the case looked like a sure winner. At his recommendation the woman had turned down a decent settlement offer and they had gone to trial. Even back then Sulli had been drinking too much, and he had prepared poorly. The defendant's insurance company brought in a team of medical "experts" who testified to the effectiveness of the pedicle screws and to the competence of the doctor. The screws, they claimed, had actually improved the woman's condition, and prevented a much worse outcome in the future.

They lost the case. Sulli had been stunned. He urged an appeal and he spent the next few days making phone calls and surfing legal sites on the Internet. He discovered what he should have known before the trial – the defendant's experts all owned stock in the company that manufactured the pedicle screws. This fact alone would have most likely changed the verdict, and was a solid basis for an appeal. Repeated calls to the woman's house were unanswered, but on the way home that evening he stopped at her apartment to deliver the good news. Thus it was Sulli who found her body. She had consumed a cocktail of every pain killer and muscle relaxant that she had in her possession (which was a lot). She died pain free.

Sulli's pain was not so easily treated, but alcohol was at least a temporary cure. Days later he woke up in an abandoned house alongside Rocky, and they had been together ever since. Sulli and Rocky got along well because they had established a dominance relationship much like that used by a pair of wild dogs. Sulli, the "alpha" individual of the pair, determined the daily routine, made all decisions and had first crack at any food or booze. Rocky was more than content with this system because he didn't have to worry about organizing his daily routine or making decisions. Sometimes he wished that Sulli would leave him more food and booze, but usually he was content.

Sulli's day was ruined by the rich woman's sympathetic comment. "Poor indeed!" he muttered to himself. In his lawyering days, each hour had been a struggle. There was always a document to file, a decision to be made, a client to call. The pressure never stopped until he was home and had a blessed drink in his hand. Now he had no worries or stress. Never again would someone take their own life because of his incompetence. He gathered up his few belongings and crossed the street to where Rocky was working. "We've got enough Rocky. Let's go."

"Plenty of time left . . ." Rocky muttered, but he gathered up his things and followed Sulli anyway.

Sulli took the money Rocky had collected. It wasn't much. Between them they had enough for a bottle of wine, but with too little left over to buy food. They would have to make do.

"How about some pizza, Rocky?" Sulli suggested, and led the way to a dumpster behind a nearby Pizza Hut. Of all restaurants, pizza joints were their favorites for trash picking. At the fancier places salads and meats and expensive sauces would be mushed together in an unappealing mess. Who needed salad anyway? Even at the burger joints the soft rolls, mayo, ketchup and tomatoes would combine with the meat and cheese to make a truly inedible pudding. Pizza was the ultimate trash food. Its firm crust and congealed cheese gave it a trash life of a couple of days. Washed down with a bottle of Gallo red (the perfect wine for the occasion) they could eat like kings. The nearly abandoned BiTech factory was a nearly ideal place to crash. The bathrooms still worked and the security guards rarely bothered them. The slipped through a flapping panel of plywood that was supposed to block a service entrance, and found a hidden nook to eat and drink.

"Hey, Rocky, looka this." Sulli waved a nearly uneaten slice of sausage pizza. "My favorite." Rocky grunted and nibbled at his scrap of greasy stromboli. Sulli could not get that woman, and her insulting comment, out of his mind. The wine had not worked. He took a bite from the cold pizza. A maggot, ghostly white and disgustingly fat, wiggled out from a hole exposed on the bitten edge. Sulli shivered and tossed the pizza across the room.

"Poor man!" Rocky shouted.

"What? What did you say?"

"I said 'Whoa man', why you toss that pizza away?"

"It's got worms."

"Don't bother me." Rocky got up and recovered the pizza. He dusted it off and picked out the visible maggots with a dirty fingernail.

Prior to the pedicle screw disaster Sulli had taken a brief shot at AA. He had quit after a few months, but he remembered vividly what had been said to him at his last meeting — that he had not yet sunk low enough, and not until he had reached absolute rock bottom would he be ready to make a serious effort to give up alcohol. Sulli looked at Rocky. He was eagerly finishing the last crumbs of the maggoty pizza, oblivious to the filth and decay of the abandoned factory that was their home for the evening.

Sulli had reached his bottom. With a certainty he had not felt in years, he knew that tomorrow he would return to his past world. There were old friends who would provide him a place to stay while he got himself cleaned up and would help him find a new job. He had once been a damn good lawyer, and he could be one again.

"Here Rocky, finish this off for me." He handed Rocky the bottle of wine, which was still half full. Rocky took it without questioning his good fortune, and quickly drained the bottle. He was soon curled up in his pile of rags and sleeping peacefully. Sulli made a pillow of his jacket and lay down, but did not sleep. Above him the sun was fading behind the filthy glass of the few unbroken windows that remained in the derelict building. Beams of light, scattered by the dusty air, fanned out from the high windows, creating a cathedral-like atmosphere. A deep peace settled over him. He knew that he was ready to go back. This would be his last night sleeping in an abandoned factory. Finally Sulli crawled under a splintered wooden bench, where he had stashed his pile of old clothes, and he too quickly fell asleep. Neither Rocky nor Sulli was awakened by the entry of a third person into the room.

13

Misha did his work quickly. From a plastic trash bag he removed the used clothing that he had purchased from the Salvation Army and sprinkled them with half of the bottle of cheap, but strong, vodka he had brought. Thieves had ripped open the wall in several places to gain access to the copper pipes and wires. He shoved the vodka-soaked clothing into one of the resulting gaps. The exposed wooden studs would burn nicely, but he wanted to be sure so he sprinkled more of the vodka on them. The rest he poured in a line along the edge of the wall. The alcohol would give a nice start to the fire, and little chance of detection by the arson investigators. If they found anything at all, it would be attributed to the homeless drunks that regularly slept in the factory. The air was already thick with the fumes and he finished his preparations quickly before the alcohol could evaporate. When he was satisfied, he touched a match to the rags. The pale, almost invisible, blue flame of the alcohol was quickly replaced by the yellow, smoky fire of burning clothes and wood. He left rapidly through a busted rear door. He never saw Sulli and Rocky, asleep in their rags, and would have done nothing even if he had.

14

As Senior Editor for biology Jean Goldman's main job was to read each article submitted to Science, and to decide which were good enough to justify further review by an expert in the field. Prior to taking her present job, Jean had been actively involved in research herself. Her experimental results at that time had led her, without intention or planning on her part, into areas that were controversial. A small number of powerful investigators, as in most areas of research, dominated her field. They had deemed her experiments to be "poorly performed" and her conclusions to be "excessively speculative." After a few years of rejected publications and unfunded grant proposals, Jean had jumped at the offer to be an editor for Science.

Perhaps she should have fought harder for her ideas, but the battle to gain professional recognition had exhausted her emotionally. The only good that had come from her battles was that it had made her a more caring and conscientious editor. Jean never forgot that a publication in a prestigious journal like Science could make or break a young investigator. Established researchers were less of a concern, since they would survive and prosper regardless of her opinion.

In the course of her work, Jean saw all kinds of manuscripts. Some were clearly from crackpots and were easily disposed of. Others were by earnest investigators with too little data and too much speculation, the kiss of death in biology. Occasionally her day was made by being the first to see a new and exciting result. She did not know what to make of the manuscript in front of her.

Until the phone call the previous day, she had never heard of Jack Keaton. From his address and acknowledgments she knew that he was at a small, but respected institution and that he had obtained independent research support. His writing was clear and concise, unlike much of the "techno-babble" that passed as acceptable scientific writing in some quarters. The data he presented was, up to a point, well documented and could be repeated by any skilled investigator. She reread the accompanying letter.

> "I am submitting the enclosed manuscript for publication in Science. The results presented should easily exceed Science's exacting standards of significance and broad interest. It is because of its potential significance that I have taken an unusual step. Important data, namely the actual sequence information of the modified adeno-virus DNA, has been blocked out. Just prior to publication (if the manuscript is accepted) I will submit the sequence to your office. I know that this is an unusual step, but the importance and potential impact of this information is such that I felt it must not be made available piecemeal. While I have full confidence in the editorial staff of Science, and in the integrity of your reviewers, I feel that withholding the sequence data until the last moment is an essential safeguard against its premature release. In addition I would request that only a single reviewer be assigned to evaluate the paper and that you do not make extra copies of the manuscript or share it with anyone else. I hope that these requests do not create an insurmountable problem for you. Please feel free to contact me if you have any questions or need further information."

Keaton's concern was certainly well justified. The results reported, if true, were revolutionary and had huge commercial potential. With the speed of modern communications news of this discovery would spread around the world in minutes. Not long ago an astronomer had predicted that a newly discovered asteroid might hit the earth. It did not matter that the calculation was based on very preliminary, inaccurate observations of its orbit, or that the astronomer had only sent his early calculations to colleagues over the Internet. The next day it was headline news around the world. The same thing could easily occur with Keaton's claims.

Jean had pride in her ability to distinguish good from bad science. But this was not her field. She needed an established expert in aging research to look at the paper before any decision was made. She opened the dialing directory on her computer and clicked on the P tab.

15

For weeks Jack had been consumed with the writing of his paper. Now that the manuscript was in the mail he had time to take care of some personal matters. The first order of business was a visit with his mother. Daisy Keaton lived in Andorra Village, a retirement home at the northern limits of the city. Its verdant gardens and rolling expanses of perfectly manicured lawn suggested a resort hotel, but inside the aroma of disinfectants and illness quickly brought one back to reality. Many of the older and sicker residents of the home would sit all day in the lobby, quiet and grim, as if expecting the hooded spirit with his scythe to walk through the door. They would look up at Jack as he entered, see that he was just another visitor, and then look away as if disappointed. He was thankful to find his mother sitting outside on a bench.

"Hi, mom. How are you feeling?" He kissed her on the cheek. She smelled of makeup and cheap perfume. What little physical energy she had went into maintaining her appearance.

"I am going to do it," she said without acknowledging his presence.

"The doctor thinks it's unwise. At your age an operation like that could be dangerous." His mother had been having dizzy spells for months, but only after she had fallen and broken an arm did she tell anyone about them. A CAT scan had revealed a tumor growing behind her right ear. The tumor was on the surface of the brain and appeared to be benign. But as it grew it was putting more and more pressure on the brain and on the nerves from the inner ear. Hence the dizzy spells. In a younger woman surgery would have been automatic, but the doctors were, justifiably, concerned about performing major surgery on a woman of eighty-two.

"Screw the doctors!" Daisy responded, her voice cracking with emotion. "This is no way to live – not being able to go anyplace without fear I will fall and break another bone." She grabbed her son's hand and gripped it with impressive strength. "You know what kills people here? Broken hips. The old ladies, they don't get cancer or heart attacks. They break a hip and spend their last days in misery in a wheel chair. I think they die of boredom."

Keaton's mother was no scientist, but she was remarkably accurate in her observation. Most people believe that the older you got the more likely it is that you will die soon. That this was not strictly true was, oddly, first demonstrated with fruit flies, a popular organism for genetics research. Most fruit flies died at an average age of about eighty days. It was not known why they died – no one did autopsies on dead flies – but most would be dead within a few days of the average fly life span. The surprise was that flies that got past the average life span could continue to live for an extended period (in fly terms), and did not die until they approached a maximum age. A similar phenomenon was true for humans. Most people died of cancer, heart disease or strokes in their sixties or seventies, but once you got past that age you could expect to live for twenty or even thirty more years. It was one of the many mysteries of aging.

Jack tried, once again, to explain the situation to Daisy. "Mom, do you understand that the operation could kill you. The risk of complications is very high at your age."

"Complications! You call dying a complication?" His mother looked up at her son. Sunlight glistened from the moisture that coated her eyes. "Living, that's the complication. I don't want to live like this, afraid to move. Afraid some days to even get out of bed. If I die, I die." She grabbed both his arms and pulled herself up. "It's a nice day. Take me for a walk."

His mother had always been decisive and strong-willed, and these traits had, if anything, become more pronounced as she aged. It would probably be futile, but Jack thought he should make sure she understood all of the ramifications of her decision. He placed a hand under her arm and supported her as they walked along. "It's not just that you could die. The doctor explained to you that crucial nerves might be damaged in the operation. You could lose the ability to walk, or to speak or even to see. Do you want to risk spending the remainder of your days as a blind cripple? You need to think about the quality of life that you may have."

"Let's go this way" she said, pointing down a walkway that led to the main building. "I want to show you someone." Just outside the entrance was a brick patio, shaded by large maples and ringed by red and white flowering Impatiens. The patio was one of the nicer areas on the grounds and several of the residents were outside, sitting on benches or in their wheelchairs. A flock of pigeons and several squirrels were gathered around a grey-haired man who was tossing them scraps of bread. Jack stopped and watched the animals for a while.

"What are you looking at?" Daisy asked impatiently. "Haven't you ever seen a pigeon before?"

"Many times, and squirrels too." There was something strangely relaxing about watching other living organisms going about the routine affairs of their existence. He looked around. Most of the elderly residents were, like Jack, looking at the pigeons and squirrels. He was reminded of the question that his friend Tom Winston had posed some years earlier. Ever since, he had been observing squirrels closely, but he still did not have an answer to Winston's question. "Did you ever wonder where squirrels defecate?" He asked his mother.

"Why should I care where squirrels shit? That's why we have scientists – to find the answers to important questions like that." She tugged at Jack's hand. "What I brought you here to see is over this way."

Daisy led him up to an elderly woman in a wheelchair, accompanied by a middle-aged woman who Jack guessed to be the older woman's daughter. "Tell me what you see?" Daisy said.

Jack looked more closely at the old woman. She was rocking gently back and forth in her chair, making a low humming sound. Although Jack and Daisy stood directly in front of her, her eyes appeared to be focused somewhere in the distance. Jack guessed, from the desiccated state of her skin and the few wisps of grey hair that remained on her head, that the woman was in her nineties. He knew his mother well enough to suspect that she had posed a trick question to him, and that the answer she was looking for was not "a very old woman." He looked at the woman more closely, and saw what his mother had, no doubt, brought him to see.

"I see an old woman smiling," he said. Not only were the woman's lips curled up into a distinct smile, her eyes were bright with life. Whatever she saw in the distance, or imagined she saw, it seemed to please her.

"Very good Jack. This is Mrs. Darnell. She hasn't uttered a word for five years and needs someone to feed her and wipe her ass. So mister scientist, who can measure the size of an atom and calculate the age of the universe, how do you score her 'quality of life?' On a scale of one to ten what do you give her?"

"I don't have a clue." Jack admitted.

"Well she looks pretty happy to me. Maybe if I am lucky the operation will turn me into a Mrs. Darnell."

Jack knew that further argument with his mother would lead nowhere. "So when do you want to have the operation?"

"Next week." She said firmly.

"I will call the doctor and make arrangements to have it done as soon as possible."

"As usual, you don't understand. The operation is next week. I have already made the arrangements."

16

The manuscript from Science was delivered to George Potts the Thursday after Labor Day. He knew Jack Keaton only vaguely. They often attended the same meetings, but Jack was a couple of rungs down, at least, on the status ladder. Potts got tired of dealing with these types. They always wanted to tell him about their latest theories, or ingratiate themselves so he would remember them when their grants came to him for review. He read the cover letter from Jean first, then quickly scanned the paper. Jean was being overly cautious. She should have rejected it out of hand. The results made no sense. It was true that the paper was well written and impeccably documented (except for the critical DNA sequence data). But anybody could invent beautiful results. Scientific frauds almost always had perfect data, which was one of the clues that the results were not real. The world was full of people who would do anything for a moment of glory, from shooting a president or, as in this case, claiming to have the key to eternal life.

The kiss of death for the paper, as far as Potts was concerned, was that the results simply could not be true. Many years of research by thousands of scientists had established how cells worked. DNA contained genes, genes contained the instructions for making proteins and the proteins did all the actual work. Satellite DNA did not fit into this picture, and no mechanism he knew of could explain how it might function as described in Keaton's paper. The concluding paragraph suggested a mechanism based upon an absurd idea. Citing that fraud Benveniste was the final straw. "This is a no-brainer" George muttered to himself, and turned to the computer to write his review.

As he was finishing his (mercifully) short critique, Liu walked in. She noticed the manuscript on his desk. "A manuscript for review?" she asked. "Would you like me to look at it?"

Her offer was not unusual. Potts reviewed a lot of papers and grant proposals, and he often called on his postdoctoral staff for help. "I've taken care of it already," he said. "But you are welcome to look at it. It might give you a laugh." Potts went over the day's experiments with Liu and she left a few minutes later with Keaton's manuscript under her arms.

17

Liu took the manuscript home with her that evening. Although she had only spent a few minutes with Dr. Keaton at the cell biology meeting, she would never forget him. How could she forget the name so closely associated with her first public humiliation at the hands of Dr. Potts? But she also remembered that he had patiently listened to her and answered her questions as best he could. Not an easy task given the poor state of her English at that time. Her overall impression was that he was a sincere and serious scientist.

His data, she recalled, was out of the mainstream, which was one reason why it had not been well received when she presented it at the staff meeting. Yet his experiments had been well documented, and Liu was surprised that Dr. Potts would reject Keaton's work by him so casually.

Liu read Keaton's paper carefully, staying up well past midnight to go over every aspect of the experiments. She was literally stunned by his results. The work was impeccable, and try as she might she could find no errors or weakness in the experiments. That night she slept little. Her mind insisted on reviewing each and every one of her own experiments. She began to see how they could fit into the new model proposed by Keaton. If his results were true, it would open up a new era of aging research. The physics that Keaton used to explain his results was complicated, but Liu had received excellent science training in China and she understood the basic concepts. To apply them to biology in the way he did was truly revolutionary, but then his results required a revolutionary theory.

As soon as she got into the lab the next morning she went to see Dr. Potts and to return the manuscript. "I read Keaton's paper last night. Did I understand right, that you are going to reject it?"

"Yes, the work is a joke."

"The experiments seemed sound to me."

"He certainly seems to know his stuff." Potts said sarcastically. "Otherwise he wouldn't have been able to construct such an impressive pack of lies."

"You think he is a fraud?"

"Just read the last section. He cites that nut Benveniste, who has been totally discredited."

Liu had read Benveniste's work before she had left China, where it had received a great deal of attention. The Chinese had a long history of doing science that was outside of the mainstream of Western practices. Acupuncture and herbal medicines had been scoffed at by Westerners because they did not have a "scientific" basis according to their tradition. Of course acupuncture and herbal medicines had eventually found their way into Western practices anyway because of the undeniable fact that they worked in certain situations.

Liu did not consider challenging Dr. Potts' views. While the Chinese were open to alternative views of nature, those in positions of power were not open to alternative views of their opinions. An American might have argued with Potts, but Liu did not consider doing so. Liu took a more indirect approach.

"Perhaps we should attempt to repeat some of his experiments. The basic observations are not that difficult."

"Liu, I have to prepare a renewal application of our BiTech grant soon. I do not want you wasting your time or the lab's resources on Keaton's absurd experiments."

Liu nodded politely, to indicate that she understood, and returned to her lab bench. In China she had learned to show deference to authority, even as she refused to submit to its demands. The democratic revolution that was underway in China had not taken place as it might have done in a Western country, with violence and bloodshed. In China the Western approach had been attempted, and it ended abruptly in Tiananmen Square. The Chinese had returned to their traditional ways — millions of individual Chinese bowing to authority, but subtly doing their own thing. Liu decided that she could easily fit some of Keaton's experiments into her own project. Potts never looked at raw data, only the summarized results. He would never know that she had disobeyed his orders.

While critical information in Keaton's manuscript was, understandably, blocked out, the basic ideas and the experimental protocols were thoroughly described. The liquid nitrogen freezer in Dr. Potts' laboratory contained an extensive collection of DNA from a wide variety of organisms. These were primarily used to compare the results of genetic analysis between different species. She was somewhat surprised to find a redwood sample in the collection – about ninety percent of the samples were of mammalian origin and most of the remainder were from bacteria or fungi.

The procedures for amplifying and analyzing the DNA, which Liu had performed thousands of times, took her just a few days. Keaton was right about the correlation. The redwood DNA was totally lacking in highly repetitive satellite DNA.

But Keaton said a lot more in his paper. He claimed to have developed a virus that would disrupt the aging function of the satellite DNA, and which greatly increased the longevity of mice. This was a remarkable claim. Genetic engineers had been attempting for years to reliably introduce genes into cells by way of a virus. Keaton claimed to have a virus that would disrupt the satellite DNA. He had used a modified adeno-virus for his work, but his paper gave no hints as to the actual DNA sequence introduced into the virus.

Liu considered her options. She had violated Dr. Potts' direct orders not to pursue Keaton's experiments. Technically she had also violated the accepted rules of confidentiality. Manuscripts were sent out for review on the understanding that the reviewers would not use the information to gain an unfair advantage. Liu knew that this rule was unenforceable and widely violated, but it could well create problems in the future.

The line of authority was clear. Dr. Potts wrote the grants and paid the bills, including Liu's salary. He was also responsible for writing the annual letters to the U.S. immigration service, essential for renewal of her visa, that claimed she had unique skills not available from an American citizen. She could not continue these experiments without Dr. Potts or someone else in the lab knowing about them. She had to tell him about her results, and their confirmation of Keaton's work.

Potts was on the phone. She stood outside the door waiting for him to finish. He seemed agitated, and she could easily hear his shouting. "I understand your problem, Bob, but I don't have anything I can give you right now . . . Of course I appreciate your support and you will be the first to know if anything practical comes from our research …I was hoping you could give us some more time …" Potts noticed Liu at the door and waved her in. "Are we still on for golf this afternoon? … Good we'll talk more then." Liu heard Potts slam the phone down, and she wondered if this was a good time to approach him.

"What do you want, Liu?" He was not in a good mood, but Liu could not gracefully back out now. Liu handed him the photographs from her analysis of the redwood DNA. She had clearly labeled each lane. Potts had insisted on this ever since one of the postdocs had committed suicide two years ago. His data was so poorly labeled that Potts had to throw out over a year of work. The lost data had upset him more than the fact that one of his staff had killed himself.

Potts spent several minutes examining the photographs. "Is this what I think it is? You repeated Keaton's experiments?" Liu nodded. "I thought I told you not to bother with his crackpot ideas."

"I had some spare time, and thought it would be worth checking out the basic results," Liu said defensively. She pointed to the lane labeled "redwood." "He was right about the correlation between satellite DNA and life span."

"But his theory is nuts, and his claim to have developed an effective virus vector is not believable. A lot of man-hours and money have gone into that effort. How could one person with limited funds do what no one else has accomplished?"

"I don't know," Liu said, "but I thought you should be aware that at least the correlation he claims is accurate. Perhaps there is something to the rest of the data."

Potts pondered this statement. He looked again at the data that Liu had brought him. "Shit!" he grunted.

Liu had never heard Potts curse. He was usually very formal in his dealing with the lab staff. "Is something wrong Dr. Potts?"

"I admit that the results you just showed me are a bit of a shock," he said. "I may have judged Keaton too hastily. Fortunately I have not yet mailed the critique of his manuscript back to Science. I will take time to go over the paper more thoroughly and I will give it serious consideration."

Liu was surprised that Potts, who was usually very stubborn in his view, had reversed himself so quickly. "Should I do more of these experiments?"

"No, not for now," Potts said. "I will be at a meeting all afternoon, but I will take another look at Keaton's manuscript as soon as I can. In the meantime you must tell nobody about his experiments or about your own results."

18

Potts had been jolted by the data that Liu had shown him. Keaton's paper had struck him as a fraud, but now he wasn't so sure. It would make little sense to report a valid result along with a false one. Why risk a significant discovery by combining it with an easily discovered fake? If the satellite DNA data was correct perhaps the rest of Keaton's results were also valid. If so, Keaton had made the most significant discovery since antibiotics. Potts felt his stomach churn.

Potts had devoted his professional life to the problem of aging, and now this young nobody may have made Potts' entire career meaningless. But what galled Potts most of all was that Keaton's discovery came from looking at redwood DNA. The idea of investigating redwood genes had occurred to Potts years ago. That was why there was a sample of redwood DNA in the freezer. It wasn't right that he should wind up with no credit for the idea, while fame and wealth would soon flow like a landslide to the previously unknown Dr. Keaton.

Potts, like many scientists, did not care much about money. He made a good income, but he could make a lot more doing other things. Science gave him a status that no amount of money could purchase. His name was cited, according to the Institute for Scientific Information, hundreds of times each month, and he was often asked to give presentations at important meetings. Reporters, political leaders and CEO's of large corporations frequently called on him for information about the latest research on aging. In a word, Potts was Important.

Not that he didn't need money. A modern biotechnology lab was expensive. A few milligrams of a rare enzyme could cost thousands of dollars, and a state of the art ultracentrifuge more than a hundred thousand. Federal agencies used to provide sufficient funds for his purposes, but they had been cutting back on support of "big" labs. Just about any young assistant professor could get a grant, but a productive researcher, like himself, could not maintain a lab with a critical mass of research assistants and postdocs. That was why he had turned to industry for support. Now Hopkins at BiTech was threatening to cut him off . . .

Potts looked again at Liu's results. If the virus was real Keaton would be famous, and whoever had the rights to Keaton's virus was going to make a lot of money, an awful lot of money. Potts took a deep breath to compose himself. He had no intention of reevaluating Keaton's paper, but the promise should satisfy Liu while Potts considered more useful options.

Bob Hopkins would certainly be interested in Keaton's work, possibly interested enough to part with some of BiTech's money. Potts played golf regularly with Hopkins. He didn't particularly care for the game, which had a way of making him feel like a failure, but he knew the value of maintaining friendly relationships with people in high places. He sent Hopkins and email, suggesting a game, and dropping a hint at some important news.

They usually played at the Bala Golf Club, not one of the best courses in the area, but conveniently located near the city. Potts did not want to seem too anxious, and he made casual chatter through the first three holes.

As they walked toward the fourth hole, Potts decided it was time to raise the issue of Keaton's experiments. "I gave some thought to your problem since our chat this morning, Bob. There is something that has come up that you should know about." Potts told Hopkins about Keaton's paper. Transmitting information about a manuscript was a serious violation of confidentiality rules, but these were something that Potts routinely ignored. The whole point of reviewing papers, for which he got no compensation, was to have the latest results first. In science, information was power, and he needed to use that power now with Hopkins.

"The key to Keaton's results," Potts explained, "is the use of a special adeno-virus that he developed. Unlike most viruses, which only invade certain cells, his AAV virus appears to go in at random."

Hopkins interrupted. "I don't need to know the details right now, George. Fax me a copy of Keaton's manuscript, but make sure to use my private office fax number." Hopkins paused to sink a short putt. "The potential applications of Keaton's results are what I care about for the moment. What kind of dose-response curve are we talking about? That will have a lot to do with potential profit margins. A drug that's too potent, like a single pill that could prevent headaches for a year, would be of little value."

"The response appears to be logarithmic," Potts said. "Low doses extend the life span of a mouse a few weeks. Higher doses add increasing time. At the highest dose tested the mice are still alive. So we don't know where the plateau is."

"Side effects?"

"Well, it's only been tested in mice. At high doses they had flu-like symptoms that lasted a few days."

"So with humans we would want to use small doses with an extended treatment."

"It would make better economic sense to give one large dose."

"For the customer maybe!" Hopkins laughed. "George, for such a smart guy you have never understood business."

Potts nodded in agreement. "That's why I leave the business to you. But what difference does all of this make. Keaton has the virus. Not us."

"How far along are you toward getting the virus?"

"We have repeated the basic observations. I had the same idea as Keaton some time ago and had redwood DNA on hand." Potts paused to get control over his emotions, and to shoot an easy two-foot putt. The ball hit the lip of the cup too hard and rolled three feet beyond the hole. "Fuck!" Potts spit out.

"Relax George. It's just a game."

Potts didn't give a damn about the game, or the missed putt. He cared about the missed opportunity. He was certain that he would have analyzed the redwood samples soon, and that he, not Keaton, should have made the discovery of its unique DNA structure.   "Anyway, we have independently confirmed the essential results, but Keaton appears to be well ahead of us on developing an effective anti-aging virus." This was more than a small exaggeration. Potts did not have a clue how to make the virus.

They played in silence for a while. "I want to make sure I understood you correctly." Hopkins said after a while. "The key information about the virus, its DNA base sequence, was kept secret in Keaton's manuscript." Potts nodded. "And as far as you know, only a few people even know about its existence?"

Potts reviewed the information in the manuscript. Keaton was the sole author. This was unusual, and he could not remember another major research paper that had just a single author. Teamwork and collaboration had become essential to modern science. Keaton's manuscript had an acknowledgment page that Potts had only glanced at, but he thought that it only contained two or three names. The editor at Science had presumably read the paper. In the cover letter that she had sent with the manuscript she emphasized the importance of complete confidentiality. It was likely that she had not shown it to anybody else.

"I would guess that no more than a half dozen people know about the work in any detail."

"Good. That's manageable." Hopkins paused to tee off. His ball flew over two hundred yards straight down the middle of the fairway. Potts hit his ball into woods. They walked up the fairway together. "I assume that the virus is in Keaton's lab at Drexel?"

"As far as I know." Potts did not like the way the conversation was going. "What are you getting at Bob?"

"Is there any chance that Keaton would give you a sample of the virus?"

Potts shook his head. "Given the level of secrecy that Keaton had constructed, I don't see him sharing it."

"So we will have to steal it."

Potts was shaken, and strangely excited by Hopkins response. While Potts had never been hesitant to occasionally fudge data (as long as he was confident the result would ultimately be confirmed), he was moving into uncharted ethical territory. He had to admit, however, that Hopkins had seen a solution to their unpleasant situation. Keaton had been too clever for his own good. By not revealing the secret of the virus, he had left open the possibility of an "independent" discovery. Potts might yet get the credit he deserved.

The discovery of HIV was an obvious parallel to the present situation. Robert Gallo, working at the National Institutes of Health, and Luc Montagnier of the Pasteur Institute in France had reported, at about the same time, the isolation of the virus that causes AIDS. It wasn't until a couple of years later that it was discovered that Gallo's virus was the same strain as the French one. In truth, Gallo's virus was the Montagnier virus. It was never made clear how the virus got from France to America. Gallo claimed it was inadvertent. It didn't matter. By the time the true origin of the virus had been sorted out Gallo was famous and it was an American company that was earning millions selling the first blood test for HIV.

The editors at Science were paranoid about preserving anonymity of their reviewers, and there was no way Keaton would know that Potts had seen his manuscript. He could easily delay its publication for weeks, or even months, while he arranged to "discover" the virus himself. With Potts' reputation, and friends in high places, he was sure to get the lion's share of credit, and BiTech the patent rights to the virus. By the time the origin of his virus was discovered, if it ever was, he would have accomplished his purpose. Meanwhile BiTech's lawyers would be perfectly capable of holding off indefinitely any challenge to their rights to the virus.

In Potts' laboratory experiments were only started when all of the required information and materials were in hand, and Hopkins' proposal called for at least that level of care. Stealing Keaton's virus was tempting, but it was also risky. Whatever they were going to do, the first order of business was to collect the essential data. "We don't even know if this anti-aging virus actually exists," he said, "or where it's stored."

Hopkins was apparently thinking along the same lines. "Is there some way you can get into his lab without raising suspicion?"

Potts recalled that Liu had met Keaton at a Cell Biology conference. "I think I have a person who might be able to do that."

The next morning, after a sleepless night, Potts called Liu into his office. "You said that you once met Keaton?"

"Just briefly, at a Cell Biology meeting."

"Hopefully he will remember you," Potts said. "I am going to arrange for you to collaborate with him." Liu looked puzzled. She would know that Potts rarely collaborated with others, and certainly not with someone like Keaton, a virtual unknown. As naive as Liu was, she was no dummy, and her puzzlement quickly turned to consternation as she deduced the reason for Potts's request.

"I doubt he will share his virus with us," she said.

Potts explained the situation. "The issue as I see it, Liu, is that Keaton's paper cannot be accepted without independent confirmation that the virus exists. If we had a sample of the virus, we could establish its biological activity. But we can't be sure that there even is such a virus." Liu was naive and easily manipulated. She would be perfect. Last night Potts had looked up Keaton's publications on the Internet. One of his earlier papers was a technical report of a new method for measuring the metabolic rates of single cells. It was common for researchers to exchange staff for brief periods to learn new techniques, and that was what he hoped to arrange for Liu.

"I am not sure we should do this," she said.

Potts explained in detail what he wanted her to do. "I am not asking you to steal anything. In good conscience, I cannot accept Keaton's paper unless I know that the virus actually exists. By confirming the existence of the virus you will be doing him a favor."

"I don't like this" she insisted. "It's unethical."

Potts had made up his mind to a course of action. He was not used to, and did not like, someone questioning his decisions. "Liu, the virus may or may not exist. If it does not exist, someone will need to reveal Keaton for the fraud that he is. If it does exist, it is not right that one person should control it. I promise you that I will do everything I can to get the virus legitimately, and I will see to it that everybody will have reasonable access to it. Keaton clearly has the intention of keeping the virus to himself and not sharing it with other investigators. That is not the way science should be done."

Liu may have suspected that he was telling her blatant lies, but they were lies she needed to hear. "You know that I will be very grateful if you will do this for me." Potts added. It would be much easier for Liu to suspend disbelief if she thought that her future career was in the balance.

"You want me just to look around his lab?" Liu said.

Potts tried to avoid smiling at his victory. "That's all. Nothing illegal or unethical." Reluctantly Liu agreed to Potts' plan. His instructions to Liu were very explicit. She was to scout the lab and attempt to find out if the virus actually existed, and if it did exist where it was stored. She was to keep the actual purpose of her visit secret.

19

Jack was at his office computer, reading once again the paper he had sent to Science. It was amazing how differently his words read now that they had been submitted for publication. Sentences that had seemed clear and precise when he had written them were now nearly incomprehensible even to himself. His carefully constructed and concisely reasoned arguments now seemed, on rereading, as if they had been written by a maniac. The last sentence – "The impact of the anti-aging virus on humans remains to be established." – was trite and pointless. Of course the virus's effect on people needed to be tested, and that would be the first order of business once his results became public knowledge.

The cat rubbed up against his leg, and he lifted her up onto the desk. Snuffles purred contentedly as Jack scratched the favored spot behind her ear. Her fur, once sleek and black, was tinged with grey, and had lost much of its luster.

"So how about you, Snuffles. Would you like to live forever?" It was a question, of course, that a cat could not answer, or even consider. But a person could, and in rereading his manuscript Jack had discovered a glaring omission – it contained no discussion of the potential ethical issues arising from his discovery.

Only recently, with the experiments behind him, had he begun to consider their consequences. The virus would be in great demand, and even before proper FDA testing and approval a thriving black market would be certain to bloom. If the virus proved effective in humans, it would still be in limited supply and very expensive for many years. The ever growing rift between the rich and the poor would become a grand-canyon.

Jack's musings were interrupted by a knock on the door. The building janitor, Lester Jackson, had come to clean the lab. Lester was a large black man with an overhanging belly and quick wit. In a different world, where people were truly able to advance on their talents, Lester might have been a lawyer or a doctor or entered some other profession where success was based upon the ability to think clearly and act wisely. Lester had, in fact, done many things in his life. He had fought as a professional heavyweight boxer, sailed in the merchant marines, preached in a north Philadelphia storefront church, served as a ward captain for the Democratic party, and helped run a drug rehab program for teenagers. His considerable energy had diminished in his later years, and today he was content to sweep floors and dump trash.

"Hey, doc, how you doing today?" Lester said cheerfully.

"OK." Jack responded vaguely, his mind still on the potential consequences of his research.

"You don't look OK to me. You look like a worried man. What you got to worry about? I had your money I wouldn't worry." To Lester all of the professors were virtual millionaires.

"Let me ask you a question, Lester. Suppose someone invented a pill that would allow you to live forever -- to be immortal. Would you take it?"

Lester didn't hesitate. "Nah. Why would I want to live forever on this earth? I'll have eternal life in Heaven soon enough."

"Think of all the things you could do, the places you could visit."

Lester leaned on his broom and contemplated Jack's question. "When I was young, Doc, I wanted to see the world. I saw enough to know that there was nothing out there that mattered to me that I couldn't find in my own backyard."

"What about watching your children and your grandchildren grow up?"

Lester pushed the broom briskly across the floor for a few seconds, and then stopped as if exhausted by the effort. "That would be nice." Les admitted. "But I see it this way, Doc. God gives us life and he gives us death. I think he has a reason for both." Les made a few more strokes with the broom and paused to rest again. "You know I love to eat." He said, and patted the broad expanse of his belly. "But if I never felt hungry, eating would be just a chore. Maybe God gave us death so we can appreciate life."

"I thought you believed in heaven Lester," Jack said. "If I follow your metaphor, our life on Earth is just the appetizer. The main course will be served up above."

"For sure, doc, and that's where you'll get your immortality. You don't need no pill."

"Perhaps God has changed his mind," Jack said. "Maybe the afterlife is filled to capacity with souls, and death can no longer be the doorway to eternity."

Lester leaned on his broom and stared at Jack as if he was a misbehaving child. "Heaven's not like a bucket that only holds so much. The Earth may fill up, but not Heaven."

"But what if there is no heaven, Lester. What if the only road to eternal life is a pill?"

"Oh, there's a heaven all right." Lester said. "You scientists think nothing exists unless you can put a ruler on it." Lester placed his hand on a nearby piece of equipment, a digital pH meter that was flashing 7.00 over and over. "But just cause your fancy equipment don't measure it, don't mean it ain't real. You believe what you want, I'll stick with my own faith."

"So you think science is nothing more than a religion?" Jack said.

"Looks that way to me," Lester said. He finished sweeping and collected the trash cans. "In truth, Doc, I guess that I might be tempted to take your pill, but God often puts temptation in our path. It's how He tests us. Perhaps He is testing you. The Devil is never far away, and all of us are sinners."

"What sin do you think I might be guilty of?"

"Greed, maybe. Lust. Why else would you want to live forever. I like you doc. You're a good man but I don't see you spending an eternity doing God's work."

Lester collected his equipment and left to finish his rounds. When he was done, the world would be fundamentally unchanged. A bit cleaner certainly, but otherwise the same. The same could not be said about Jack's efforts, and like it or not, he was about to change the calculus of life on Earth.

Jack understood, as a biologist, that the underlying goal of organic evolution is eternal life for genes, not individuals, who are simply the tools by which genes gain immortality. If people quit dying they would eventually have to quit reproducing. For the earth, as Lester had suggested, was like a bucket of finite capacity, and it would eventually overflow with immortals.

People naturally held onto what they had, life being no exception, and came to consider it their God-given right. By this philosophy the living had a kind of "right of possession" over those who would never be born and would never even experience life. But could you actually say to somebody "You have seen enough of life, and now it is time for you to give way so someone else, not yet born, can be given a life of their own?" This question went well beyond the usual "right-to-life" arguments of the abortion issue. The child not yet conceived had no legal standing, not even among the anti-abortion advocates, but did that mean it had no moral existence?

Then there were the practical issues. "Saving social security" had become a popular topic of discussion for politicians and economists, but they worried about a future in which there would be too few young workers to support the growing population of the old and retired, not a world in which there were no young people at all.

But it was neither the ethical nor practical issues that bothered Jack the most. He remembered how he and Mary had talked shortly after their marriage about having children, but had decided that they were not "ready" yet. Then she became ill and had to undergo the rigors of radiation and chemotherapy. Under those conditions, pregnancy would have been profoundly unethical. When it became clear that she would not be cured of her cancer, the decision to postpone children became one of their deepest sorrows. Now, Jack realized with a shiver, he had made a discovery that could well lead to a world of childless families.

Jack's thoughts were broken by the ringing of the phone. He was surprised to hear George Potts, from Thomas Jefferson

University, on the other end. Jack could not imagine why he would be calling.

"Jack, I thought you might be able to help us." Potts' voice oozed with sincerity. "I greatly admired your work on the measurement of single-cell metabolic rates. It seems that we have a need for this technique, and I was hoping that you could show one of my postdocs how to do it." Over the years Jack had taught this technique to a handful of students and postdocs and even to a professor on sabbatical. Potts' request was unusual only because it had been a few years since anyone had asked.

"I haven't actually used this protocol myself for quite a while. I am sure there must be others who are using it and have even improved on it."

"I really hope you'll help us out on this," Potts pleaded. "Our lab does little but DNA sequencing and biochemistry, and we want to expand our cell biology capabilities. I know elsewhere your technique is considered old news, but it will be an entirely new approach for us."

"I'm rather busy right now, with the start of the fall semester."

"I'm sure it won't take much of your time. The postdoc I want to send over is very bright and will need no more than a few hours to pick up the technique. I think you met her at a Cell Biology meeting a few years ago. Her name is Meiling Liu."

Jack remembered well the young Chinese women who had salvaged what had been a miserable day, and the memory of her smile ruled the day. With his manuscript in the mail, he could easily afford to take time off from the work that had totally consumed him for so many months. Jack agreed to spend the next afternoon with Liu.

20

Liu was upset with Potts' plan to spy on Keaton. She hated that he had placed her in such an awkward position, and she hated herself even more for caving-in to his demands. But then she hated many things that he had made her do during the past five years. It began when Potts' had requested that she eliminate some data from the first paper she had coauthored with him. A minor experimental result had weakened the conclusions that he wanted to emphasize. Liu felt that the experiment should be included in the manuscript.

Potts had disagreed. "It's a marginal experiment and the result is probably wrong," he had argued, "and we would need to repeat it several times to confirm the result. Why weaken the paper unnecessarily? Once it is published, we will have plenty of time to firm-up the results."

Against her better judgment, Liu had succumbed to Potts and the paper was published without the conflicting data. She had hoped to confirm or disprove the results, but Potts had never let her perform the needed experiments. Later, when his conclusions had been proved to be wrong, he had shrugged it off. "How could we have known?" he said.

Similar incidents had occurred in the following years, and each time Liu had given in to Dr. Potts. Now she was being asked to go beyond the misuse of data, and to engage in a plot against a fellow scientist. In China intrigue and deceit were common as the powerful attempted to cling to their power, and the powerless attempted to get it. That was one reason she had left. In spite of her qualms, Liu had agreed with Potts's plan, and now her remaining hope was that Keaton would not agree to teach her his technique. However, Potts came back just minutes after talking to her with the information that she was scheduled to visit Keaton's lab tomorrow afternoon.

The next morning she fretted over what to wear for her visit to Keaton's lab. Her normal attire was casual, jeans or shorts and a simple blouse, but she thought that this occasion called for a more "professional" look. Her limited wardrobe did not allow much leeway. Eventually she selected a dark-blue cotton skirt and a silk blouse that she had brought with her from China. She showed up promptly at Keaton's lab at one o'clock.

Liu was surprised by how young Dr. Keaton was. Apparently her memory had added extra years to his age since their only prior meeting. He was dressed casually in blue jeans and a short sleeve knit shirt. Liu suddenly felt overdressed. Jack showed her around the lab. It was a typical biology research lab. Every square foot of bench space was occupied by research equipment. Water baths, power supplies, chromatography racks, mixers and assorted glassware were scattered as if a tornado had passed through. Most of one wall was taken up by racks of clear plastic cages in which individual mice could be seen scurrying about. Available floor space was also heavily used. An old model Hercules centrifuge was squeezed next to a scintillation counter at one end of the lab. At the other end sat a CO_2 incubator and a sterilizer. She looked around for an ultra-low temperature freezer. None was visible. Only a standard kitchen refrigerator-freezer, shoved against a bench appeared to be present. The virus, she knew, would be stored in a special freezer that could go down to -80°C, or in a liquid nitrogen freezer, which was even colder. Perhaps there was no virus and Keaton was, as Potts had suggested, a fraud.

"Are you ready to get started?" Keaton asked.

"Sure."

"This can be a rather messy procedure."

Liu felt herself blush at the implied insult. "I am a very careful worker."

"I'm sorry. I didn't mean to suggest that you weren't. It's just that your clothes are much too nice to risk ruining by an inadvertent splash of dye or acid."

"Of course, you're right. Perhaps I could borrow a lab coat."

"Sure, I think we are both about the same size." Keaton stepped behind the refrigerator. A white lab coat was draped over a large apparatus, whose function Liu could not make out. A black object lay on top of the lab coat.

"Shoo," Jack said and brushed the object with his hand. The object moved.

"My god, it's a cat!" Liu said in surprise. The cat slowly stood up and stretched its legs.

"I call him Snuffles. Since I mostly work alone, I keep her around for company."

Snuffles seemed irritated at being awakened, but quickly perked up at the sight of company. She jumped down from her perch and began rubbing against Liu's leg.

"She's adorable." She bent over and scratched the cat behind its ears. The cat purred contentedly. "Does she always sleep there?"

"On hot days. She likes the coolness from the nitrogen." Keaton picked up the lab coat, revealing the squat cylinder of a liquid nitrogen freezer. Liu took a quick glance around. A clipboard hung from a hook on one side. This would list the contents of the freezer.

Keaton handed her the lab coat. "Put this on. We need to get started if we are going to finish today." Liu was nervous and distracted throughout the procedure. Keaton was wonderfully patient and calm as she blundered through each step. Unfortunately the equipment needed was at the end of the lab opposite the liquid nitrogen freezer and she was unable to get a closer look at the clipboard.

"I'm sorry. I am so clumsy today!" Liu confessed at one point as the contents of a flask splattered as she attempted to transfer its contents to a small test tube.

"That is why we wear lab coats." Keaton said patiently.

Finally they were done. Liu unbuttoned her lab coat. "I should put the cat's bed back." As she walked across the lab she felt that Keaton was watching her, but when she looked back he was busy cleaning up the bench. Instead of walking directly to the nitrogen freezer she took the short detour to the side of the lab where the mouse cages were stacked. An identification card had been inserted into a slot, provided for that purpose, on the front of each cage. Key information, such as the age and treatment history of the animal within, would be recorded on these cards. Afraid to stop, she was only able to read one of the labels as she walked past. At the top of the card was written 317C, presumably the animal's code number, and below that was a date and the notation "AAV-X32 0.1 ml."

AAV stood for the adeno-associated virus, the one that Keaton claimed to have modified for his experiments. She remembered from the paper that he had gone through thirty-two trials before developing a virus with the right properties. The date indicated that the mouse was more than four years old, well past its normal life span, but the animal, visible behind the clear plastic of the cage, looked young and vigorous.

She reached the freezer. The clipboard was attached by a piece of string tied to the handle of the lid. It was hanging on the opposite side, facing the wall a few inches away. It would be impossible to read without picking it up, or kneeling down. She saw that the cat had followed her, perhaps anxious to get her bed back. "What a nice pussy cat." She cooed, and bent down to pet it. As she stroked the cat's back, she glanced at the clipboard.

"She's a wonderful cat, but she is addicted to back rubs." Liu jumped to her feet. She had not heard Keaton walk up behind her. "No need to stop, it's a harmless addiction. At least to the cat, but sometimes she drives me nuts."

"You gave me a start. I didn't hear you come up behind me."

"I just wanted to check the level of nitrogen in the freezer before the cat went back to sleep." He pulled open a nearby drawer and took out a key, which he inserted into a padlock that held the lid in place. "You might want to stand back," he said. "Liquid nitrogen is very dangerous. If some splashes into your eyes, it can freeze the tissue instantly."

Liu stepped back, insulted that Keaton assumed that she was unaware of the dangers of liquid nitrogen.

"Of course I'm sure you know that already," he said.

"Yes, of course," Liu said, smiling. "We use liquid nitrogen for storing all of our DNA stocks." Keaton put on a pair of safety goggles and then removed the foam lid from the freezer, which he placed on a nearby bench. A wooden yardstick was leaning against the wall, and Keaton picked it up and stuck it into the opening. The location of the frost line would indicate the amount of nitrogen remaining in the freezer.

The clipboard was hanging on the side of the lid facing Liu. Keaton pulled the yardstick from the freezer to check the frost line, and Liu used the moment to glance at the clipboard. To a molecular biologist most of the entries were familiar, but among the HIND-IIs and Deoxy-ATPs the letters AAV-X32 jumped out at her. She made a mental note: The virus was in rack two, box three.

"The nitrogen level is fine. You can give Snuffles her bed back." Liu managed to avoid jumping this time. She placed the lab coat back over the freezer. The cat quickly leaped back up, and after a few quick turns lied down and fell asleep.

"Are you allowed to have a cat in the lab?"

"I don't know. Nobody in authority apparently never thought to ban lab cats, and until they do, Snuffles stays."

Liu smiled. "You would do well in China. The bureaucrats keep attempting to control what people can do, the people keep finding new ways to do what they want."

"We call them loopholes."

"What?"

"A loophole is a gap in a law. If you can find the loop hole, you can violate the spirit of a law, but not the law."

"So you like loopholes?"

"Don't you? I would guess you are here in the US because our immigration laws are less than perfect."

Liu smiled. "Maybe so, or maybe no US citizen can do what I do. That's what Dr. Potts said on my visa application, and I would never disagree with one so famous."

Keaton laughed. "A good philosophy," he said. "You should do well in America."

The cat stirred. It rose to its feet, made a couple of perfunctory turns and lay down again. "Aren't you worried the cat will knock something over?"

"Cats are naturally careful. I think it comes from their skill as stalkers. You could never catch a mouse if you kept bumping into things. In any case she usually sleeps during the day, and comes home with me in the evenings. It's the house she makes a wreck of."

"Your wife doesn't mind?"

"I'm not married," he said. He seemed about to say something more, but then the door of the lab opened. A large black man entered, carrying a broom and pushing a janitor's cart ahead of him.

"Hey, Doc, get yourself a new assistant?" the man said. He put down his broom and held out his huge hand to Liu. "Hi, I'm Lester." Liu bowed politely and let her hand get engulfed by his. "I hope Doc's treating you good girl. He gives you any trouble you just come to me. I'll put him right."

"This is Meiling Liu," Keaton said. "She is just here for the day, Lester, so don't get your hopes up."

Les laughed, causing his belly to shake ominously. "I always have my hopes up Doc. These days that's about all I am able to get up."

Liu blushed and Keaton moved to save her from further embarrassment. "Don't mind him, Liu. Ever since my wife died he has been telling me that I should get a new woman."

"Man's not whole without a woman," Lester said. He turned to Liu. "What do you think?"

Liu shook her head. "A woman can't make a man whole. He must be a whole man already if a woman is to love him."

"I think you have a bit of the truth there," Lester said. "Been telling my wife for years she got to love the whole me, and to quit ragging me to lose weight." He looked at Liu and made a show of eyeing her. "Now you girl, you got to put some meat on your bones. Not healthy to be so skinny."

"Don't mind Lester," Keaton interjected. "He gets his kicks trying to embarrass young ladies. It just means he likes you." He looked at his watch. "I'm getting hungry. Are you?"

In truth Liu was famished, having been so nervous before coming to Keaton's lab she had skipped lunch. Liu had accomplished her purpose, and knew she should be leaving. Potts would be anxiously awaiting her report, but Keaton was an interesting man. Perhaps she should find out more about him – information that could be valuable when Potts tried to convince Keaton to share the virus. Liu agreed to join Keaton for dinner, and they left the lab together.

Keaton led Liu a couple of blocks to where his car was parked. "The restaurants around here are all jammed at this hour. I know a nice quiet place that's not far."

They drove across the Schuylkill River and north along Kelly Drive. A few minutes later they pulled into a parking lot. "Do you like Korean food?" Keaton asked Liu as they entered the restaurant.

"Korean?" Liu said. The sign over the entrance read "West River Japanese Restaurant."

"The name is a bit confusing," Keaton said. "The restaurant is actually owned by a Korean family, and most of the menu is Korean."

"But aren't we on the east side of the river?"

"Yes, but apparently the term 'east river' is associated with bad luck in Korea, so the owner felt the need for a virtual move." They were led to a table that was next to a small indoor fountain. Water sprayed from a statue that appeared to be of Italian origin.

"I have never had Korean food, or Japanese," Liu said, as she looked over her menu. Jack expressed surprise to learn that Liu had never eaten Japanese food. "There are few Japanese restaurants in China, or of any other foreign country. I think even McDonalds would have difficulty making money there."

"But you've been in the US for, what … about five years?"

"Almost six." Liu admitted. "How did you guess?"

"I remember you from the Cell Biology meeting a few years ago. Your English is much better now. You were just off of the boat when we first met."

Liu was surprised, and flattered, that Keaton remembered her. Their discussion had been very brief. "You really remember me?"

"Sure I do. Don't you remember me?"

"Yes, but you were a famous scientist and I was just a young postdoc."

Keaton laughed "You thought I was famous?"

"I read your papers in China. To me you were famous."

An elderly woman came out of the kitchen and spied Jack. "Ah, Mr. Jack. Where you been. You not come for months. I get you some kimchee?"

"Not today." Keaton said. "Liu, this is the owner, Kimmie Wee."

Liu shook hands with Mrs. Wee "You must come here often Dr. Keaton," she said as Mrs. Wee scurried off to welcome other customers.

"Please call me Jack. If someone hears you call me doctor they may want me to remove their appendix."

"OK … Jack." She said awkwardly.

"I've actually only been here three or four times. Mrs. Wee is famous for remembering the names of everybody who eats in her restaurant. If you come back a year from now, she will remember your name, what you had eaten and make you feel guilty for not coming back sooner." Mrs. Wee reappeared with a platter of steamed dumplings.

"No charge," she said, placing the complimentary serving of dumplings on the table. "Fish very good today. I get sushi for both?" Liu had never eaten sushi, and was hesitant to eat raw fish, but yielded to Jacks assurances that it was delicious. The combination sushi platter that Jack ordered was shortly delivered to their table. Liu found the sweet rice delicious. She picked up a bit of the green paste that sat in a mound next to a pile of pickled ginger. The fumes from the fiery material exploded in her mouth, and up into her nose. Tears flowed from her eyes.

Jack handed her a glass of water which she gratefully swallowed. "I guess you weren't kidding about never having Japanese food. The green stuff is wasabi, a spicy horseradish powder." Jack showed her how to mix the wasabi paste with soy sauce to use for dipping the sushi. The spicy, salty mix was a perfect balance to the sweetness of the rice. Jack picked up a piece of sushi with his chopsticks. Liu noticed that he was struggling to grip the sushi properly and she was not surprised when it slipped from his grasp and fell onto his lap. "Damn" He muttered.

"You are not holding the chopsticks properly." Liu held up her chopsticks and displayed the proper grip. "Hold the lower stick steady and move just the upper one to grab the food." Jack attempted to use the same grip, but botched it badly. Liu placed her hand on his to demonstrate the proper position. If asked, Liu would have been hard-pressed to say when she had physically touched another person, man or woman. No doubt she had made some casual contacts – the handshake with a complete stranger, the brushing of bodies in a crowd – but nothing like she now experienced. Not since her departure from China, when she had been hugged by, and hugged in return, her family and her friends had she had meaningful human contact. Her heart pounded as she moved her fingers over Keaton's hand and positioned the chopstick correctly.

"Try it now." She said, as calmly as she could, and removed her hand from his.

Jack picked up a piece of sushi between the tips of the chopsticks and transferred it to his mouth. "That works much better. Thank you. Someday I'll show you how to use a fork properly."

Liu stiffened, but before she could reply Jack was already attempting to recover from his clumsy attempt at humor. "I'm sorry," he said. "That was a terrible thing for me to say."

"Not at all," Liu said. "It took me years to stop holding a fork like this." Liu picked up a fork and held it across her palm, like one might hold a hammer. "Then one day in a restaurant I saw a mother yell at her child for holding his fork wrong, and I realized I was holding mine the same way."

"You have very soft hands," he said. "You must take good care of them."

Liu blushed. "Thank you. It must be the gloves. Dr. Potts insists that we wear latex gloves whenever we are in the lab, even if we are just writing notes. Sometimes I wear gloves ten or twelve hours a day."

"Potts is very strict?"

"He has his rules. That is why he is so successful. Everyone has a specific job to do and if everyone is productive we get the results we need."

"That doesn't leave much room for creativity."

Liu sighed. She hated working for Potts, who had sucked the pleasure from science. She could not, however, admit this to Keaton.

Keaton appeared to sense that Liu was bothered by his question. He changed the topic. "Do you remember what you said to me when we first met?"

"No, not exactly."

"'You are very brave.' I have always wondered what you meant by that."

Liu remembered how she had been struck by how unorthodox Keaton's results had been. The idea that satellite DNA could have a function in controlling aging was without precedent. She must have realized even then that Keaton would be subject to disdain and professional attacks. This was dangerous territory. She would need to be careful not to reveal how much she knew of Jack's experiments. "That was a long time ago." She said. "What I remember was that your results were very controversial." Liu knew that, as one scientist talking to another, she should ask about his work. "Did you ever publish your results?" Her voice cracked as she said this, and she thought that the falseness of her question must be obvious to Jack.

"No, not yet." Liu did not ask for further clarification, which Jack must have found a little strange. A popular topic of dinner conversation among scientists was the trials and tribulations of getting papers published. Every researcher had a favorite story of how they had been screwed by an incompetent reviewer or editor. Liu did not request, and Jack did not offer, any further explanation of his failure to publish his results.

For the rest of the dinner they chatted aimlessly about various non-consequential topics. Liu learned a bit of Keaton's life and experiences, while Liu told him about her family back in Beijing. She remembered few of the details, which were of little importance, but found herself entranced by the conversation. It had been months, perhaps years, since she had engaged in the mundane and ordinary act of social conversation with a man.

After dinner Jack suggested a walk along Main Street in the nearby Manyunk section of the city, which Liu quickly agreed to. They walked along the street stopping to enter the various arts-and-crafts stores that were scattered among the restaurants and tony women's shops that featured Gucci-designs that were beautiful if impractical. Liu was fascinated by the art work in a shop that specialized in American Indian crafts. A glass shelf was lined with small rocks, about the size of a quarter, each of which had been sculpted into the image of an animal.

"These are beautiful," Liu said. She picked up a bluish stone, flecked with white quartz, which had been carved into an exquisitely detailed image of an eagle.

"That's a Zuni Indian fetish." Jack explained. "Traditionally the fetishes were carried by hunters and warriors to bring good luck. Nowadays they are a major source of income to the tribe. Would you like one?"

"Of course, they are wonderful."

Jack took the stone from her. "It's yours then." He turned and walked to the checkout counter. "How much is this?" he asked the young woman who was managing the shop.

Liu was stunned. She had interpreted Jack's question to be hypothetical, not an offer to buy it for her. Struck speechless, she could only watch as Jack paid for the stone. Liu had very little experience with men – her life had been focused on her career – but she knew that accepting a gift such as the carved stone was taking their relationship to a new level. "You shouldn't have" she said weakly, as Keaton returned with the stone. That she should reject the gift was obvious. She had just finished spying in his lab for Dr. Potts, and the last thing she should do now was become entangled in a relationship with him. Yet she held out her hand and took the stone. "You shouldn't have," she said again.

"Don't worry. It didn't cost very much and I could see that you really liked it. Maybe I could come and visit it sometime."

When fear and desire collide, fear almost always wins. A biologist might argue that this is a natural consequence of Darwinian evolution. Faced with the choice between a tempting bit of fruit hanging at the end of a branch, and the possibility of a long fall to the ground if the branch should break, it is wise to choose caution. Liu's fears were as indefinite as that of the child in a dark room and as immediate as the soldier's on the eve of battle. It was the fear of the unseen and the unknowable, and it carried the day.

Liu thrust the stone back into Keaton's hand. "I am sorry," she said coldly. "I really can't take it. Would you take me back to my car now? I should be going home."

21

The next day, Potts met Hopkins for lunch at an expensive steak house in Manyunk. They each ordered a grilled Porterhouse, and made small talk while they waited for their food. It wasn't until they had eaten that Hopkins got to the point of the meeting.

"So George, what have you got for me?"

"I have done some research," Potts began. He would not explain how he had obtained his information, and he knew that Hopkins would not ask. The previous evening he had gone to Liu's apartment, something he had never done before, when she had failed to answer her phone. Liu had been out to dinner with Keaton, who apparently had been attracted to her. She did not want to talk about her visit in detail, but when pressed she provided him with enough information to justify a meeting with Hopkins. "It appears that the virus is for real. There are apparently mice in his lab that are twice as old as one would normally live."

"Did you find out where the virus is stored?" Hopkins asked.

"There is a liquid nitrogen freezer in his lab, and the log book suggests that's where the virus is."

"Can we get it?"

"What do you mean? Buy the virus from Keaton? I'm sure that Keaton will not part with his precious virus for any money we can give him. Why should he, when it will be worth millions to the man with the patent? I thought we discussed this already."

"We did, but I am not interested in buying it, not if we can get it some other way."

Potts was prepared for Hopkins suggestion, and had decided that he would not participate in an outright theft of the virus. After their discussion at the golf course, Potts had carefully considered his options. He had never been shy about using whatever techniques were necessary to achieve success, and while sometimes they were on the ethical borderline, they were always legal. Potts considered himself typical of most scientists in his peer group, those who had reached the top levels of their discipline. They all, or so Potts believed, published only selected data in papers, made photographs 'clearer' with creative use of computer technology or made use of confidential data that were in grants and papers they reviewed. These and similar acts were so common among scientists that they hardly seemed unethical anymore, but stealing experimental materials was not only scientifically unethical, it was criminal. He could not afford to be sucked into Hopkins dangerous schemes. Nevertheless, he wanted Keaton's virus. Fortunately there was an alternative approach.

"You don't need the virus itself." He explained. "All you need is the DNA sequence that Keaton introduced into the virus. If I had the sequence data I could put my lab to work and have a functional virus in two, maybe three, months."

Hopkins considered this information. "That may still be too slow. It is likely that Keaton will have his paper published before then, and once the data is public we have lost our opportunity."

"You forget. The paper was sent to me for review. I could easily hold on to it for a month or two before the editor insists on a response. Even then I could demand revisions that could take several more weeks."

"If you had the DNA sequence data, and I gave you the resources, could you construct a virus in less than a month?"

"Yes, if I had an unlimited budget and access to the facilities at BiTech," Potts admitted.

"You've got it," Hopkins said. "But all of BiTech's money and resources won't help if we don't have the sequence. Keaton had the foresight to remove that critical data from his manuscript. How do you propose to get it?"

"It's possible we can get the sequence information from his lab. He may have a copy of the full manuscript lying around, and even if he does not, the data must be in his computer. My postdoc, Liu, apparently hit it off with Keaton. I am sure she can get back into his lab."

"Get it done," Hopkins said.

Potts returned to the lab and immediately called Liu into his office. "I want to thank you for the information that you brought back from your visit with Keaton. Your skills as a scientific observer are very impressive indeed."

"Thank you," Liu said coldly.

"As I explained to you, the information you got was necessary for me to make a judgment on the validity of Keaton's results. The labels on his mouse cages and his freezer inventory were useful information, but I find it suspicious."

"Why is that? The labels corresponded exactly to the information in his manuscript."

"That's the point. Here is a guy that keeps the most critical part of his work secret, and yet anybody can walk into his lab and see that he has made an unbelievable discovery. Furthermore, it is a routine practice in well-run labs to use encrypted labels on research animals. I always insist on this in my lab, as you well know. Using a blind protocol is simple, and important, so why didn't Keaton do it?"

Liu considered this argument. "I don't know." Liu admitted. "He seems to be an excellent researcher. Perhaps he thought it was unnecessary to use encrypted labels."

"Perhaps." Potts grunted in disbelief. He got to the point. "The key information in the manuscript is the sequence of the virus DNA. He claims that he kept it secret because he didn't want it revealed prior to the actual publication of the data. But maybe there is no such sequence. Perhaps he blocked it out of the paper because he hasn't come up with a believable lie yet."

Potts picked up a USB flash drive from his desk and handed it to Liu. He had abandoned the thought of looking for a complete printed version of Keaton's manuscript. Even if Keaton was careless enough to leave one lying around, it would be too risky to steal it. Fortunately, the needed data were certain to be on his computer's hard drive, and could be copied without leaving a trace. He explained the situation to Liu. "If the sequence data actually exists, it will be stored in his computer, either by itself or in the file that contains the original version of his paper. I want you to get a copy of the sequence and bring it back here."

Liu looked stunned. "I can't do that," she said as firmly as she could.

"You did excellent work so far obtaining information, but I need more facts."

"That was information openly visible to anybody that cared to look. Now you are asking me to break into Keaton's computer files."

Potts fully expected Liu to object, but he thought he could turn her around. The key was to find the right approach. He knew that threats alone would not work, although they could be important, and that she would have to believe that what she was acting for good reasons. He could only hope that his tactics would succeed. "Consider my problem, Liu. A manuscript, reporting an incredible result of shattering importance, is sent to me for review. But the most significant data is not given. If I reject it, I may become the intolerant fool that blocked publication of the most important discovery of the century. If I accept the paper, and it turns out the results are false, I become the idiot that accepted a manuscript without even seeing the most important part of the data. Keaton has placed me in a no-win situation."

"Why don't you call him and demand the sequence data?"

"You know that confidentiality of reviewers is critical to editors. I would never review another manuscript if I did that." Potts made his voice as pleading as he could. "I really need your help here Liu. You know that I have done everything I could to be of help to you. It was my pleasure to bring you over from China and to see that you got your visa renewed each year." The threat was unstated, but Potts assumed Liu would make the obvious connection. "Now I need you to do me a favor. I know you are concerned about the ethics here, but this is a tricky situation. It is not my fault that Keaton chose not to reveal all of the data in his manuscript. All I am asking for is a chance to review the full document, and to keep confidentiality intact. I don't see how this can be considered unreasonable."

"You may be right Dr. Potts, but I don't see how I could possibly get access to Keaton's computer."

Potts tried to refrain from smiling. Potts had enough experience with various academic and government committees that he had discovered one of the secrets of getting his way. You try to get your opponents to move from the position that a course of action is "wrong" to the position that it is "impossible." Then you describe a course of action that could succeed, putting them in an untenable position. It had been almost too easy to get Liu to step into his trap.

"I don't think it will be that difficult. You said that Keaton wanted to see you again. Call him and suggest a lunch date. It will have to be on a Tuesday or Thursday."

"Why those days?"

"Because those are the days that he teaches. I checked the class schedule on Drexel's Web page. He teaches from ten to eleven thirty in the morning. You show up for lunch before he goes to class. Tell him you have to write a letter, or some such thing. From what you have told me about Keaton, I am sure he will not hesitate to let you use his computer."

22

Liu left Potts office and went to her lab bench. A dozen DNA samples set in an ice bucket, waiting to be analyzed. Using an automatic pipette, she removed five microliters, a barely visible drop, of the first solution. The tip of the pipette, barely thicker than a needle, shivered in her hand, and refused to find its way into the narrow slot at the top of an electrophoresis gel. She put the pipette down and took a deep breath to calm herself.

"Damn," she muttered. "Damn, damn, damn." The curses were strangely calming, like an ancient Buddhist chant. As much as she hated the thought, she would do as Potts wanted. Like most complex decisions more than one factor went into the equation. Liu could not have said if she made her decision because Potts had maneuvered her into a corner, or because she was afraid he would carry out his implied threats, or because she wanted to see Keaton again. For whatever reason, she had agreed to Potts' plan to get the data from Keaton's computer.

But that was not the only decision she made at that moment. She vowed to herself that this would be the last job she would do for him. It was time to step up her efforts to find another research position. The one positive outcome of the unethical task that Potts was demanding of her was that it gave Liu, for the first time, a lever to use against him. He would *have to* help her find a new job!

After transferring the DNA solutions, Liu phoned Keaton. She began by apologizing for her behavior the previous day. "I am not used to receiving presents."

"I understand," Keaton said. "It was presumptuous of me. But believe me, I didn't have any ulterior motives."

"I wouldn't be upset if you did." Liu felt the warmth of embarrassment spreading through her cheeks, and quickly changed the subject to the reason for her call. She explained that she had an errand to run near Drexel the next morning, and could meet him for lunch. Keaton was happy to agree.

"I do have another favor to ask," she said. "My errand will be done by ten in the morning, and I have some letters to write. Would it be possible to borrow your computer for a few minutes?"

"Sure, that would be no problem. I have to teach from ten to eleven thirty and you are welcome to use my office while I am gone."

Liu showed up at Keaton's lab just before ten o'clock. This gave him just a few minutes to greet her and to show her to the computer. "I hope you don't need to print your letter. I may be low on ink."

"Thank you. I brought a flash drive to save it on," Liu said, and removed the thumb-sized device from her pocket. Keaton left and Liu sat down. For a few minutes she sat, hands on her lap, doing nothing but staring at the computer on Keaton's desk. A "Star field" screen saver was running. Bright dots formed, as by magic, in the center of the screen and flew outwards, growing larger and larger, until they disappeared at the edges. The flying dots on the screen were very relaxing, even hypnotic. Liu considered just sitting there and watching the dots fly until Jack returned. Yes, that was just what she would do. When she reported to Dr. Potts she could simply say that, try as she might, she couldn't find the sequence information on the computer. Keaton, she would argue, may have the data stored on a CDROM or a flash drive, which could be hidden almost anywhere, or even locked up for extra security. She could also suggest that Dr. Potts was correct when he proposed that the virus did not exist at all. Potts would just have to accept her word.

She was brought back to reality by the sudden appearance of the cat who, apparently tired of watching the mice, had jumped up on the desk. The cat walked up to Liu, hoping for some attention. As Liu moved her hand to scratch the cat's ears, she brushed the hanging cord of the computer mouse, moving it just slightly, but enough to alert the computer. The flying dots disappeared, to be replaced by the familiar Windows screen.

It would be worthwhile while she was here, Liu decided, to at least check if the virus sequence actually existed. She could still tell Potts that she couldn't recover it. She double-clicked on the Word icon and waited for the program to load. Clicking on "Files" pulled down a list of commands, at the bottom of which were the names of the last ten files that had been worked on. The first four files were labeled as "exams" or "letters" but below them were two files named "Science ms v1" and "Science ms v2" that caught her eye. She clicked on the "v2" file and the text of Keaton's Science paper appeared on the screen. Quickly she scrolled down to the section in which the virus sequence was supposed to be. The sequence shown was a string of X's, just as it was in the submitted paper. She closed the v2 file and clicked on v1, but instead of a document a box appeared with the instructions "Enter password." Liu was both disappointed and relieved. Disappointed because she was hoping to find independent confirmation of the reality of the immortality virus. Relieved because she would not have to decide to withhold the sequence information from Potts. The truth, in this case, would suffice.

Keaton would not be back for more than an hour and Liu looked for something to occupy herself. The cat walked in front of the computer and offered up her backside for a scratch. Liu petted the cat for a while until both she and the cat tired of it. The dialog box, with its request for a password, was still on the computer screen, demanding her attention. She would close the program before Jack returned, but it would be interesting, since she had nothing else to do, to see if she could guess the password. No doubt it would be a simple number-letter combination that would be easy to remember. If she knew Keaton's birthday or social security number, she could try permutations of those. Of course it could be something simpler.

She placed her hands on the keyboard and began typing. Various permutations of Keaton's name were the logical thing to try, but none of her guesses were successful. She might as well give up. Below the desk the cat had found Liu's leg and she felt the soft caress of its fur against her ankle. Liu entered SNUFFLES into the password box. The box disappeared and was quickly replaced by the familiar words of the title page of Keaton's manuscript. She scrolled down and quickly found the page where the virus DNA sequence should be. The string of A's, T's, G's and C's filled several lines of text.

Liu hands shook as she attempted to insert the flash drive into its narrow receptacle in the computer and it took a few tries before she was successful. When the drive was properly installed, she clicked on File, then on Save As. Finally she selected the flash drive and hit the enter key. She was rewarded with the familiar flying folder, indicating the transfer of the file. After a few seconds the light went out and she removed the drive. She was about to place it in her pocket, when it occurred to her that the drive was unlabeled. In Dr. Potts laboratory everything must have a label. Even a flask that held nothing but waste water had to be labeled "waste water." Liu looked around for a pen. Nothing was visible on the desk. She pulled open the narrow drawer in the front and found, as expected, an assortment of pens and markers.

As she picked up a marking pen a flash of color caught her eye, and she pulled the drawer open another inch. The Zuni Indian stone with its exquisitely carved eagle stared up at her. Out of guilt, she had rejected the gift from Keaton. Perhaps she should have taken it. Placed in a conspicuous spot, the carved stone would have served as a daily reminder of her failings.

In China every neighborhood had at least one person (always, it seemed, an old woman with deep winkles and white hair) who would interpret omens for a small fee. To the Chinese almost anything could be viewed as a sign of a coming event or as guidance for a course of action. The implications of a dropped cup of tea could make even a rational person fear to leave the house. As a scientist Liu had always laughed at these superstitions. Yet she was herself ingrained with the Chinese traditions and now the Indian stone spoke to her. Liu placed the flash drive back into the computer. She opened Windows Explorer and selected the flash drive. She hit the delete key and watched with satisfaction as the file name disappeared from the screen. After removing the drive she closed all of the active programs and returned the computer to its original status. Keaton returned from teaching about twenty minutes later.

23

Jack returned from class to find Liu sitting at his desk with Snuffles curled up on her lap.

"Did you get your letter written? I hope the cat didn't bother you too much."

"She was no trouble. Thank you for the use of your computer."

"My pleasure," Jack said. "Are you ready for lunch?"

Jack and Liu left the lab together and walked down Spruce Street to the K.C. Steak House, an inexpensive chain restaurant popular with students and faculty. As he strolled alongside Liu, he thought how strange it was that he could still feel the adolescent nervousness of a first date, if that was what this was. He wondered how she felt. Since he had come back to the lab from teaching, Liu had said only a few words to him, and seemed tense and distracted. Jack hoped this was not a bad sign.

At the restaurant, a line of people, mostly young and dressed in jeans and carrying bulging knapsacks, stretched out the door. "It appears to be crowded," Jack noted unnecessarily.

"There must be other restaurants nearby that aren't so popular," Liu said. "I am not particular what I eat."

"Neither am I, but I hate waiting in lines." Jack waved his hand up 34th Street, where the campus buildings and store fronts gave way to houses and apartments. "My house is only a few blocks from here. I can whip us up a decent meal in minutes."

Liu hesitated. "I don't want you to go to any trouble. We could just grab a sandwich from one of the food trucks on campus."

"We would still need a place to sit down to eat."

Jack lived in an aging three-story brick townhouse typical of the Powlton neighborhood. It was not the best part of town, or the best of houses, but it had been all he and Mary could afford when they had come to Philadelphia. Mary hated the house, and their plan had been to move as soon as he got tenure and the raise in salary that would come with it. Now that he had more than enough money to live in a better location, he had no reason to do so.

Inside the house, Jack led Liu directly to the small kitchen and dining area at the rear, hoping to minimize the impact of his disheveled living room. "Please ignore the mess," he said. "I am not much of a housekeeper."

"I think it's fine. It looks lived in."

In the refrigerator Jack found six carrots, a head of broccoli and some mushrooms. He began to doubt the wisdom of having offered to make lunch, but he would do the best he could. "Not much here," he muttered. "I wonder what Sara would do with these?"

"Sara … " Liu said, looking puzzled. "Was that your wife?"

"No," Jack said, smiling at the misunderstanding. "I was referring to Sara Moulton. She has a television cooking show that I watch sometimes."

"Oh," Liu said. She glanced around the room. "When did your wife die?"

Jack realized that she must have taken note of the flowery curtains and the pink tones of the kitchen. "About six years ago."

"I'm sorry," Liu said. "I shouldn't pry."

"That's OK." Jack removed the vegetables from the refrigerator, and quickly changed the subject. "Would you like pasta with these?" He asked.

"That will be fine."

Jack wasted little time and he quickly prepared a dish of linguine and vegetables with a sauce made of canned chicken broth and flour. He did the best he could to make the table setting attractive, breaking out the cloth napkins for the first time in months and using the "good china." (The china had been Mary's idea, since Jack thought it silly to spend so much money on something too fragile to go in a dishwasher.) Just fifteen minutes after he had started the water boiling for the pasta, they sat down to eat.

"This is delicious," Liu said. "Do you cook a lot?"

"Not anymore. When I was married I did most of the cooking, but it is not much fun cooking just for yourself."

Liu sighed in agreement. "Yes, I know what you mean. It's like scientific research. Without the recognition and intrest of others it's hard to keep up your enthusiasm."

"I looked at some of your recent research publications last night," Jack said. "You do very nice work."

"Thank you." Liu said, blushing. "But I wasn't fishing for a compliment."

"I was serious." Jack had, in truth, been impressed with the quality of Liu's work. It displayed evidence of creativity and intelligence. There were also some inexplicable weaknesses. "One thing did bother me however." Jack continued. "In your experiments on the mechanism of DNA repair, you never looked at the temperature dependence of the reaction. The double helix may have started to unwind at the temperature you used. If so, wouldn't that change your conclusions?"

The color went out of Liu's face, and her eyes filled with moisture. "Maybe," she said, her voice tense.

Jack was stunned at her response to what, he had thought, was a minor criticism. Was she that sensitive? "I'm sorry," he said quickly. "It's not important. Many people would have missed the significance of that experiment."

"I didn't miss it," Liu said, her voice barely audible across the tiny kitchen table. "I told Dr. Potts that we should test the effects of temperature."

"What did he say?"

"He said there wasn't time for more experiments, and that he needed to get whatever results I had published as soon as possible." Liu paused to take a sip of water and to finish the last of her meal. "Dr. Potts is always concerned about his rate of publication. Granting agencies pay a lot of attention to that. I'm sure you understand."

"Yes, I certainly do. You can't run a large lab without money, and that means producing a constant flow of papers to keep the grants coming in." Jack saw in Liu's face that it was time to change the subject. "Would you like some dessert? I think I have some ice cream."

"No. I'm fine," Liu said softly. She stood up and started gathering the plates. "I'll help you clean the dishes."

Liu washed the few dishes they had used, while Jack dried. When Liu was finished, she wiped her hands with a paper towel and turned to look at Jack. "I did that experiment," she said.

"Yes, I thought you must have."

Liu sighed and gripped the edge of the sink. "After the paper was submitted, I tested the effects of temperature, even though Dr. Potts had said not to. Your concerns were well placed. The new data proved that we had misinterpreted our earlier results."

"What did you do?"

"I took the results to Dr. Potts ..." Liu paused to wipe her face with the towel. "He told me to forget about it. I said we should submit a correction."

"I don't remember seeing anything in your publications ..."

Liu interrupted him. "Potts said that if I ever told anyone about the results ..." She paused to gain control over her quivering voice. "that I would never work as a scientist in this country again." Liu covered her face with the towel and behind this thin protection began to sob.

Jack could think of nothing to say. Wordless, he moved to Liu and took her in his arms. She let the towel fall from her face and buried her cheek in his shoulder. He held her close, but loosely, allowing her chest tremble against his. After a few moments her sobbing eased, and the trembling was replaced by easy rise and fall of breathing.

After a while, but all too soon, Liu pushed herself away. "I'm sorry," she said, and wiped her face once more.

"You have every reason to be upset." He reassured Liu gently. Jack took the towel from her and used it to blot some moisture from her cheeks that she had missed. "Why didn't you leave Potts? You could find another job."

Liu sighed. "It's not as easy as that. There are visa problems. Letters of recommendation …" She seemed on the verge of tears again.

"I could help."

Liu forced a weak smile. "Thank you," she said. And then, "I think I should be going home now."

They walked in silence back to the campus. When they reached the entrance to the biology building, and the time to part, Jack said, "Can I see you again?"

"Yes. I would like that." Liu said, and smiled the smile that Jack remembered so well.

24

Potts was not pleased with the report that Liu brought back from Drexel. He suspected that she had not done a thorough job of examining Keaton's computer files, but there was nothing Potts could do about it. The bitter fact was that it was Keaton, and not Potts, who had made the scientific breakthrough of the century. The pill was bitter indeed, but would just have to be swallowed. There was no point in delaying the inevitable, and Potts called Hopkins to give him the bad news.

Hopkins listened quietly until Potts had finished. When he spoke, he was brief and to the point. "We need to talk about our options. But not over the phone. Do you know how to get to Valley Green?"

Potts had never been to the Wissahickon section of Fairmont Park, which was mostly known for its forested trails and was of little interest to him. He joined Hopkins in the parking lot and then followed him across a stone bridge and onto a dirt path that led into the woods.

"Beautiful, isn't it?" Hopkins said. "Hard to believe we are still in Philadelphia."

Potts nodded politely. He did not understand the charm that some people found in dirt and trees, but they were completely alone on the trail, and Potts quickly got the point of their excursion into wilderness. "So what do we do now? Either the sequence data is not accessible, as Liu claimed, or she did not make a serious effort to find it. Either way, I can't send Liu back to Keaton's lab."

"There must be a way to get the virus's DNA sequence before it becomes public knowledge?"

"Sure, if we had a sample of the virus," Potts replied.

"How much would you need?"

"A small amount, less than a drop, would be more than enough for DNA analysis."

"If we took some of Keaton's virus, would he be able to detect that it was gone?"

Potts shook his head. "Not likely. The amount that we would need would never be missed. In fact, it would be nearly impossible to prove that any of the virus had been taken. " Potts did not like the direction the conversation had taken. "If you are thinking about stealing the virus, count me out."

"I thought you wanted it."

"Of course I do, but not if I risk ruining my career … and going to jail."

"I am not suggesting you do it yourself. Send your Chinese girl back to Keaton's lab to finish her work."

Potts shook his head. "Liu would never do it, and I won't ask her. She can be manipulated or coerced, but only to a point. In my judgment, she would never agree to steal the virus, and even if she did, could not be trusted to keep her mouth shut."

Hopkins response was immediate. "We will have to use other resources to get our hands on the virus. Liu thinks the samples are stored in a nitrogen freezer in the lab?"

"Yes, based on a notation in the logbook. It also makes sense that he would keep the virus in liquid nitrogen to maintain its activity."

"Where are his 'immortal' mice?"

"They are in his lab also."

Hopkins expressed surprise at this. BiTech and all of the major Universities that Hopkins dealt with were equipped with separate, dedicated animal facilities.

"Drexel is a primarily a teaching college," Potts explained. "They do relatively little research there. Keaton has a small lab, and it appears that everything is in that one room."

Hopkins seemed to like what he was hearing. "Where is his office?"

"It's in a small room attached to the lab."

"This was almost too good to be true. Where is his secretary?"

Potts almost laughed at this question. A private university like Drexel, which was barely able to meet its costs each year, did not provide individual faculty members with personal secretaries. He explained this to Hopkins.

Hopkins visibly brightened. "This should be an easy assignment for Misha."

"Who is Misha? What assignment are you talking about?"

"He is a guy who has done sensitive jobs for me in the past. I want you to meet him and give him the necessary details."

"Sensitive jobs?" Potts repeated. "What sensitive jobs?" Hopkins did not respond, and didn't have to. "I told you, I have no intention of getting involved in something illegal."

"The risk is minimal. Misha is a professional, and there will be no trail that leads to you, or to me."

"That's irrelevant." Potts said, although he saw that it was quite relevant. Ethical arguments, particularly from Potts, would carry no weight with Hopkins, and Potts tried a different approach. "Even if you succeeded in getting a sample of the virus, Keaton is too far ahead of us. He would still have the remainder of the virus, and the documents to prove that we created the virus first."

"What if we take all of his virus, and make sure that his records, and his lab animals are … unavailable."

"That would make it harder for him, of course, but how do you expect to accomplish that?"

Hopkins hesitated. They had arrived at a wooden bridge that passed over a small, rocky stream. Hopkins stared down into the water for a while. "I am going to tell you some things that I have never told anyone else before," he said after a while, his voice barely audible over the sound of the water. "Nobody, within or outside the company, knows about this, but if we are going to work together it is essential that you are fully informed. Can you handle secrets?"

"Of course."

"Do you know about the fire at the St. Louis BiTech facility?" Potts shook his head. "It was in an old, obsolete building. It was costing us more to keep it open than it was worth. The fire destroyed an unused part of the factory and did enough damage to the working portion that we will need to tear the entire structure down." Hopkins paused for effect. "The fire inspector concluded that the cause of the blaze was careless smoking by a couple of homeless men who were living in the abandoned section of the factory. Of course we will never know for sure, since both men died in the fire."

Potts stared at Hopkins for a minute as he digested this information. "You're telling me that your man Misha was responsible for the St. Louis fire?"

Hopkins just smiled in response, a wordless admission to having conspired to commit arson and murder. This was a dangerous moment, and Potts could not risk being sucked into Hopkins schemes. "Destroying an old factory is one thing, they burn all the time. A lab fire will certainly lead to a serious investigation. Keaton will not overlook the disappearance of his virus, and he will know the fire was not an accident, no matter how good this Misha is."

"That's easy to take care of. We will remove his immortality virus from its container, and replace it with our own version of the adeno-virus. As far as Keaton will know the fire will be an ordinary lab accident, and it will be months before he discovers that his precious virus is just an ordinary cold germ. "

Potts was stunned by Hopkins proposal, which was, Potts had to admit, brilliant. The virus, protected by its liquid nitrogen bath, was likely to survive the fire. Keaton would certainly assume that the material in the vials was unchanged, and begin another series of mouse injections. Only when his treated mice began to die off at their normal life span would he become suspicious and do the DNA analysis that would reveal the substitution. By then Potts and Hopkins would have their own experiments well underway, and it would be too late for Keaton to do anything but complain.

They were crossing another bridge, over a larger stream, and Hopkins paused again to admire the view. Islands of fall color, like splashes of dried blood, had begun to appear here and there in a sea of dense green foliage. Below them the water ran brown from recent rains. Beauty was indeed in the eye of the beholder, Potts decided, as was right and wrong. "I want to us to be clear about one thing," Potts said in a tight voice. "Nobody gets hurt."

"The two bums in St. Louis were an accident, and there is no reason for any violence in this case. We just need to get the virus and remove as much as we can of Keaton's supporting evidence. The worst thing we could do would be to harm Keaton and create an investigation where none is called for."

"It is important that the fire looks like an accident."

"Misha is a professional. He can cause a fire that will fool even the most skilled arson investigator." Hopkins explained how to get in contact with Misha. "Remember no paper records, and no unnecessary contacts or phone calls."

"I am not stupid," Potts responded defensively. "The less I have to do with your man, the better I'll like it." A building appeared around a curve in the trail. Hopkins had apparently led them on a circular route and they were almost back to Valley Green Inn and the parking lot.

"Stop by the house, and I will give you the cash for Misha. He gets paid as soon as the job is finished."

"How much money are we talking about?"

"That's not your concern. Just make sure that you don't lose it or get mugged before making delivery."

25

Jack dragged himself out of bed at six a.m. and drove to the retirement home to pick up his mother and take her to Penn for surgery. She was in her apartment packing a few belongings. "Will you take care of all this while I'm gone?" She said, sweeping her arm around the room.

"What do you mean?"

"You know. Some real vultures live here. Every time somebody leaves, or dies, they swoop into the vacated apartment. They take whatever they want."

"Why don't you give me your jewelry and other valuables? I'll take care of them until you get back."

Daisy laughed. "You mean if I come back." She picked up a string of pearls that lay in a heap on top of her dresser. "If you are worried about these trinkets, don't bother. The vultures don't come for the jewels. They are not much use to a ninety-year-old broad who is half blind and hardly ever leaves her room. Plus the other vultures, the children – not you of course, dear – will raise a stink if anything of monetary value is missing." Daisy opened a drawer and lifted up a box of Whitman's chocolates. "This is what they come looking for. Believe me some of them would drop their panties in a second if you waved one of these in their face."

Jack was no longer shocked by his mother's crudities. She had once explained to him that after more than seventy years of being a proper lady she had a lot of catching up to do. "Let's go mother. You are supposed to check into the hospital by eight." He helped Daisy to the parking lot and into the car.

"So, how is your work going?" She asked as he turned onto Henry Avenue. "You don't talk about it like you used to."

"Not much to talk about," Jack lied. What was he supposed to tell his mother – that he had discovered the secret of eternal youth, but she was already too old to take advantage of it? One thing was certain, if he even hinted at his discovery to Daisy the news would spread through the retirement home in hours, and probably be the talk of the elderly from coast to coast in a few days. Jack had spent enough time with his mother and her friends to know that they talked about little but their health. The daily "organ concert" was Daisy's term for it. Other than the state of their various body parts, their favorite topics were the incompetent doctors and nurses who cared for them, or of miracle cures they had recently read about. While they often complained about the bad food and their ungrateful children, health and medicine, understandably, formed the core of their discussions.

"You should have kept your job when Mary was ill. You had that big lab and all those smart people around you."

Jack sighed, and forced himself to stay calm. When Mary had entered the last stages of her cancer Jack was working at the University of Pennsylvania as an untenured assistant professor, and he had let his research lag to spend as much time as possible with his wife. Both Mary and his mother had urged him to continue to work on his research, but he had not considered that as an option. He knew, however, that this meant that Penn, which put a heavy emphasis on research productivity, would never grant him tenure.

Fortunately Drexel had offered him a job, and had agreed to consider his years at Penn for their tenure consideration. Jack was happy to accept since it meant he would not need to move from the house that he and Mary shared. The Drexel position required more teaching than Penn, but it included laboratory space, however small, and a chance to do a limited amount of research. The irony was that had Jack stayed at Penn, with its pressure to publish, his career would probably have taken a different track, and he would not now be sitting on the biggest discovery in decades.

"I have a good job, mom, and I am doing just fine," Jack said. "And you know that I have never regretted the last few months I had with Mary. They were worth more to me than a Nobel prize." During the rest of the drive to the hospital his mother became pensive and said little. She remained silent, not even complaining about the long wait, until she was called to be prepped for surgery.

It was not until she was stretched out on the gurney and ready to be pushed into the elevator that she spoke to him. "Jack . . . ." Her voice trembled with emotion. "Jack, I did the best I could." Jack tried to respond but his throat had suddenly become constricted and no words would come out. Before he could compose himself, the elevator doors closed behind her. Jack had not been fooled by his mother's earlier bravado. She knew that this could well be the last day she would spend on this earth. If she survived the operation, Jack vowed to tell his mother that he loved her.

Jack did not see any point in waiting in the hospital. It would be several hours before the surgery would be over and she would be out of intensive care. He drove to the University to take check on the animals and grade some exams. He also had to finish a letter of recommendation for a student that he had started yesterday morning. It had been a difficult letter to write because the student was, in truth, not very good. Students had the right these days to see their letters, so Jack had to be careful about his words. Damning with faint praise was a lot harder task than writing a recommendation for a truly good student. After opening Word he clicked on "files" and found the file name for the document among the list at the bottom of the pull-down menu. As he opened the file it occurred to him that something was not right, but he shrugged off the feeling and concentrated on writing the letter.

The doctor called about five o'clock. He thought the operation had gone well and that Daisy should have a full recovery. Jack made sure that Snuffles had plenty of water and a clean litter box. He expected to be with his mother most of the night and the cat would be happier in the lab where she would have the mice, at least, for company.

26

It was about seven p.m. when Misha entered the biology building at Drexel. The security guard at the entrance barely glanced at the fake business card that Misha flashed. Nor did he look inside the small red cooler that Misha carried. A label on the side of the cooler read "BIOLOGICAL SAMPLES," but inside were an assortment of tools that might be needed for tonight's job. The few students still in the building at that hour ignored him as he made his way to the third floor. A glance at the door to Keaton's lab confirmed Misha's suspicion that security was not a high priority at the school. The lock would be easy to pick.

Misha found a men's room and made himself as comfortable as he could in one of the stalls. In a few hours the evening classes would end, and he should be able to carry out his mission without distractions or interruptions. It was after midnight when Misha finally left the men's room. His first task was to ensure that he had a safe exit. As expected a side door was secured with nothing more than a simple switch and a sign that proclaimed "EMERGENCY EXIT" and "Alarm Will Sound if Door is Opened." He disabled the alarm and made his way back to Keaton's lab. The lock yielded in a few minutes, and he pushed the door open, then carefully closed it behind him. Briefly he scanned the room with the beam of his flashlight. He turned the light off and pocketed it. One of the secrets of his success was a photographic spatial memory. But even without his memory the profusion of instruments in the lab with their illuminated dials and indicator lights provided ample light for his purposes. Potts had been able to give him only the most rudimentary information about the lab, but it was all he needed to know. The lab was like most such working spaces — a hodgepodge of bottles, equipment, papers and things that Misha could not identify. The racks of sawdust-filled plastic animal cages along the far wall were an arsonist's dream. Conveniently Dr. Keaton had left a partially used bottle of 95% alcohol sitting out on a bench. A spilled bottle of alcohol and a source of ignition from one of the pieces of electrical equipment would create a convincing accidental fire. He walked quickly to an object in the far corner that looked like a squat beer keg. This, he guessed, would be the liquid nitrogen freezer.

The lid was sealed with a standard padlock. Potts' spy had reported that the key was kept in a nearby drawer, although she had been uncertain as to which one. Misha found the key on his third try. He was not surprised that Keaton would bother locking the freezer, and then conveniently leave the key in an unlocked drawer. Most people did not take security seriously until it was too late. He could have picked the lock if necessary, but finding the key made his work much easier.

As he removed the lid from the freezer, a dense fog flowed up over the lip and descended to the floor where it spread out in an undulating cloud. The cold vapor chilled Misha's feet. A clipboard with a log sheet was, as expected, attached to the lid. His target, according to the notations on the clipboard, was in Rack 2, Box 3. Four stainless steel handles protruded from the freezer, each of which had an attached, numbered tag. A pair of thick insulated gloves hung from a wall hook, but the leather driving gloves he had on would provide sufficient insulation for his purposes. He grabbed the handle labeled "2" and pulled it out.

A stream of liquid nitrogen poured from the storage boxes. Misha had been warned about the dangers of liquid nitrogen, which could instantly freeze human tissue on contact, and he waited until the nitrogen had quit flowing before carrying the rack to the nearest lab bench. The rack held four white plastic boxes, arrayed vertically in the steel frame. A layer of frost had quickly formed over their frigid surface, hiding any markings they might have. "Which was Box 3?" Logically they would be numbered like the floors in a building. He removed the third box from the bottom and placed it on the counter. While the vials thawed, he made preparations for the accidental fire.

His instructions had emphasized the importance of destroying the mice. The building was equipped with smoke alarms, but these were located in the hallways. The building appeared to date from the fifties, and was constructed of concrete block. He thought it unlikely that a fire would spread much beyond Keaton's lab. He scanned the ceiling, and was pleased to see no sprinkler heads. If the fire was started close to the animal cages, even a rapid response by the fire department should be too late. A large open bag leaning against the bottom row of cages caught his attention. He couldn't help smiling when he looked inside and found it full of wood chips. This would be spare bedding material for the cages, and excellent kindling.

Among his supplies was a frayed extension cord, which he now arranged to contact the bag of wood chips. The setup was clumsy, and would not fool an astute arson investigator, if one was called to the scene. The fire needed to appear accidental so that it would get only a casual investigation. The frayed extension-cord trick would have to do.

The contents of the small plastic vials had now melted, and he carefully transferred the resulting liquid to an identical set of vials he had brought with him. As instructed, he filled each of the original vials with a solution that Potts had given him. Misha did not know, or care, what was in the vials, but he understood the goal of his efforts. Once the freezer was re-locked, no visible evidence would exist that someone had been inside. To Misha's eyes, the original and substitute solutions looked identical, and it would be a while before Keaton would deduce that his precious samples had been stolen.

Before he could complete his mission, he needed to remove a small amount of liquid nitrogen to refreeze the vials. A nearby shelf held a variety of laboratory glassware and he selected a large glass beaker. He carefully dipped the beaker into the liquid nitrogen, causing it to boil violently and sending another cloud of fog streaming over the floor. His leather gloves were, he realized, too thin and his fingers began almost at once to sting from the coldness.

Something brushed against his leg. Startled, he kicked at it with his foot, hitting a soft object that responded with a harsh screech. Misha spun around. He caught a brief view of a cat as it darted away through the fog, and then the liquid nitrogen, tossed from the beaker by Misha's rapid movement, hit the side of his face. The beaker crashed to the floor, and Misha beat at his face with both hands, but he was already too late. The frigid liquid, with a temperature of minus 320ºF, had instantly frozen the outer layer of skin and the delicate tissues of his eye. In his violent life Misha had been shot and stabbed, but this pain was worse than anything that he had ever experienced.

Misha stumbled across the lab. There would be no time to arrange an "accidental fire." Misha grabbed the bottle of pure alcohol he had observed on the bench and tossed it on the floor. He gritted his teeth against the pain as he pulled a lighter from his pocket and ignited the alcohol. He grabbed the cooler, his pain was because of what was in it, and bolted from the lab. The nitrogen had hit the right side of his face, but he could still see out of his left eye. With one hand over his frozen eye and the other carrying the cooler he raced from the lab. As he slammed the door behind him, he heard another screech. "Damn cat. Serves you right." Misha muttered. Potts would be upset that he had not switched the solutions, or set a fire that would appear accidental, but not every operation went perfectly. He had the vials, which was the important thing.

The short drive to the rendezvous, an isolated parking lot behind an office building, was agony. Misha was glad to see Potts' Mercedes sitting, on schedule, in the middle of the parking lot. He would make the exchange, collect his money, and get himself to the nearest emergency room.

27

Potts was shocked to see Misha careening across the parking lot. He was driving like he was drunk. Misha braked with a squeal and stumbled out of his car.

"Here's your stuff, give me my money." Misha was holding his face and was clearly in pain.

"What happened to you?" Potts took the cooler from Misha and opened it.

"Some of that damn nitrogen splashed in my eye."

Potts was irritated. He didn't care about Misha's injury, but the project had apparently not gone according to plan. "How did you do that? I warned you about the risks of liquid nitrogen."

"You didn't tell me to expect a cat! The fucking animal scared the shit out of me." Misha groaned with pain. "I hope it died slowly."

Potts looked inside the cooler. At least the vials were there. "You made the transfer?" Misha nodded. Potts noticed that there was no nitrogen in the cooler. Now he would have to rush back to his lab to get the virus frozen again.

"Where's my money man?" Misha groaned. "I have to get to a hospital."

It occurred to Potts that Misha must have splashed himself before he had completed the transfer of the vials. Misha must be lying about the transfer. "Did you swap the samples?" Misha only moaned in response. "What about the lock, did you replace the lock on the nitrogen freezer?"

"You got your fucking virus, so pay up."

Now Potts began to get angry. It was essential that the swap of the virus samples went undetected, at least until Potts could produce his own version. Keaton would certainly notice the missing lock. "Did you burn the lab?" Misha nodded. "So it will look like an accident?" Misha just stared at him.

Potts's mind raced. Even if Keaton failed to notice the missing lock, the deliberate burning of the lab would set off an intense investigation. If Misha went to a hospital, they would want to know how he managed to freeze one side of his face. Nothing but liquid nitrogen could cause such injuries. The break-in and arson at Keaton's lab would be discovered, the spilled nitrogen deduced and Misha would be quickly tracked down. Misha was nothing more than a mercenary and he would quickly make a deal with the prosecutor. Potts felt like vomiting.

"I'll get your damned money." Potts hissed. He got in the car and opened the glove compartment. The money provided by Hopkins was in an envelope. On top of the envelope was a gun. Because he was carrying such a large amount of cash Potts had taken the 45-caliber pistol that he purchased after getting mugged a few years ago. He realized within hours of buying the gun that it had been a stupid idea. He wasn't going to walk around packing a pistol, and even if he did so he was not going to outgun a determined criminal. The gun had sat for years in a drawer next to his bed, and had never been used.

To get to the money, Potts had to move the gun. The mass of the weapon was strangely calming. Potts' hands would shake when giving a simple lecture at a conference, but they were steady now. Potts hesitated only briefly. Cold logic said that Misha had to be eliminated, a logical deduction strengthened by Potts' anger over the bungled theft of the virus. Misha was standing alongside his car, holding his throbbing face in both hands.

Potts was barely conscious of the tightening of his fingers and was truly surprised by the sudden explosion of the gun and the violent upward jerk of his hand. Misha collapsed without a sound onto the pavement, blood spreading from the hole in his head. The viscous liquid, nearly black under the yellowish lights that illuminated the parking lot, took on the shape, familiar to Potts from his days as a biology student, of a hugely magnified, crawling amoeba. Potts was strangely empty of emotion, and felt neither guilt nor elation at what he had just done. It occurred to him that Misha was himself a murderer and deserved to die, but that was a purely academic thought. The truth was that he cared nothing for Misha, or his death, one way or the other, but he did care about his own safety. Potts quickly returned to his own car and drove from the parking lot.

He called Hopkins' private number at his home. "I have the virus samples."

"Great!" Hopkins replied. "Did everything go smoothly?"

Potts hesitated. Hopkins would be furious, but there was no way to hide the disaster at Keaton's lab, or Misha's death. "Not exactly."

"What happened? I hope Misha didn't screw up. He always does good work for me."

"Not anymore. Look, I don't think we should talk about this over the phone. I'll bring the samples to you. Did you get the ultra-low temperature freezer?" Potts and Hopkins had agreed that it would be unwise to store the virus in the lab at Jefferson. Too many people routinely had access.

"Yes, I got the freezer. It's in my basement. I told the staff it was for storing fish that I planned to catch during my next trip to Rio."

"I'll be there in about forty minutes," Potts said, hoping that Hopkins would not wonder why it would take him so long to make the short trip from west Philly to the Main Line.

28

After Hopkins got the virus sample from Potts and had tucked it safely away in the freezer, he insisted on a complete accounting of the evening's events. Potts was severely shaken. Hopkins poured a glass of double malt scotch for Potts and one for himself. The drink helped calm Potts down and he explained how Misha had botched the operation. "I hadn't planned on shooting him." Potts said. "It just seemed like it was necessary."

"You did the right thing." Hopkins reassured Potts. "Misha had to be eliminated."

"I suppose you're right." Potts' hands were shaking, causing the ice in his drink to clink against the side of the glass. He steadied the glass with both hands and eagerly gulped the soothing liquid. "Still, I never expected to become a murderer. I should never have let you talk me into your dangerous scheme, and I am not going to be involved in any more of them." "Relax, George. We have the virus, and Keaton will be out of business for quite a while." Hopkins spoke calmly, but inside he was seething. The original plan had been nearly foolproof. Keaton would have needed months to get his lab working again, and would not even know that his precious virus was gone. From Potts' description of the events in Keaton's laboratory nearly everything had gone wrong. Misha had not re-locked the freezer, and Keaton would soon realize that the fire was deliberate, and that his virus had been stolen. Quick action was needed to salvage the situation. Potts, who actually thought that stealing the virus would be the end of it, was humorously naive. Fortunately, thanks to Keaton's obsessive secrecy, only a few people were aware of the existence of the virus.

Prior to today's fiasco, Hopkins could have arranged for Misha to perform the additional tasks that now had to be done, but as a result of Potts incompetence these would no longer be accomplished – at least not by Misha. He had relied on him for too long, and now he had no one else available. Hopkins would have to do the work himself, but he would also need Potts's help.

"I think we need to change our plans," Hopkins began. "My original thoughts were based upon Keaton having been effectively neutralized. Because of tonight's screw-up the police will know that his lab was torched, and that someone was into his nitrogen freezer. We need to speed things up. How long will it take you determine the base sequence of Keaton's virus? "

"A couple of months at least." Potts knew he could extract the sequence in a few weeks, but it was always good to leave some leeway in case of unexpected problems.

"That is still too long."

"Why?"

"If we had the sequence we could easily cook the books to explain how we came up with the idea and constructed the virus. But with the screw up in Keaton's lab, investigators will be looking into our records sooner than we would want them to. It is too bad that your girl Liu was not able to get the sequence out of Keaton's computer. Is there any hope of still getting it?"

"I drove by his lab before coming here, and his office appeared fully engulfed in flames. I doubt his computer survived."

"Would the information be stored somewhere else?"

Potts was about to respond in the negative, when he remembered that Keaton had acknowledged help in coming up with the idea of the virus DNA sequence. "There is someone. Keaton worked with a computer expert named Winston."

"What do you know about this Winston?"

"Nothing, really, other than that he helped Keaton deduce the pattern in the satellite DNA base sequence "

"Would this information still be on his computer?" Potts admitted that it probably was. "You need to retrieve it," Hopkins said firmly.

"He is not going to just give it to me."

"Then you need to find a way to get it. Find out what you can about Winston – where he lives, if he has a family, his financial status, anything that might be useful. But do it soon, or the information will be of no use to us."

29

Potts had not slept well. He had killed a person, and you didn't need to be a rocket scientist to know the potential complications that could come from that. He didn't feel sorry for Misha, and he did not regret his actions, which he viewed as necessary based upon the information at hand. Both the shooting of Misha and the fire at the college had made the morning edition of the newspaper – the fire on the front page and the murder of Misha on page two of the Metro section. This made a kind of sense according to the logic of the news media, murders being much more common, and hence less newsworthy than a fire in a university lab. The information provided was sketchy, but Potts was pleased with what he read. Misha was known to be "associated" with the mob. The killing was being viewed as drug related, and the damage to his face was assumed to be the result of torture. Although the killing occurred only a few miles from the site of the fire, there was no hint that the police considered them to be related.

It was time to begin the process of cleaning-up the mess caused by Misha's incompetence. The next morning, Potts called Liu into his office. "Did you hear about the fire in Keaton's lab?" Liu shook her head. Potts pointed to the Philadelphia Inquirer on his desk. "It was in the morning paper."

"Somebody keeps swiping the paper from my apartment building." Liu read the article. "They think it was arson?"

"Yes. The fire was started by a combustible liquid."

"Do they know who did it?" Liu finished the article and placed it back on the desk.

"I suspect that Keaton did it himself." Potts saw her shock. "Think about it. Who had something to gain? If Keaton was a fraud, he was sure to be found out. A fire would be a convenient way of destroying the evidence." Potts was confident that it would not occur to Liu that her boss, a well-respected scientist and figure of authority, might be involved.

"I thought you now believed that the immortality virus was real?"

"Not really. The only evidence we have are some notations on a clipboard and the dates on some animal tags. Now all of his records and his experimental animals, even his cat, are destroyed or dead. If he wanted to hide his tracks he couldn't have done a better job. In any case, the fire means we will not know for sure anytime soon if there is any truth to his claims."

Liu stood up and headed to the door. "I just can't believe that Keaton would burn down his own lab."

"You can never be sure about people Liu."

Later that afternoon Liu tried calling Keaton at his lab, but not surprisingly got an out-of-service recording. A call to his home was picked up by an answering machine, and she left a message.

30

Keaton received the call from the University security office at about four in the morning. By the time he got to his lab the firemen had finished their work and were packing up. Fortunately, the hallway sprinklers had done their job and the fire had been confined to just his lab and office space. The inferno had raced through the lab, feeding voraciously on the many sources of combustion it contained. The plastic mouse cages, filled with wood-chip bedding and neatly stacked like logs on a grate, had burned ferociously. Nothing remained of the animals they had contained but blackened mummies. Jack's lab, unlike modern research facilities with their cold, steel furniture, was furnished with wooden cabinets and benches. He had liked the warmer and more pleasant working environment created by the wood furnishings, but now they were little more than charcoal. In his office, years of accumulated paper – journals, reprints, books, old exams and countless memos from the University administration – had all been turned into ashes.

To his untrained eye there was nothing that revealed the cause of the fire. A fireman, wearing plastic gloves and equipped with a clipboard and flashlight, was examining the wreckage. His name tag said "K. T. Cotter, Inspector." Jack introduced himself. "Do you have any idea what caused the fire?" Keaton asked.

"I'll need to do some more analysis Dr. Keaton, but right now I would have to guess arson." He pointed to some barely visible streaks of soot along the base of a wall. "The blaze started here, and was initiated by a flammable liquid." The remnants of a bottle of alcohol were lying on the floor. Inspector Cotter placed the bottle in a plastic bag and made some notations on his notepad. "I would guess this was what was used to start the fire. Do you have any idea why someone might want to do this to you?"

"No. I can't think of a reason anyone would want to destroy my lab," Keaton said, but even as he said this he knew he was wrong. He glanced to the corner of the lab where the ash-covered hulk of the liquid nitrogen freezer set. The freezer itself was made of stainless steel and was intact, but its plastic lid was missing. It was possible that the lid had been consumed by the fire, but the sick feeling in his stomach told him otherwise.

Jack waited until the fire inspector had left to get some more equipment, and then went to check the freezer. The nitrogen had long since evaporated, but it had lasted long enough to protect the contents of the freezer from the worst of the fire. The plastic storage boxes were covered with soot, but were otherwise intact. Jack was hardly surprised to discover that the box that should have contained the virus samples was missing, but the fact nevertheless hit him hard.

A few more minutes of searching uncovered the other thing he was immediately concerned about. He found the body of Snuffles behind the freezer, which had offered protection from the heat of the fire, but could not save her from the smoke. Jack felt the pangs of guilt. He should have taken the cat home last night instead of going straight to the hospital.

Lester Jackson walked into the lab. "Whoa, what a mess Doc. You've been burned out good. It's going to take me a bit of time to sweep this up."

"Don't worry about it, Les. The university has hired a company that specializes in fire cleanups. They will take care of everything." He led Lester over to the freezer. "Do you have a trash bag? I would like to take care of Snuffles myself."

"Oh man, that's a shame. She was a nice cat. That shouldn't happen to anyone, and for sure not one of God's innocent creatures." Les got a trash bag from his cart and held it open while Jack carefully placed the body of Snuffles inside.

Les sealed the bag with a twist and tied a knot in the end. "Do you want me to take care of this?"

"Yes. See that it goes to the incinerator." The University sent its organic and hazardous waste to special high-temperature incinerator for disposal. Snuffles would at least be properly cremated. "If they ever find the person that did this I will happily shove him into a furnace with my own hands."

"Vengeance is the job of the Lord, Doc. I am sure the guilty person will suffer an eternal hell. You should take comfort in that and find your peace." Lester placed the bag in his cart and Jack watched silently as he walked away, pushing the remains of Snuffles ahead of him.

Inspector Cotter returned with a box of glass vials and a small scoop. "I need to take some ash samples to see if we can identify the chemical used to set the fire. Until we are done with our investigation, nothing should be disturbed. Why don't you come back tomorrow to see what you can recover?" Jack was too depressed to argue and in any case he still had classes to teach.

After teaching his two classes (a lecture to a couple of hundred bored humanities students taking their required science, and a senior seminar on cell biology) Jack spent the rest of the day sorting out various problems associated with the fire. He had to arrange for a new office and telephone and to fill out a host of insurance and university forms. The fire inspector had also demanded an hour of his time for questions. Jack had no idea who might have set the fire, and told the inspector as much. No one had threatened him and he had no enemies that he knew of. Of course every student that he had ever failed in a course (or if they were pre-meds, given less than an A) could be considered a potential enemy. A request for his class records had brought a laugh from Jack.

"Any paper records I had were reduced to ashes." He pointed to the blackened hulk of his office computer. "And I doubt if you will get anything from my hard drive. The University will have all of my past students and their grades on their system. Check with them."

Throughout the questioning, Jack said nothing about the open nitrogen freezer and the missing virus samples. When the fire investigator asked directly if anything was missing, Jack simply shook his head. What was he going to say – that a virus that could make a person immortal had been stolen? Jack was not prepared, for the moment, to deal with the string of consequences that would result from such information.

He did not need the fire inspector to know that the fire was a case of arson, the missing virus samples proved that, but he was puzzled as to who could have started the fire and taken the virus. Only a handful of people knew about his work. He could not believe that either Peter Cooke or Tom Winston had anything to do with it. Since his wife's death he had been a virtual hermit, and he could think of no one else that he might have told about the existence of the virus.

As far as Jack was aware, the only other people who knew about the virus were those who had seen the manuscript he had submitted to Science. One of his first steps was to call Jean Goldman. She was shocked to hear about the fire, but would not reveal who his paper had been sent to. The rules of peer review were firm, and anonymity was sacred. Given this restriction, the most she could do was to contact the reviewer, tell him about the fire and ask for permission to release his identity.

Jack finally got home after six. After showering and eating a light snack, he listened to his phone messages. Pete and Winston had both called to express their concern. Liu had also called, and the sound of her voice was the first pleasant experience of an otherwise miserable day.

<h1 style="text-align:center">31</h1>

Hopkins watched as Potts dove away and then slammed the door shut. Potts surprised him. Who would have thought that such a weak-kneed excuse for a man would have the balls to actually shoot someone? It was the right thing to do, of course. Misha would sell any information he had to save his own ass. Nevertheless, Hopkins now had to deal with the unpleasant and risky task of finding someone else to take over for Misha. This was going to be a problem.

It had been a pure stroke of luck to find someone like Misha in the first place. Hopkins socialized with scientists and other CEO's, not with hired killers. The options were limited. One solution was to simply abandon any hope of using the stolen virus. He was not prepared to do that, at least not yet. The bitter truth was that the likely consequences of claiming the virus as their own were not good. A virus that could prolong life would trigger a huge media event. Keaton would claim that the virus was his discovery, and he would have the backing of a senior editor at Science. She was the critical person. His ex-student and his friend Winston would be a mere nuisance by comparison. It was fortunate that so few people appeared to have any direct knowledge of Keaton's work, but together they could create serious doubt about BiTech's claim to have developed the virus first. Even the most carefully faked lab notes would not stand up to serious scrutiny.

Misha had generally worked alone, but once he had hired two thugs from North Philly, who Hopkins knew only as Rusty and Spike, to help him on a simple breaking and entering job. But Rusty and Spike were common criminals with no special skills. They were certainly not killers. Even if they would agree to do the work that needed to be done, they could not be relied upon for the important tasks.

There was, in the end, only one person whom Hopkins could trust to do the job he had in mind. The foul-up at Keaton's lab could not be undone, and it would now it would be up to Hopkins himself to see to the necessary … repairs.

Hopkins reviewed the facts. Based upon the information in Keaton's manuscript only two people, other than the editor at Science, knew about the existence of the virus. The student, Peter Cooke, should not present a problem. He was essentially a nobody, and young men of that age died violently, from auto accidents, drug overdoses and suicides, all the time. Winston, the computer person, would have to be left alone for the moment – at least until Hopkins got the needed information from him.

The real problem would be the editor at Science. There was no way of knowing what kind of records she had kept, or whom she had talked to. A person at that level could not be killed without leading to a massive investigation, an investigation that could get into areas that Hopkins wanted left untouched. How would Misha have handled the situation? He would certainly have established a false lead, a logical suspect for investigators to focus on. Hopkins quickly formulated a plan.

He began by writing a letter on the computer, tossing in the usual fanatical charges and a few grammatical errors. The result was no masterpiece, but Hopkins was confident it would do the trick:

Death to America! Death to the US Satan! No more
will america invent new weapens to kill innocent peoples.
The Jew scientist devils responsible for weapens of mass
killing will be brouht to justice. This is just the first blow in
our struggle. The Arabic Peoples Liberation Front.

Hopkins knew that the American Association for the Advancement of Science had no connection with the government, and did no weapons research, but it was reasonable that an Arab terrorist might think that it did. A few minutes on the Internet gave him plenty of ideas for constructing a bomb. As a high level executive for a large corporation Hopkins could have easily obtained some potent high explosives, but these could be all too easily traced. Nor could Hopkins make full use of his engineering skills, since the device had to be something that a poorly trained person might construct. As an experienced engineer Hopkins would need to make a conscious effort to keep the device simple. He could not afford to behave like the overpaid technicians at BiTech who all too often would turn a simple assignment into a Rube Goldberg monstrosity.

His small basement workshop contained everything he needed. The device he constructed that evening took less than an hour to complete. It was amazing, he thought, what one could do with a flattened coffee can and the contents of a few shotgun shells. The design of the trigger was the tricky part. He wanted something that was not too complicated – this was supposed to be a bomb from an unsophisticated person – but which would be reliable. The final device consisted of an AA battery connected to a detonator wire with a half inch gap that would prevent current flow until the package was opened. Attached to the flap of the envelope was a strip of aluminum foil. Opening the envelope would drag the aluminum foil across the bare ends of the wires and close the circuit.

When he was done, Hopkins sighed with relief. It had been a delicate operation to attach the trigger in a way that allowed the envelope to be properly sealed, while not setting of the explosive prematurely. He took a moment to admire his deadly creation. It was a shame, he thought, that there was nobody he could show the bomb too. Nevertheless, he felt a sense of satisfaction at a job well done. Misha would have been proud of him.

"Nice work," he said to himself, as he placed the bomb in a UPS overnight delivery box, stamped conspicuously with "CONFIDENTIAL: TO BE OPENED ONLY BY ADDRESSEE" labels. It was unlikely that the package would be X-rayed, and even if it was, the opaque rectangle of the flattened can would give little hint of its contents. He drove downtown, where he mailed both the bomb and the letter, ensuring that the letter would be taken seriously.

It was past midnight by the time Hopkins had finished mailing the bomb. He tried to get some sleep, but there was too much on his mind for rest to come easily. Coming up the corporate ladder he had made decisions that had cost thousands of people their jobs, and a few, such as the corrupt official in Russia and the homeless pair in St. Louis, had even died. Hopkins supposed that he should feel guilty for the harm that he had caused, but he had always acted for sound, logical reasons. He remembered an argument he had with his ex-wife.

"You have no remorse for anything, do you?" she had screamed at him. Hopkins could not remember what it was he was supposed to have been remorseful for, but he did remember his response.

"Only for marrying you." He had said. "Everything else has turned out pretty good."

Eventually he had, with Misha's assistance, taken care of that one mistake.

It was not guilt for what he had done, or was about to do, that kept him from sleep. It was excitement. He felt energized and strangely elated by the impending sense of danger. It was a feeling that he rarely experienced lately, but which in his youth had been more common.

While still in college he had taken up white-water canoeing, and it had taught him that danger could be loved and cherished, much as most men loved safety and security. When canoeing a wild river he would pause just above the first rapids and let the roar of cascading water engulf him, until the sense of risk, even the possibility of death, became palpable. Where the river crashed over the rocks a fine mist would rise and, with a flick of his paddle, he would plunge into the mist to be swallowed up by the boiling turbulence. The ride itself typically lasted just seconds, and he would be spit out on the other side of the rapids, exhilarated, and at the same time strangely disappointed, that he was still alive. A similar anticipation filled him as he lay in bed and went over and over again in his mind the plans for the next few days. They should work, he decided.

32

Jean Goldman had still not heard from George Potts. Yesterday Jack Keaton had called to inform her of the fire in his lab, and to request the name of the reviewer of his manuscript. The apparent arson at Keaton's lab was a serious matter, but maintaining confidentiality of reviewers was, for editors of scientific journals, also serious. It was hard enough to get reviewers. It was difficult work and their only compensation was an annual letter of thanks. If reviewers thought that their identity, and the source of their often harsh and insulting criticisms would be revealed, most would refuse to contribute.

She had called Potts to get permission to release his name, but he had refused her request. After more urging he had promised to think about it, and to call her back later with a decision. It was highly unlikely that Potts was involved in the fire, but that was not for her to judge. If she did not hear from him by that evening she would call Keaton and, for the first time in her tenure as editor, violate the confidentiality of a reviewer.

With that difficult decision out of the way she turned to the stack of manuscripts on her desk. The mail had come early, and it looked like it would be a busy day. On her desk were several thick envelops, each containing the fruits of months, and often years, of labor. The authors, she was certain, were all convinced of the importance and quality of their results, and would be devastated to have their precious papers rejected, but that was just what was going to happen to most of them.

The third item on her desk was a UPS box that raised immediate suspicion. She routinely glanced at the return address of each envelope before opening it. This one had an acronym she had never heard of before. Was APLF a university? It was common to get submissions by overnight mail – authors may have spent years doing the research and months writing a paper to describe the results, but once they were done they wanted instant publication. The box had been sent from Philadelphia and from there even regular mail took only a day to get to Washington. Her secretary had opened most of the mail (it was her job to record the submissions), but she had obeyed the confidential label on this one. The box did not feel right to her – it was too heavy for its thickness and more rigid than a stack of papers should be ...

How many of us have done things that we later regret? Situations that turn out badly where afterward we tell ourselves, "I should have followed my instincts. The signs were obvious." This was one of those situations, but Jean Goldman would not live to have regrets. The explosion shredded the coffee can into razor-sharp fragments that tore through her body, killing her instantly. Her office, like that of most editors, was a jumbled mass of paperwork, most of which was quickly consumed by the resulting fire, including her only copy of Keaton's manuscript.

33

The day after the fire in his lab, Jack returned to see what could be recovered. The intensity of the fire, and the flood of water used to extinguish it, had left hardly a scrap of paper intact. His desk had been transformed into a pile of ashes, in the middle of which sat the blackened box of his computer. He poked through the ashes with his toe. All that was left were paper clips and other metallic odds and ends. An odd shape caught his eye and he picked it up and dusted off the ashes. Jack shook his head in strained amusement. Just about the only thing in the lab that had survived unscathed was the Zuni Indian carving. The one that Liu had refused to accept from him. He placed it in his pocket and continued his inspection.

In the lab itself the situation was even worse. He had hoped that one or more of the experimental mice were sufficiently unharmed to allow some intact cells to be recovered. In principle the virus could be recovered from their DNA, but the high temperature of the fire had consumed all of the living tissue. No doubt, nothing more than isolated fragments of DNA would be recoverable. He inspected the liquid nitrogen freezer again. The remnants of the lid were on the floor alongside the freezer. The lid consisted mostly of plastic foam and had been consumed except for a few metal parts. Jack kicked at the ashes with his toe and heard a metallic clink. He pushed the ashes aside to reveal the padlock that had held the lid in place. The key protruded from the bottom of the lock.

Jack was surprised to see that the key was in the lock. He had assumed that the arsonist had simply broken into the freezer, which after all was not designed to function as a safe. A crowbar or even a strong screwdriver would have easily served to gain entry. It was true that the key was not exactly hidden, but how would the arsonist even know that the key was in a nearby drawer? The key could just as easily be on Jack's personal key chain, or be otherwise unavailable. It was, of course, possible that Jack had simply forgotten to put the key back in the drawer. The last time he remembered going into the freezer was a few days ago when Liu last visited the lab.

He took the Zuni Indian stone that he had bought for Liu from his pocket, and stared at it as if it could deny what he was starting to think. He remembered that something had seemed odd the day of Liu's second visit. That morning he had started work on a letter and which he had subsequently finished after having lunch with Liu. The word processing software was set up to keep track of the most recently used files, listing the last open document at the top of the list. But the first file name listed when he had used the computer that afternoon was not for the letter that he had been working on. He remembered clearly that he had to move the cursor two or three file names down to open the letter of recommendation.

Liu said that she had written a note and that she had stored it on her flash drive, but Jack was certain that he had not seen any unusual file names listed. Her document should have been at the top of the list. He closed his eyes and tried to visualize the list of file names. What he saw made his stomach turn. At the top was the file name of the full version of his Science manuscript, the one with the base sequence of the virus' DNA. Jack was certain of one thing – he had not opened that file for several days.

Liu had been alone in his office for over an hour, more than enough time to uncover the simple password that he had used to block casual access to the manuscript. Perhaps he should have used a more complex password, but that was beside the point. Liu had come that day not to see him, but to obtain the virus sequence. She had succeeded and then someone had come to the lab, someone who knew where the key to the freezer was, and the virus samples had been stolen and the lab destroyed.

The foul smell of smoke and burnt insulation was beginning to make Jack ill and he fled the building to clear his head. He began to walk through the campus, heading in no particular direction. It seemed impossible Liu could be involved in the fire and the theft of the virus. Perhaps he had forgotten to put the key back in its drawer. Perhaps his memory of the list of file names was wrong. In the phone message that she had left on his answering machine she had seemed sincerely upset and sympathetic.

Then something that Liu had said in that message came back to him, and he knew for a certainty that there could be no doubt as to her guilt.

He found a bench and sat down, feeling incredibly tired. That Liu was involved in the fire and the theft of the virus was now clear, but he was also certain that she would not have acted on her own. George Potts, he of the esteemed reputation and constant stream of bad research, had to be behind everything. Keaton was truly shocked. Potts was typical of many overrated big-name investigators, with their questionable ethics and self-promotion, but fudging data and taking credit for someone else's work was a long way from arson and theft.

What to do next was the issue. Going to the police was an obvious choice, but there were a couple of reasons to delay that option. First of all, he would have to reveal the existence of the anti-aging virus, and under the worst of conditions. He could imagine the firestorm of news reports that would result, which wouldn't be so bad if he actually had possession the virus or his records. No doubt he would be labeled as a crank and they would certainly wonder why he had not mentioned anything to the investigator the day of the fire.

His only hope was that the police could find the virus in Potts' possession. But the handful of small vials would be easy to hide. The virus would need to be frozen, but the vials could easily be repackaged and relabeled in such a way that they would never be identified without expensive and time-consuming tests. Potts was many things, but he was not stupid.

Even if Potts had been incredibly careless and the police found the virus in his possession, Keaton would have no way to prove that it had been stolen. Jack had worked alone, and in secret. This had seemed, at the time, the right thing to do, but now there was little hard evidence to link the virus directly to himself. Before he went to the police he would need as much confirmation of the facts as possible. The first thing he needed to establish was how

Potts had learned of the existence of the virus, a fact that was known to only a few people; Peter Cooke, Tom Winston and the editor of his Science manuscript.

It was inconceivable that either Tom or Peter had told Potts about the virus. The only way that Potts could have learned about Keaton's discovery was if he had received the Science manuscript for review. This would be easy to confirm through Jean Goldman, the editor at AAAS. When he called her yesterday, she had agreed to talk to the reviewer and attempt to gain his permission to release his name. She had not called back, indicating that such permission had not been granted, but now that Jack had specific evidence that Potts was involved, she would have to respond. It was too late to call her now, but he would do so first thing in the morning. Jack could not face the ruins of his lab again, and decided to go back to the house. As he entered, the phone began to ring.

34

Liu was puzzled and upset by Jack's behavior. She had finally gotten through to him on the phone. He had listened to her without responding and then said, "Please don't call me again," and hung up. They had gotten along so well together that Liu had come to think of him as a friend, and had almost forgotten why she had gone to his lab in the first place. Keaton had good reason to be angry about the fire in his lab, but why was he angry at her? Could he have discovered that she had been spying for Dr. Potts?

Liu went over the two occasions she had been in his lab and could think of no clues that she might have left behind. Perhaps his attitude toward her had nothing to do with her spying. Maybe she had said or done something else that had upset him. Whatever had happened, Liu was convinced, was her fault. A natural consequence of her own failings.

Liu considered her options. She had gone against her better judgment when she had spied for Potts, and the best she could do now was to try to make amends. She would go to Keaton and tell him what she had done and apologize. Potts would be furious, which could well mean the end of her job, and her US visa, but she would do it anyway. She considered calling Keaton back, but feared he would just hang up again. It was too late to go to his house, but she would go to see him in the morning. For now she was exhausted and needed a good night's sleep.

35

Hopkins' next turned his attention to Mr. Cooke. Thanks to the wonders of the Internet, he knew quite a bit about this young man. Cooke had apparently gone on to medical school after graduating from Drexel and was now an intern at a hospital in Baltimore. The hospital had, conveniently, posted pictures of the medical staff on their Web site. He found Cooke's home address listed in the on-line Baltimore directory. Hopkins would have to go to Baltimore to carry out the second stage of his plan. The third stage would have to wait until he returned to Philadelphia.

He drove to Baltimore without any clear idea of how he would take care of Mr. Cooke. His plan, such as it was, was to follow Cooke for a while and learn something of his routine. What mattered most was that he use entirely different methods to eliminate each of his "problems." They would then be linked only by their remote relationship with Keaton, a fact unlikely to be picked up by investigators. Hopkins brought along a gun, but he hoped to avoid such a crude method -- loud and messy and which would never be confused with an accident. It was not in Hopkins nature to act without careful planning, but it was critical that he act quickly, even if it meant increased risk. His targets needed to be eliminated before they began to talk to each other, and to the authorities. That was the real risk.

As it turned out Cooke had attempted to walk across a major road that ran alongside the hospital where he was an intern. Given the opportunity, Hopkins had not hesitated. When the Subaru struck Cooke it was going at about twenty miles per hour. He wished at that moment that he had taken a car with more acceleration, but the speed had been sufficient to throw Cooke's body into the air and into the path of an oncoming SUV in the other lane. There was a panicky "beep-beep" from the SUV and then the ugly thud of a collision between metal and flesh. The resulting spray of red convinced Hopkins that Cooke was unlikely to have survived the impact.

Driving back to Philadelphia, Hopkins began to plan the next stage of his operation. Potts was a fool to think that Liu could be trusted. There was nothing so dangerous to their success as that young woman. Liu knew too much, and could not be relied on to keep her mouth shut. The speed of events had left Hopkins little time to make plans. It had been no problem finding out where Liu lived – she was in the phonebook – but many details of her life were still unknown. He had to be particularly careful in how he took care of Liu. She was the only one with direct links to Potts, and through Potts to Hopkins.

The key, once again, was to deflect attention toward someone else. In this case the best approach would be to make the killing look like a random act, one not directed at Liu in particular. Rape-murders of young women were all too common, especially in a crime-ridden city like Philadelphia, but successfully staging one would not be trivial. Hopkins was not about to leave a sample of his DNA behind.

A solution occurred to Hopkins just before crossing the Ben Franklin Bridge into Philadelphia. The Fantasy Adult Bookstore boldly advertised its presence with a large sign that must have cost the owners a healthy bribe to the Camden City officials in charge of approving such things. He purchased a pack of condoms from the machine in the hallway that led to the video booths. Only moments later the door of a booth opened and a man, still adjusting his fly, stepped out. The condom in Hopkins pocket, with its dab of semen from the floor of the video booth, would ensure that he would never be identified as the rapist.

Hopkins arrived in Philadelphia in time to see Liu enter her apartment building. The old brownstones on the narrow center-city street had once been desirable homes for middle class families, but most had long since been subdivided into apartments. Many of the buildings on the street, including Liu's, were in poor repair, and probably had primitive locks and minimal security. A few minutes after Liu had disappeared into the building, lights went on in a third floor corner room. A first floor apartment would have been more convenient, but there was nothing he could do about where she lived.

The lights went out again about an hour later, but Hopkins waited patiently for another hour before getting out of the car. He shoved the few items into the pocked of his jacket that he might need. Inside the grimy lobby of the apartment building he paused to check the mailboxes. Liu's name, and only her name, was pasted to box 3C. This was good. A roommate could have made his task much more difficult. Like most old buildings of its kind, the security system, such as it was, consisted of an intercom and a buzzer system that controlled a latch on the front door. He pressed the button labeled 3C.

"Who is it?" The young woman's voice was distorted by sleep and the cheap acoustics of the intercom but had a recognizable Chinese accent.

"Liu, It's Dr. Potts. I need to talk to you. It's urgent." Hopkins knew his attempt to imitate Potts's voice was lousy at best, but he counted on the poor sound quality of the intercom to camouflage the difference. Liu would also be disoriented from having been awakened, and the lateness of the hour and the urgency of his words would combine to erase any doubt she might have about the importance of her visitor. The buzzer of the latch sounded and Hopkins pulled the door open. He did not have to worry about fingerprints on the door handle. His would be one of hundreds of smeared prints. However, once inside he slipped on a pair of latex laboratory gloves and put on a baseball cap with the brim pulled down over his face. There was no point in taking unnecessary risks.

Liu might not open the front door for him, but he considered that unlikely. Most people, particularly the young, paid little attention to the most basic rules of personal security. Once, as a young college student living in a rundown apartment much like this one, his doorbell rang and he had opened it to find a young black man he had never seen before. The man asked for "John" and when Hopkins had replied that "No John lives here," the man had politely apologized for being at the wrong apartment and left. Hopkins thought nothing more about it until he stepped out his door the next morning to find the hallway swarming with cops. A young woman, just four apartments down from his, had been raped and killed. There had been no signs of forced entry and the police theorized it had been done by someone she knew. Hopkins suspected otherwise, but never spoke to anyone about the young man knocking on doors and asking for "John."

Hopkins climbed the stairs, and found the door to Liu's apartment. He took a deep breath, flexed his fingers, and prepared himself mentally for what he was about to do.

36

Liu could not imagine why Dr. Potts, who had been to her place only once before, would come to her apartment in the middle of the night. His voice sounded urgent, but why didn't he use the telephone? The news must be something that he felt needed to be given in person. Liu's heart sank. Her mother had been ill lately, but it was so expensive to call China that Liu had not kept close track of her condition. It was possible that she had died and the authorities called her employer to give Liu the news. Liu removed the security chain and turned the doorknob.

The door flew open violently, flinging Liu backwards. The man who was rushing at her was not Potts! He was on her in seconds, giving her no chance to scream or even defend herself. His hands went around her neck, the thumbs pressing painfully against her larynx. Instinctively she grabbed for his hands, but she realized at once that he was too big and too strong. She had taken martial arts lessons for the exercise, not in the expectation that she would ever need its skills. However, the movements she had practiced so often were indelibly recorded in the wiring of her brain, and now they triggered her into action.

She let go of the hands that were cutting off her breath. Quickly she drew her right arm back and just as quickly, and with all the strength she could muster, thrust it toward the exposed throat of her attacker. The final twist and stiffening of her hand just before striking its target served its purpose. The edge of Liu's palm struck the base of her attacker's windpipe with enough force, and pain, that she thought her hand had been broken.

Her attacker let go and stumbled backwards, gagging. Liu gasped for breath herself, unable to run. He was rushing toward her again. This time with his fist raised and aimed at her face. Another sequence of learned movements was activated. She raised her arm to deflect his fist and stepped to the side, simultaneously grabbing his elbow and pulling herself around his onrushing body. The momentum of his rush carried him past Liu's hips and across the leg she thrust into his path. He stumbled and crashed against the cheap glass coffee table that filled the center of the room. The table shattered and he fell heavily into the sharp fragments. He yelled in pain, but quickly pushed himself up from the glittering mess.

"Damn you!" he shouted. He reached into his jacket and pulled out a gun. Blood dripped from the glass cuts on his hand. "Let's see if your karate will stop a bullet."

"Why do you want to kill me?" Liu screamed. "What have I done?" Her attacker said nothing, but raised the gun. The black pit from which the bullet would emerge stared at her from a few feet away. It seemed, Liu thought, like an awfully small hole for death to squeeze through. She heard a metallic clink.

"Fucking safety," her attacker cursed. He lowered the weapon to adjust something. Liu had recovered her breath and her wits. The apartment door was still wide open and she turned and fled through it. She ran down the hallway to the unmarked door that led to the stairs, and out to the street.

Liu, expecting to feel a bullet enter her back at any minute, rushed out of her building. The street lights, which had always seemed so dim to her, now glared like miniature suns. In the adjacent building the blackness of a recessed doorway beckoned her and she dashed into its shelter. The door of her building creaked open and then slammed shut. She cowered in the doorway, not daring to look. Footsteps echoed down the deserted street. They grew louder, and then stopped. A few seconds, an eternity, passed and the footsteps began again. But now they were gradually fading. Liu dared a glance. He was getting into a car, a small Japanese import Liu guessed. As he drove away, she stepped out onto the street and watched his car disappear down the road.

Only when she was sure that her attacker was truly gone did Liu return to her apartment. The police came within minutes of her 911 call. She quickly described the attack to them, and then handed the policeman a scrap of paper with lettering on it. This was the license number of her attacker's car. As the car sped away it had paused briefly at the first intersection, just long enough for Liu to read the license plate.

They wanted to take Liu to a hospital to be checked out, but she assured them that she was fine (except for a bruised hand that she was now certain was not broken). The detectives assured her that with the license number, and DNA from the blood on the broken glass, they had a good chance of identifying her attacker.

It was almost dawn when the police finally left. Liu was exhausted, but too agitated to go back to sleep, and decided to go to the lab early to catch up on paper work. The worst part of her job was the tedious business of maintaining accurate notes, of making sure every piece of data was thoroughly and accurately described, of keeping an inventory of consumable supplies and ordering new supplies as needed. She seemed to have less and less time for the things that she enjoyed most about science – reading the latest research and planning new experiments of her own.

It was still early when she got to the university and no one else had come in yet. Normally she relished these times when she was alone in the lab, and she could read and think in peace. This morning, however, she could not get her mind off the attack. It was strange that her attacker had known that she worked for Dr. Potts. The detective had suggested that someone from the University was involved, someone who knew Liu and who may have been stalking her for some time. Liu was certain, however, that she had never seen her attacker before. Of course it was no secret that she worked in Dr. Potts lab. The university phone directory listed her name and room number, and anybody could have obtained that information.

Unable to concentrate on her lab work Liu decided to treat her attack as if it were a scientific problem. When confronted with a difficult research topic Liu would make a list of facts, in order of their importance and in the confidence she had in them. From each fact she would attempt to formulate an explanation and then construct a hypothesis that seemed to offer the best explanation for all of the facts combined.

Her initial list of facts was depressingly brief. The attacker had known her name and place of work. She wrote down on her paper "Attack not random – directed at me specifically." He had worn latex gloves. This implied that the attack had been planned in advance, and that he was worried about detection, but that could be true of any rapist or burglar. Burglary made no sense, since Liu owned nothing of value (any extra money she had went to help her family in China). Rape also made no sense. Liu was convinced that the initial assault was meant to kill her. But why would someone want to kill her? She had no enemies that she knew of, and in truth she had very few friends. Liu had been in America long enough to know that it was not uncommon for young women to be murdered for no apparent reason, but this did not appear to be one of those cases. The attack on her had been for a reason.

Liu never got a good look at her attacker's face, but he appeared to have been in his fifties, which had been a surprise to the police. They had questioned her very closely about her estimate of his age, presumably because they expected such attacks to be perpetrated by younger men, but she was certain about his age. The attacker was strong and appeared to have a suntan – he was not a bum off the streets.

The logical conclusion from these facts, as the police had concluded, was that the attacker knew Liu. But Liu did not recognize him. What were the "facts" in this case? Liu's thoughts were interrupted by the ringing of the telephone. It was the detective in charge of her case.

"Do you know someone named Rebecca Maxwell?"

Liu had no memory of somebody with that name. "Is she related to the attack on me?"

"Probably not. The license plate number you gave us was registered to a Rebecca Maxwell on Greene Street. She's a sixty-year-old woman, and her car, a Subaru, does not appear to have been driven recently. We think your attacker may have used a fake plate."

"Perhaps I got the number wrong. It was a dark night."

"We think you got the right plate number," the detective said. "Is the name Peter Cooke familiar?"

Liu thought about this for a few seconds. The name was strangely familiar, but she could not remember where she had come across it. "Not really," she said finally. "Who is he?"

"He was a medical student living in Baltimore. Yesterday he was struck and killed by a hit-and-run driver. A witness was alert enough to get the license number. It was the same number as from your attacker's car."

After she finished talking to the detective, Liu considered the latest information. If the information was correct, somebody ran over Peter Cooke in Baltimore, left the scene of the accident to drive to Philadelphia where he then attempted to kill her. Liu and Peter Cooke were linked in some way.

She was almost certain that she had seen the name Peter Cooke somewhere, but try as she might she could not remember where, or when. With the stress of the morning she had not had an appetite and had skipped breakfast. Maybe she would think clearer after a cup of tea. Liu walked down to the cafeteria. She bought tea and a doughnut and sat at a table near the television set that was attached to one wall, and which was always tuned to CNN. The sound was turned off, it was usually too noisy in the cafeteria to hear it anyway, but it was programed to display subtitles, and Liu read the scrolling words as she sipped her tea. This morning the lead item was about an explosion in the offices of the American Association for the Advancement of Science. The explosion was being blamed on a previously unknown terrorist group that was accusing the United States of developing weapons of mass destruction. Liu knew that the AAAS had no association with the government. Their major activity was the publication of the journal Science. The TV showed a posed publicity photograph of the woman killed in the explosion, and identified her as the biology editor and mother of two.

"Oh no ..." Liu muttered to herself. In the short span of a couple of days there had been a fire in Keaton's lab, an attack on her, and now an explosion in the office of the Biology editor of

Science. No doubt the woman killed in the explosion had handled Keaton's paper. Liu suddenly knew where she had seen the name Peter Cooke. He had been named in an acknowledgment paragraph on the last page of Keaton's manuscript. Somebody wanted to eliminate all traces of Keaton's discovery.

But how would they know about her. Only Dr. Potts knew about her attempt to reproduce Keaton's results, and of her visit to his lab. But it was not Potts who had attacked her. Nor was it believable that Potts would have burned down Keaton's lab, made a bomb to send to AAAS, and hired someone to kill her. He certainly could not have driven to Baltimore to run over poor Peter Cooke. He had been in the lab all day yesterday.

Could Potts be right? Had Keaton burned down his own lab to hide his scientific misconduct? Could he have discovered that Liu knew about his claims to have developed an anti-aging virus? Logically, scientifically, this was the strongest theory, but Liu discarded the idea as absurd. The Jack Keaton she had come to know could not have done this. Perhaps she was reacting emotionally, she certainly was attracted to Keaton, but his sincerity and commitment to science were unquestionable.

This left Dr. Potts as the only other person who had all of the relevant information. Perhaps Potts had communicated with somebody else. As was his custom, he had asked her to compile her results and write a preliminary report. The next day she had seen him at the fax machine. He had been holding Liu's report in his hand – and a copy of Keaton's manuscript.

Liu returned to the lab. The fax machine was in Potts's office, but was used by all of his senior personnel. Potts did not like people going into his office, but sometimes he wanted the latest results faxed to him while he was attending important conferences. A key to his office was located in a drawer that held a collection of keys to various common rooms. Liu went into his office. She activated the fax machine and pressed the button labeled "Redial."

The number that appeared in the digital display was a local number, but not one that she was familiar with. The first three numbers were 215, the Philadelphia area code, but the next three,

715, were ones that she could not remember seeing before. Identifying the owner of the number might prove difficult. She couldn't just call, nor could not even be certain that the fax machine had not been used recently, in which case this would not even be the number to which her report had been sent.

Whom would Potts have sent the report to? It would be someone important, Liu was certain, most likely the director of a large lab at a major university or research institute. They would no doubt have the use of several numbers beginning with 715, but the main office would be likely to have a number that would be easy to remember. She picked up the telephone and dialed 715 and then 1000. A computer generated voice informed her that the number was not in service. She tried 715 followed by 2000. Same result. When she got to 5000, a different, more pleasant, computerized voice responded. "Welcome to BiTech Industries. Please press one if you know your extension. If you wish product information press two …"

37

The explosion at the offices of the AAAS was the main item in the morning news and Potts watched the television with growing dismay. The letter from the "Arab Peoples Liberation Front" might fool the police, but Potts knew all too well who was responsible for the explosion.

Things were moving too fast for Potts, and in the wrong direction. It was one thing to conspire to get Keaton's virus – by all rights it belonged to Potts anyway – but to kill innocent people was unacceptable. The death of Misha was unfortunate, but he was hardly an innocent bystander, and the shooting had been unplanned. Potts viewed it as more of an accident than a murder. Jean Goldman was guilty of nothing more than doing her job. Potts knew Jean only casually, but she was a real person to him. She had a face and a voice that Potts could remember clearly. Furious, he phoned Hopkins.

"Did you have anything to do with the Washington explosion?" Potts expected a lie, but Hopkins didn't respond to the question directly.

"You sound excited, George. Why don't we get together and talk? It's a nice day, let's say the Bala Golf Club at ten." Potts could understand Hopkins reluctance to talk on the phone and he agreed to the meeting and hung up. Just seconds later the phone rang.

"Bob, I thought you said not to use the phone." But it wasn't Hopkins, it was Liu.

"Dr. Potts I have to tell you something," she said excitedly.

Potts listened to Liu with growing concern and anger. Hopkins was completely out of control. He had apparently not only killed Jean Goldman with a bomb, but he had also murdered Keaton's ex-student and he had attempted to kill Liu. And now Liu had deduced that someone at BiTech was involved.

"What should I do Dr. Potts? Should I call the police or do you think it is better if you do it?"

"No, don't call the police!" Potts struggled to stay calm. "I will take care of it." He continued in his most reassuring voice. "The person I work with at BiTech is a highly respected administrator there, and I can assure you that he would not be involved in what you are suggesting. Any number of other people at BiTech may have seen the fax I sent. It is possible that many people have seen Keaton's manuscript, or know about his work from other sources." Potts paused for effect. "And we cannot eliminate the possibility that Keaton himself was attempting to eliminate the evidence, and the people, who know of his scam."

"I understand what you are saying, but I think the police should know about the person at BiTech."

"Liu, let me explain something to you. I don't know what it is like in China, but I suspect it is not much different there. You do not casually tell the police to investigate a person in a high position. Not unless you are very certain of your facts. I will make some further inquiries, and if anything turns up I will inform the authorities. In the meantime you do nothing."

38

At the Bala Golf Club Hopkins led Potts to a table on the clubhouse deck that overlooked the pond. It was too early for lunch and the deck was deserted except for them. Normally the sound of the fountain that fanned out in the center of the pond, and the graceful motion of the ducks across the water, would have been relaxing to Potts, now he found them an irritation. He got right to the point. "Did you send the bomb that killed Jean Goldman?" Hopkins responded with a thin smile that further increased Potts' anger

"And why do you want to know?" Hopkins said. "Assuming I was involved in some way, of what possible use would this information be to you. I suggest you don't involve yourself with matters that are peripheral to your tasks, but that you concentrate instead on getting the information we need from Winston."

"What about Peter Cooke?" The smile disappeared from Hopkins' face.

"How do you know about Cooke? There was nothing about that in the local news." Hopkins' smugness was unbearable. "Perhaps you would be interested to know that Liu not only survived your attack on her, but that she knows that someone from BiTech was involved." This got Hopkins attention. The smile had been replaced by a look of grim seriousness. It was a look that frightened Potts. "Don't worry. She doesn't know that you were personally involved."

"Understand something, George, and don't forget it. Not for a second. We are in a high-stakes game and there are only two possible outcomes. Think of it as a pass-fail exam, but we are not college students, and if we fail we do not get to retake the course. I for one, do not plan to fail, and I will do what I think is necessary to succeed. I suggest you consider doing the same. Get the information we need from Winston, and don't worry about Liu. I will see that she is taken care of."

"I didn't sign on for murder."

"Tell that to Misha," Hopkins responded.

Potts shivered. The image of the blood spreading like a black amoeba from the hole in Misha's head was still vivid in his memory. "That was different. Misha was a murderer himself."

"George, think about it. You're a scientist; you know all about cause and effect. I don't think I need to spell it out for you." Hopkins paused for several seconds to let the menace of his words sink in. "The screw-up in Keaton's lab has put us at risk. It was unplanned, but now we have to deal with it. Our only hope is to remove, as much as possible, the traces of Keaton's experiments. I have taken care of Goldman and Cooke, but now we need to deal with Winston and with Keaton himself. Neither of us wants to spend the rest of our lives in jail."

Potts could not allow himself to be sucked any deeper into Hopkins schemes. "I agree that we need to use our brains here, but I am not sure you have analyzed the situation correctly."

"So, what is your analysis?"

"You did a brilliant job with Goldman and Cooke." Potts almost choked on the words, but what was he going to do – tell Hopkins that he was a homicidal psychopath? "It is very unlikely that anyone will link their deaths. After all, they did not know one another, and their common connection to Keaton is rather remote. But if Keaton dies, and his best friend Winston, the police are likely to examine other connections. We don't need them dead, we need them neutralized."

"I assume that you have a plan."

Potts in fact had no plan, but as he began to respond an idea emerged. "Winston's only connection with Keaton's work is, apparently, some computer analysis. It is safe to assume that the sequence data that Keaton gave him is still on his machine. Without that data they have no physical support of their story."

"So we erase his hard drive?" Hopkins sneered. "For your information, George, deleting a computer file doesn't get rid of it, and any skilled person could recover the erased data. And he probably has back-up disks."

Despair fell over Potts like a dense, dank fog. Potts didn't care if Keaton and his friend were dead or alive, but he knew that their deaths would open a floodgate of investigation. Liu would never keep quiet. A fact that would certainly occur to Hopkins, who would want to complete the botched job of killing her. Hopkins was a maniac. He talked of killing Goldman and Cooke with pride and excitement, as if he had just successfully scaled a difficult mountain. Now he was looking for other challenges. If Potts was not careful, he could himself become one of Hopkins' trophies. A possible solution occurred to him.

"We need them alive," Potts said firmly, trying to hide the fear that made his mouth dry.

"Why is that?"

"Because we can use them. The fact is, we do not know how many people are aware of Keaton's work. He must have other friends. Maybe he talked to his bartender. I would not be surprised if copies of his manuscript, and his data, exist that were not destroyed in the lab fire. We will never be certain that we have eliminated everyone and everything that could reveal the existence of Keaton's experiments. But we can discredit them." Potts described his plan to Hopkins, who made him go over it several times for clarification and to suggest different approaches. In the end, after more than an hour of discussion, Hopkins agreed that the plan was feasible and that they should proceed with its execution as soon as possible.

39

Jack had a restless night, and slept little. It was nearly ten when he finally dragged himself from bed. He made himself a cup of coffee and then called the editorial office at AAAS. A secretary answered. "Dr. Goldman please. Tell her it's Jack Keaton."

"I am sorry Dr. Keaton. She can't come to the phone."

"Would you tell her that it's urgent, and that she should call me as soon as possible."

"I am sorry." The secretary's voice cracked. "She can't come to the phone because she is dead."

Keaton took a deep breath. Jean was not that old. "What happened?"

"There was an explosion. Apparently from a letter bomb sent by an Arab terrorist organization. Is there anything I can do for you?"

"No, nothing . . . " Keaton hung up. As a scientist Jack had learned to be alert to coincidences. Most coincidences were meaningless, but it was the odd coincidence that often led to the most meaningful breakthroughs. Science was full of stories of researchers who had made major breakthroughs because they followed up an unusual correlation. The discovery of antibiotics had come from just such an observation. Of course one never heard about the researchers who saw the same phenomenon, but failed to follow up.

The arson fire in his lab and the murder of the editor who had handled his manuscript could be a chance occurrence, but Jack had to assume that they were related. The conclusion was clear. As hard as it was to accept, Jack had to believe that George Potts was not only a dishonest scientist, but was also an arsonist, a thief and a murderer. And Liu was his accomplice. It was possible that other people were involved, but the trail began with Potts and Liu.

Jack considered his options. Eventually he would have to approach the police, but without confirmation his story of an immortality virus would most likely be viewed as the ravings of a crackpot. An opinion which could only be further reinforced by the suggestion that one of the most distinguished scientists in the city was a murderer. In the movies people in danger almost never called the police, a plot device that perhaps made dramatic sense, but always irritated Jack as implausible behavior. He preferred fictional characters who acted intelligently, as Jack believed he would do himself.

Now he could imagine the questions the police would ask. "So, you created this virus that will let people live forever, but it was stolen and all records of its existence have disappeared and the one person who can confirm any of this was killed by a terrorist bomb, and now you want us to investigate one of the most prestigious scientists in the city because you think that his assistant may have fooled with your computer?" Even if the authorities did believe his account of events, it was not clear that it would bring Potts, and Liu, to justice. While there was an outside chance the police would take him seriously, it was more likely they would not, and either way it was certain that the story would leak out. No doubt his photograph would soon appear on the front page of a supermarket tabloid underneath a screaming headline; "SCIENTIST DISCOVERS SECRET OF IMMORTALITY."

Jack needed to accumulate as much supporting information as possible before he went to the authorities. The only others directly involved in his work were Peter Cooke and Tom Winston. His phone book had been destroyed in the lab fire and it took a few minutes with directory assistance to obtain Peter's number. There was no answer on his home phone and Jack left a message.

Next he dialed Winston's number. The phone rang and rang with no answer. Each ring was like a dagger into Jack's heart. Had Potts killed Winston too? Jack was about to hang up to call the police when the ringing stopped.

"Heh?"

"Tom? Is that you?"

"You were expecting the tooth fairy?" Winston said in a sleepy voice. "Why are you calling so early in the morning?"

Jack had forgotten that Winston often worked late into the night. "It's after ten." He said. "I am sorry I woke you but this is important." Jack told Winston about the explosion that had killed the editor of his Science manuscript. "The torching of my lab and the explosion that killed Jean Goldman is too much of a coincidence. Your name was in my manuscript and I think you might be in danger too."

"I think you have been watching too many Mel Gibson movies."

"Maybe I am overreacting. But I think you should go stay somewhere else for a while."

Winston sighed. "I'm up to my eyeballs with work here. I have clients who want software fixes yesterday and a friend who thinks I am in mortal danger from a deranged scientist. Don't take this personally, but I think I will take my chances with the deranged scientist."

There was nothing more that Jack could say that would change Winston's mind. "Tom, just be careful, on the outside chance that I am right."

"I'll be careful, Jack. I promise," Winston said. "Can I go back to sleep now?"

40

Potts returned to the lab after his meeting with Hopkins and called Liu into his office. "I have a job for you." He handed her a newly purchased flash drive, still in its plastic bubble. "The fire in Keaton's lab, and then the attack on you, got me thinking about our own work. I want to backup all of the experimental data files and notes from the past two years."

Liu took the drive with a look of dismay. "Everything is pretty well backed up now," she said.

"I know, but I think we should keep a separate set of backup data offsite."

Liu sighed but took the drive. She returned two hours later with the flash drive, which was now unwrapped and neatly labeled in her distinctive handwriting. "Just place it on the desk. I'll take care of it later." When Liu was gone, he put on a pair of latex lab gloves and placed the flash drive into a plastic bag. The bag went into his briefcase. Liu's fingerprints would be the only ones on the drive when it was discovered at Winston's house. It had been Hopkins' suggestion to stage a robbery to gain access to Winston's computers. Over Potts' objections this had meant bringing in two additional people into the plan. Rusty and Spike were two young black men from north Philadelphia who had worked with Misha on a project that had required some additional muscle. Hopkins would take care of briefing Rusty and Spike on their duties and Potts would have to meet them only briefly, which was fine with him. The previous evening he had driven past Winston's home on Willow Lane to examine the layout (and in the process almost blew a tire on an unmarked speed bump). The setting of the house was perfect. Willow Lane was a narrow road that ran through a heavily wooded area. There were no street lights, and the houses were well separated on lots that were an acre or more in size.

At six that evening Potts pulled his car up behind a large tree about fifty yards from Winston's house. Just five minutes later another car, an old, rust-streaked Cadillac, pulled into Winston's driveway. Two black men got out. One of them carried a large flat object that appeared to be a pizza box. The man with the box went to the door and knocked, while the second man positioned himself flat against the wall alongside the entrance. The door opened part way.

"Who's there?" Potts assumed it was Winston.

"Pizza delivery."

"I didn't order a pizza."

"This is 4270 Willow Lane, isn't it?"

"Yes, but I still didn't order a pizza."

"Damn, that new girl that takes the orders is always screwing up. Can I borrow a phone for just a minute so I can find out where this pizza is supposed to go?" There was a momentary silence and then the door opened wider. The second man stepped into the light and swung something at Winston. Potts heard the muted, but sickening thud, and the two men disappeared into the house. A minute later the door opened again and one of the men waved toward Potts.

Potts quickly walked to the house. He was greeted by a large black man wearing a blue knit cap. To Potts's surprise, the hairs showing around the edges of the cap were distinctly red. "I assume you're Rusty."

"Yea. Your guy is securely tied up and locked in a bathroom."

"He is alive I hope."

"Sure. Spike just gave him a little tap to calm him down." A second man, carrying a small television set, came from a rear room.

"Man, this guy has shit. Be lucky if I get ten bucks for this." He placed the TV alongside the door and returned to the room he had come from.

"You've already been well paid. Just take a few things and go." Rusty and Spike worked quickly, accumulating next to the door a small pile of electronic devises, a camera and some hand tools. As instructed, they left the computer equipment in place. "Why don't you take this stuff right to the car?" Potts asked.

"That would be stupid. Never make more than one trip to the car. Somebody's more likely to see you." Spike returned, this time with a couple of bed sheets. In seconds the pile of loot was distributed into the sheets which were then tied into bundles. Potts had little contact with the "underclass" and assumed that they were pretty much an unintelligent bunch, but Spike and Rusty impressed him with their obvious skill and efficiency. When they were gone with their bundles of loot, Potts made a quick search of the house. He found the office in the rear, facing the woods. Several computers, including a few laptops and even an ancient IBM, were scattered on benches around the room. A newer desktop, with a large LCD monitor, occupied the center of the room, and Potts guessed this would hold the virus data. Potts opened his briefcase and put on a pair of latex gloves.

The first order of business was to find the virus sequence. He was not surprised to find dozens of folders listed on the computer's hard drive, but this would not make his work easy. The file he was looking for would most likely have a name that would include the term DNA and a search quickly rewarded him with half dozen files with those three letters. He opened the first file and was pleased to see the expected string of A's, T's, G's and C's. He began to copy the sequence onto a blank flash drive that he brought for that purpose.

The plan that he and Hopkins had put together was risky, but offered an excellent chance of success. During the afternoon and early evening Potts had falsified computer data outlining his discovery of the anti-aging virus. A matching set of handwritten entries went into a notebook. When he was done, he copied all of the computer data onto the flash drive that Liu had returned to him.

In a few days a press release would be issued through BiTech that they would be initiating animal trials on a treatment to extend life span. No doubt Keaton would come forward to press his claim, and maybe even suggest that the deaths of Goldman and Cooke were linked to the theft of his virus. Potts and Hopkins would issue statements bemoaning the prevalence of conspiracy nuts in the country. Then he would call the police and tell them that somebody had stolen a flash drive from his lab which crucial and important scientific data. He would tell them how his Chinese postdoc had been acting strangely, that she had been seeing a competitor called Keaton, and a friend of his called Winston. He would suggest to the police that Keaton had burned his lab to hide the fact that he did not do the experiments himself. The stolen data, Potts would suggest, might still be found in Winston's computer files.

Hopkins had at first argued against the plan. He pointed out, correctly, that Liu would tell a different story and that it would be difficult to support the claim that Potts had developed the anti-aging virus without anyone else in the lab being aware of it. Potts had to remind Hopkins that Liu had, in fact, secretly analyzed the redwood DNA. "Both Keaton and Liu acted in secrecy, which is what makes this plan feasible." The presence of data from Potts' lab on Winston's computer, complete with Liu's fingerprints on the flash drive, would be impossible for them to explain away. The most difficult part of the plan would be getting access to his computer without raising suspicion. It was Hopkins who had come up with the idea of using Spike and Rusty.

While the DNA sequence was being copied onto a separate flash drive, Potts picked up the phone. There was one more critical part to the plan.

41

The phone call, from Peter's roommate in Baltimore, came while Jack was making dinner. It shattered any doubts that Jack still had that the fire in his lab and in the explosion that had killed Jean Goldman were linked. Peter Cooke was dead.

This was information that Winston needed to hear, and this time Jack would confront his friend in person. The drive to Winston's house seemed to take forever, and he was relieved, as he pulled up, to find the lights on and Winston's beat-up Saab parked in the driveway. Jack was about to ring the bell when he noticed that the front door was ajar. Winston had tens of thousands of dollars of computer equipment in the house, and he always kept his doors locked. An open door was not a good sign. Briefly Jack considered calling 911, but that would take precious time and Winston might need his help now. He nudged the door open wider and slipped inside. A glow of light was visible in the rear, in the direction of Winston's office.

Jack looked for a weapon. There was a fireplace in the living room and Jack selected a heavy iron poker from the set of tools. He hoped that whoever was in Winston's office did not have a gun. A man, not Winston, was at the computer with his back turned to the entrance. Jack stepped gingerly into the room.

Jack moved as carefully as possible, but nothing he could have done would have stopped the floor from creaking under the pressure of his foot. At the sound the man spun around. He stood up and thrust a hand into the pocket of his jacket. When the hand reappeared it was wrapped around a gun.

"Hello Jack. Nice of you to stop by." He waved his gun at Keaton's head. "I suggest you drop that primitive weapon."

"What are you doing here George? Where is Tom?" Jack tightened his grip on the fireplace tool.

Potts sighed. "Unfortunately what I was doing here is now irrelevant. I was hoping to avoid more violence."

"You murdered Goldman and Cooke."

"I had nothing to do with their deaths."

"And the fire in my lab?"

Potts shrugged. "Not my doing either, but a necessary nevertheless." Potts had let the gun drop slightly, as if its weight was too much for him. It was no longer pointed at Jack's head. "The redwood DNA experiments were something that I had been thinking about for years. I was not about to let a nobody like you get all of the credit for the discovery. My entire career has been dedicated to aging research and this result belonged to me as much as anyone. Just because you got lucky does not make you a great scientist. You have to pay your dues, as I did."

Potts spoke with a conviction that was at odds with the absurdity of his words. "And you think this gave you the right to steal my work?" Jack tightened his grip on the poker, hoping that Potts would become distracted long enough for him to act.

"It was your choice not to share the results and to keep the details of your experiments secret. This was too big a discovery to leave in the hands of someone who obviously did not understand its importance, and who had no experience working with the government or with major pharmaceutical companies. I will see that the virus is properly tested and marketed."

From the far end of the room came the sound of a door opening. Jack and Potts both turned toward the noise. Standing in the brightly lit doorway was a ghostly figure encircled by a shimmering white halo. The ghost stepped into the room. Liquid dripped from its arms.

"What the . . ." Potts grunted. In his astonishment he let the gun drop to his side.

"Run Jack, for god's sake run!" the ghost shouted. The voice was Winston's. He was soaking wet and was covered head-to-toe, Jack now realized, with what appeared to be soap suds. Winston shouted again and lunged toward Potts.

Potts appeared to be stunned into immobility at the apparition running toward him. Winston was almost upon Potts when the gun, still held low, went off. Winston groaned and fell to his knees. Blood gushed from his leg.

The immediate shock at seeing Winston had passed and Jack knew he had to act. He swung the fire poker and let it fly in the general direction of Potts. Instinctively Potts raised his free hand to ward off the oncoming missile and Jack used the opportunity to rush toward him. The plan was sound, but he was not quick enough. Jack heard the explosion of the gun and felt the fire in his belly as the bullet found its mark. The poker was well aimed however and smashed into the side of Potts face, driving him back against the wall. Potts was stunned, but still standing.

The shock of the bullet had driven Jack to the floor, and now he pushed himself up, using all of the will power he could muster. Potts was on the other side of the room and Jack knew he would never reach him before he could fire again.

Potts recovered quickly from the glancing blow of the poker and he raised the gun again. Jack turned and began to run. The gun exploded behind him and splinters flew from the door frame he had just passed through. Jack raced, as best he could, out the front door. His car was just yards away, but he knew that it would be a death trap. It would take several seconds to get the key out and to start the engine. Potts would not wait that long. Instead, Keaton darted instinctively toward the blackness of the nearby forest. He glanced back to see Potts, as expected, running toward the parked car.

Jack ran into the woods, stumbling over roots and rocks, until the pain in his belly became unbearable. He stopped to rest against a tree, gasping for breath. Warm fluid poured from the hole in his stomach and ran down his leg. Behind him, between the shadows cast by the trees, moonlight glistened from the splashes of his spilled blood. Farther back a dark shape moved through the trees. Jack ran on, but soon realized the hopelessness of further flight as his remaining energy drained from the bullet wound in his side. No matter where he went, the trail of blood would lead Potts directly to him. He found a melon-sized rock and picked it up. It would have to do. There would be just one chance to surprise Potts, and he would have to make the most of it.

He pressed his back against a large tree and tried to still his heavy breathing. In a few minutes he heard the scuffling of feet through the leaves. He raised the rock over his head, gripping it as tightly as his remaining strength would allow. The footsteps reached the tree that hid Jack, and he stepped out and swung as hard as he could toward Potts's head.

42

Potts had assumed that Keaton would head for his car, but when he got there he found the car empty. Keaton must have gone into the woods. Even with a nearly full moon hanging overhead, the forest presented itself as an impenetrable black wall. He knew, from the pool of blood in the house, that Keaton was badly wounded, and it was unlikely that he could find his way through the woods to safety before he bled to death. With luck he would die in the woods and animals would consume his body. Any thought of going after Keaton ended when he saw car lights coming down the narrow road that led to Winston's house and the handful of others scattered along the edge of the park.

Potts was glad that he had parked his car off of the road, well hidden by the trees. He ran to his car and crouched behind the hood. The oncoming car pulled up in front of Winston's house and a woman got out. It was Liu! Potts had expected to be gone by the time Liu arrived, but the confrontation with Keaton had delayed his departure. Fortunately she had not recognized Potts' car in the darkness. The plan was for her to come to Winston's house (although she thought that it belonged to a friend of Potts) and to leave her fingerprints in as many places as possible. The call to her house from Winston's phone, and her presence when the police came in response to the theft would establish a direct connection between Winston and Liu. But she was supposed to find Winston tied up, not shot.

The gun was still in Potts hand, and now he raised it so that it rested securely on the hood of his car. Although no street lights illuminated the road, the white blouse that Liu wore stood out sharply in the bright moonlight. He placed the black V of the gun sight on the center of her chest.

His options had suddenly become limited. The plan had been to establish a believable link between Liu, Keaton and Winston. Nothing had to be proven with any certainty, but with the planted data and flash drive a reasonable case could be made that Liu had conspired to steal Potts' discovery. BiTec's lawyers would wear down Keaton with a blizzard of lawsuits if he attempted to contest Potts' claims.

The shootings, however, changed everything. Before tonight there had been nothing to link Potts directly with either Keaton or Winston, but Keaton's unexpected appearance and Winston's escape from the bathroom had led to gunfire. Even if both of them died, Liu would lead police directly to him, and even if he killed her it would only delay the inevitable. He considered for a moment talking to her. After all she needed his yearly approval to stay in this country, but although he had a lot of power over Liu, he knew that she would not go so far as to help him cover up a murder.

Liu disappeared into the house and Potts lowered the gun. It was time to leave. Liu would certainly call the police, if Winston had not already done so. He drove slowly to avoid making noise and kept his car lights off until he was out of sight of Winston's house. Nothing in Potts' experience had prepared him for this moment. Things had not turned out as planned, and he could see no way out of the trap that he had been led into by Hopkins' schemes. The best he could do now would be to minimize the damages. Fortunately he had something valuable to sell – Robert Hopkins. And while he was at it he would throw in that bastard Keaton, free of charge. Before he did anything though he needed to make a quick stop at the lab.

43

Liu never saw the rock, but felt the breeze as it flew by her face and smashed harmlessly into the side of the tree.

"Jack, it's me!" Liu shouted.

"Liu, what are you doing here? Did you come to finish me off?"

"No! I came to help you."

"Like you helped burn down my lab."

"Why do you think I had anything to do with that?"

Jack sighed in the pain and slumped to the ground. "The cat Liu. The cat. The cat was supposed to be home with me. Only the one who set the fire could have known about the cat."

"But it was in the news." Even as she said it Liu realized that there had been no mention of a cat in the newspaper coverage of the fire. Potts had told her about the cat, and that meant that Potts had started the fire, and that he must be involved somehow in the deaths of Goldman and Cooke. Even, Liu realized with a shiver, in the attack on her.

She wanted desperately to tell Jack that she was sorry, and that she had been a fool to trust Potts, but there was no time for that now. The blood pouring from Jack's side would soon kill him. She needed to stop the bleeding. Acting instinctively, she ripped off her blouse, not taking the time to undo the buttons, and pressed the wadded fabric against the wound. The sound of police sirens was audible in the distance and she pressed as hard as she could, praying that Jack would live.

44

One of the secrets of Hopkins' success was that he kept close track of world and local news, and he could often respond to situations before others were even aware they had taken place. His Internet server sent a continuous stream of local and national news bulletins to his home computer. The shootings of Keaton and Winston, and the arrest of a distinguished scientist were deemed sufficiently important to make the national news services.

Hopkins knew he had little time to waste. Potts would be cutting a deal with the district attorney and Hopkins would be his main bargaining chip. He could probably deal with Potts if that was all the prosecutors had, but the throbbing pain in his hand was an unavoidable reminder of the blood he had left behind at Liu's apartment. Ever since the OJ Simpson fiasco police had learned to handle DNA evidence with proper care, and he would not be able pull off the miracle that the OJ defense team had accomplished so brilliantly. The only salvation for Hopkins was that it was likely to take a day or two for the District Attorney to negotiate the fine points of an agreement with Potts' lawyers.

Hopkins had begun preparations for this moment several years ago after one of his more risky plots had nearly come undone. It took just minutes to gather his fake I.D.s and to collect the cash that was well hidden in various locations around the house. His major bank accounts were still active, indicating that the police either did not know about him or had not yet tracked down his assets. He electronically transferred the bulk of his funds to his Swiss account. He packed lightly (he could buy whatever he needed later). There was just one more thing he had to do. He headed for the basement where the ultra-low temperature freezer, and Keaton's virus, was stored.

The trip to Cuba, through Mexico, was uneventful. For years he had been sending valuable American dollars to Cuba to maintain a large beachfront estate that was left over from the pre-Castro era.

In Cuba he could live like a king on the interest from his Swiss investments. As long as he did not touch the principal he would have enough money to live forever. Which was a good thing, since he had injected all of Keaton's virus into his veins before leaving home.

45

Jack was unconscious for most of the day after being shot. He awoke into the bright glare of his hospital room feeling worse than he thought was possible. The events of the previous evening were a blur to him, and the last thing he seemed to remember was Liu leaning over him, naked from the waist up. An image that was, he assumed, a hallucination brought on by shock of his injury or by pain medication he had been given. In his imagination she had small put perfectly formed breasts. That image of Liu, and the thought of her betrayal, brought a pain that was different, but as unbearable in its own way, as that from the wound in his belly.

He had needed several units of blood and some serious surgery to repair his damaged intestines. In addition he was placed under arrest. Potts had concocted a story that he and Keaton had conspired, along with Winston and Liu, in a plot directed by Robert Hopkins, the CEO of BiTech Pharmaceuticals.

According to Potts there was no anti-aging virus. "The very idea is ridiculous" Potts had said. Their plan, he claimed, was to run up the price of BiTech stock and make a killing when they sold out just before "revealing" that the virus did not work in humans. Winston (whose wound had been minor) and Liu had supported Keaton's version of events, but the District Attorney was concerned that Potts might be telling the truth. Potts had been truthful about Hopkins, and he saw no reason why he would lie about Keaton. Accordingly he had Keaton arrested and charged with conspiracy to commit fraud and murder, and he was placed in a solitary hospital room, with a twenty-four-hour police guard outside the door.

The door opened and Winston walked into the room. Keaton was surprised, and pleased, to see him. Except for a slight limp he looked good. For some reason he was dressed in a suit and tie and had his hair neatly tied back. "Who let you in? I'm supposed to be a mass murderer. I thought that I was not allowed visitors."

"It's good to see you too," Winston laughed. "It's true that you can't have visitors, but you are allowed to see your lawyer."

"Since when were you a lawyer?"

"It's one of the side benefits of being a computer nerd." He pulled an official looking document from his pocket. Jack had never seen a Pennsylvania State bar license, but his was convincingly real.

"If you are going to be my lawyer, then I might as well kill myself now and save the state the electric bill."

"I'll get you a real lawyer soon. I just wanted to see how you were doing, and see if I could help in any way."

"I don't know how. It looks like it's going to be my word against Potts'." Jack felt suddenly weak and sank back down into his bed. The pain in his abdomen was not as bad as the total sense of helplessness and despair. He had no one to blame but himself. In his zeal for secrecy he had doomed Jean and Peter and now, very likely, himself. "I have no hard evidence, and no witnesses that any of the work I did was real."

"Were you able to salvage anything at all from the fire in the lab?" Winston asked.

"Not much." An image of the Zuni Indian carving flashed through his mind, followed by a painful spasm in his stomach. "Every scrap of paper was consumed. My lab notes and animal records are just ashes."

"A smart guy like you should know enough to make backup copies."

"I did," Jack sighed, ignoring the insult. "All of the data on the hard drive of my office computer was backed up on CDROMs. The computer and the discs were all destroyed in the fire."

"How badly was the computer damaged?"

"The keyboard was melted and the monitor shattered."

"They don't matter. What did the CPU look like?"

"A large charcoal briquette."

"But it was physically intact?"

"Superficially, yes."

"Good, I can probably get your files back," Winston said firmly. "Where's the computer now?"

"I assume it has been disposed of. The university hired a fire cleanup company, and the last time I was there they were transferring the entire contents of the lab to a trash dumpster." Jack watched the drips falling, like clockwork, from the plastic bag that fed his IV. Watching the drips made him sleepy. "Can you really get the files back?"

"Maybe. Hard drives are a funny thing. A speck of dust can ruin them, but they can survive fairly high temperatures. But I can't do anything if the trash-man gets the computer first. And I will need you to direct me to the proper files." He was interrupted by shouting from the hall way. The door opened and the policeman came in, pushing a wheelchair in front of him.

"Excuse me." The policemen said. "This lady claims she is your mother." Keaton was thrilled to see Daisy. Because of the rapid sequence of events he had not had a chance to check on her recovery from the operation that had removed her tumor. She was wrapped with a surgical bandage that covered one half of her head, including her right ear and eye. An IV bag was hooked up to her arm. Other than that she looked pretty good.

"It's OK officer," Winston said. "I can vouch that this is Dr. Keaton's mother. How are you feeling Daisy?"

"He is not allowed visitors, except for his lawyer." The policeman was still clutching the handles of the wheelchair.

"Young man, if you know what is good for you, you will let me spend a few minutes with my son."

The policeman sighed. He could hardly arrest an old lady in a wheelchair, and he couldn't just let her sit outside making a ruckus. "Fifteen minutes," he said as he closed the door and returned to his post in the hallway, closing the door behind him.

"What a jerk off." Daisy said.

"He is just trying to do his job, mom."

"Then he should have arrested my ass. It's good to see you son. How did you get into this mess?"

Jack ignored the question. "I can assume, apparently, that the operation was a success."

Winston interrupted. "Jack, I am sure that you and Daisy have a lot to discuss, but we should think about recovering your computer."

"You could call the police. Maybe they can find it."

"Maybe, but it could take a day or more before I get them interested enough to get a search warrant and another day before they send out someone to actually look. I don't think we have any time to waste."

"You could look for it yourself," Jack suggested.

"I could really use you . . . "

"In case you didn't notice, I am a prisoner."

Winston considered this information. He glanced at Keaton's mother, who had sat quietly (for a change) listening to the discussion.

"Oh oh." Jack said. "I know that look in your eye. You have some kind of a plan."

"Indeed I do," Winston admitted. "I was noticing that you and your mother are about the same size. You even have matching IV bottles."

It was clear what Winston was getting at. "Tom, I think you've lost your mind. I am not going to dress up like my mother and try to sneak out of here. That cop is not blind."

"You would be amazed what a little bit of misdirection can accomplish." Winston turned to Daisy. "Do you need help getting out of the chair?"

"Nope." Daisy said emphatically. She stood up, wobbled for a moment, but quickly recovered her balance. She shoved the wheelchair toward Jack's bed. "They made me use the chair — they're afraid I might fall and sue the hospital — but I don't need it." Winston nevertheless moved to Daisy's side, grabbed her elbow and helped her to the bed. He removed Daisy's IV bag from its hook, and switched it with the one leading to Jack's arm.

Jack sighed. "OK, I'll give it a try, but if my mother goes to jail, you will pay." Winston helped Jack into his mother's wheel chair. The costume, such as it was, consisted of a gauze bandage wrapped around his head and a hospital blanket tossed loosely over his shoulders. Fortunately his mother had brought her purse, and she was able to complete the effect with a touch of lipstick and a liberal dousing of rouge to his cheeks.

Jack looked at himself in the mirror that hung from the closet door. He had not shaved for two days. He could not help but laugh out loud. "This is absurd."

"Not to worry," Winston said. He gave Jack his handkerchief. "You will need this. Remember you are a grieving mother."

Daisy stood by the door and, at Winston's cue began to sob hysterically, and theatrically. "Oh! My poor boy! How could this happen? Oh!" Keaton had never felt so close to his mother as at that moment. He had also never felt so embarrassed. Winston went out to the hall and asked the cop how to get to the cafeteria. He needed to be told three times to go to the second floor and turn left.

Jack pushed the wheelchair out the door, keeping his head down and turned away from the officer. He managed a halfhearted sob, but he was not the actor his mother was.

"Oh, let me help you Mrs. Keaton," Winston said and stepped behind the wheelchair. He quickly pushed Jack down the hallway, not once looking back. As anticipated the policeman had barely glanced at the departing wheelchair. The bandaged head and flash of rouge corresponded to his expected picture of Mrs. Keaton. She had every right to be upset about her son, who could be facing serious charges.

No one paid any attention as Winston pushed Jack out of the hospital to the parking lot. "How long do you think we have before they find your mother?"

"A couple of hours, when the nurse comes in to check the IV." Jack stripped the tape from his arm and pulled out the IV needle. He would survive for a few hours without its assistance. Winston helped Jack into his car. They pulled up behind the biology building a few minutes later (leaving a few irate drivers behind them). The dumpster was empty.

Jack slumped in the car seat, his hopes dashed. "We're too late."

Winston did not want to give up. "We could go to the city dump. Maybe we will get lucky."

"There's no chance. The city uses several landfills scattered around the area. Some are out of state. Even if we went to the right place, this load of trash would be just one of the thousands coming in today." The doors to the loading dock opened and Lester Jackson came out, pushing his janitor's cart in front of him.

"Yo, Doctor Keaton!" Les shouted and walked over to the car. "I thought you had been arrested. Did the cops finally figure out you couldn't have done those things they said you did on the TV, or did they just decide you weren't black enough to keep in jail?"

"Actually we broke out. I guess I am a fugitive from justice."

"Well you may be a smart professor, but you're not a very smart con. Why'd you come back here? You want to get caught?"

"We were looking for the trash from my lab, but it's been carted away already."

"Yeah, they came this morning. I'm afraid you just missed them."

Winston stared out of the car window. "Why is there a bio-hazard sticker on the dumpster?"

Jack perked up. The government's rules about waste from research labs were very strict. Scientists worked with a huge variety of hazardous substances, from cancer causing benzene to AIDS viruses. Everything except routine waste had to be specially disposed of. Even though the junk from his lab was either harmless, or made so by the fire, the authorities would treat it as if it was all poison. Jack knew that there was just one high temperature incinerator in the city that was licensed to handle laboratory waste, the one where Snuffles had gone to be cremated. It was a faint hope, but the incinerator was just a few miles away. He told Winston about the possibility that they could yet recover the computer and gave him the directions. Winston raced from the parking lot.

"You might want to slow down Tom." Keaton suggested as they careened down the narrow streets of West Philadelphia. "Remember you are carrying a fugitive from justice."

"True, but remember we are in Philadelphia. When was the last time you saw a Philly cop stop a speeder?"

"I have been meaning to ask you something." Jack said. "How did you get covered with soap suds the night I got shot? I damn near dropped dead on the spot when I saw you."

Winston laughed. "The thugs Potts hired to stage the robbery knocked me out and then tied me up. I was tied up real good – hands behind my back, legs bent under my butt and tied to the hands. About the only thing that I could move was my head."

"So how did you get loose? I know you have many talents, but I never thought of you as a Houdini."

"The bad guys made one big mistake," Winston said. "They tossed me in the bathtub. Fortunately I have one of those modern faucets, the ones with a lever to push instead of a knob to turn. I was able to use my head to turn the water on. Then I knocked an open bottle of shampoo into the water – one of the benefits of being single is that I never have to close things – and pushed the lever down to plug the drain. When the water got high enough, it soaked the ropes and let me to stretch them slightly. That, and the lubrication provided by the suds, allowed me to get my hands free."

At the incinerator a dump truck had just finished depositing its load on the conveyer belt that led to a shredder which would reduce everything to fine chips to feed the fire. As they pulled up next to the truck, they could see on the belt the unmistakable hulk of the computer moving inexorably toward the shredder. The incinerator staff could only look on with amazement as Winston jumped from the car and dived into the black, ash-covered debris on the belt. When he returned to the car his smile, gleaming white against his soot-covered face, said that he had been successful.

They took the blackened hulk back to Winston's house. Keaton had little hope, but his mood brightened when Winston removed the screws that held the case in place. The inside of the computer was remarkably intact. The heat had melted some of the insulation where the wires made contact with the case, but it looked otherwise undamaged. Winston removed the hard drive and then transferred it to one of his own computers. After about fifteen minutes with a soldering gun he was ready to test it.

"OK, let's give it a spin," Winston said as he powered up the computer. He made a few mouse clicks and the monitor filled with symbols. None, however, were names that Jack had used for his various files.

"I guess it was worth a try," Jack said. "Let's get back to the hospital before they arrest my mother for abetting my escape."

"Don't be so negative." Winston highlighted one of the meaningless file names and pressed the mouse button. The screen filled with a document that Jack immediately recognized. It contained the treatment details and lifetime data of one of the experimental animals. "Your FAT is screwed up, but the drive seems to be otherwise intact."

"My fat?"

"File Allocation Table. All of your records are just as you left them, only the names have been lost." Jack had many more questions, but their conversation was brought to an end by the sound of a siren, and of the police knocking on the door.

46

Liu awoke in the grey light of her bedroom. Above her, one of the water stains appeared to have taken on the grim countenance of a human skull. It had been two days since the shootings at Winston's house, and Liu could remember little that had taken place after she had stumbled from the woods with Jack's limp body draped over her shoulders. In desperation to save him she had tried to staunch the flow of blood and then somehow, finding a strength she did not know she had, carried him back to Winston's house.

Later, after the ambulance had come, she had put the blood-soaked garment back on. A policeman had kindly offered her a coat to cover her nakedness, but she had irrationally insisted on her own blouse. The wet fabric had clung to her skin like a shroud, chilling her until she began to shiver uncontrollably, but even then she had refused the policeman's coat. She could vaguely remember throwing up, and then someone from the ambulance giving her a shot of medication. The next two days, filled with police interrogations and lawyers, were little but a fog to her.

Now Liu could feel the fog begin to lift. It was time to face the new realities of her existence. Her betrayal of Keaton had led to his shooting and nearly to his death, and her guilt would never go away. She wanted to rush to the hospital and throw herself at his feet to beg forgiveness, but it was a forgiveness that she was unworthy of. The humiliation of even seeing Jack again was more than she could bear to think about. She could not imagine that he would forgive her, nor did she deserve his forgiveness. In a strange way she wanted him to hate her, since only his hate could be adequate punishment for her betrayal.

Liu got out of bed. The past couple of days she had eaten little, and her stomach was churning with hunger. She made a cup of tea and some toast, which turned to sawdust in her mouth. One thing was clear; she would not see Jack again. That this was a minor issue anyway. With the arrest of Dr. Potts her job and her visa had become instantly worthless, and she would soon be returning to China. Amazingly, she had not been arrested herself. The authorities had concluded that Liu's behavior, improper as it was, did not constitute a crime. In her own mind, however, she was as guilty as both Potts and Hopkins.

In a way she was more guilty than they were. They had acted according to their intrinsic nature, while Liu had acted in profound contradiction to all that she believed in. She had worked with Potts long enough to know that he was greedy and ambitious and without ethical standards. Yet she had agreed to be a spy for him, and lying to herself that she was doing nothing wrong. Scientists as a group were ambitious and competitive, but they were also intolerant of anything that gave even the appearance of scientific misconduct. Her actions had become public knowledge and Liu knew that she would never work as a research scientist again, at least not in America.

There was little point in waiting for the immigration service to revoke her visa. She would make arrangements to return to China as soon as possible.

47

The police were not amused by Keaton's escape in drag and when he was back in the hospital they doubled his guard and the only visitors they allowed were medical staff and the real lawyer that Winston hired for him. Fortunately the data from the restored hard drive quickly convinced the authorities that he was telling the truth. When Potts was confronted with the data, and the threat of losing his plea bargain, he changed his story and admitted that Keaton was innocent. The police guards were removed and Keaton was allowed to have visitors. His mother was still in the hospital, not in jail thankfully, and visited him every day. Actually she did more than visit, she took over all of his routine care, allowing the nurses to do little more than change the IV bag and take his temperature. Jack found it amusing that he was once again a baby under his mother's loving care.

"Tell me about the girl." She asked on the third day of his stay.

"Which girl?"

"You know, the one who saved your life. The Chinese girl."

"She didn't save my life. In fact she worked with Potts, the man who shot me. She was his spy."

"The policeman said you would have died if she hadn't acted as quickly as she did."

Jack thought about his Mother's words. He had little memory of the events that occurred after he had swung the rock at Liu and missed. One moment he was running through the woods bleeding, the next he was waking up in a hospital room surrounded by police and doctors. "What did she do exactly?"

"For one thing she stopped the bleeding by stuffing her blouse in the hole in your belly. Then she carried you through the woods back to Winston's house. Imagine that little girl carrying you all that way."

"She took her blouse off . . . " Jack laughed out loud, not minding at all the pain it brought to his abdomen. "And I thought I was hallucinating!" He explained to his mother about the image he had of Liu leaning over him, naked from the waist up.

"Well, she must really like you! Exposing herself like that. I hope you thanked her." Jack, of course, had not talked to Liu since the shooting. He knew from the news reports that she had been questioned and released without being charged with any criminal offence. She had not called him, nor did he expect that she would.

His discussion with Daisy was interrupted by the appearance of Winston. "You're looking much better Jack," he said cheerfully. "Apparently all you needed was a bit of TLC. I am very jealous. It almost makes me sorry I only had a flesh wound."

"Believe me. It is not a fair trade."

Daisy began clearing away the lunch dishes. "We were just talking about that nice Chinese girl that saved Jack's life. What was her name?"

"Her name was Liu, mother, and it was her fault I got shot in the first place."

Winston had watched the news reports and knew just a little of what had taken place outside of his house. "I thought she saved your miserable life?"

"She spied for Potts. She told him where the virus was and she copied the DNA sequence data from my computer."

"She copied files from your computer?"

"Yes."

"That doesn't make sense. When you interrupted Potts at my place, he was in the act of transferring the DNA data from my computer onto his own disc."

"But he had it already . . . " Keaton was certain that Liu had made a copy of the sequence files the day she was alone in his office. Their conversation was interrupted by the ringing of the telephone.

The call was from Henry Norton, the Chairman of the Molecular Biology department at Jefferson. "I hope you're feeling better." He said. "You know we are all praying for your quick recovery. It was a total shock that one of our own could do something like this."

"I'm feeling better every day. Thanks for your concern. I know that no one at Jefferson knew anything about Potts' illegal activities."

After some more pleasantries Henry got to the real point of his call. "As you might imagine, we have a bit of a problem here. Potts had a large laboratory with almost a dozen people working under several different grants. We need someone to take over his position as soon as possible. You were the consensus choice of the department."

Keaton was stunned by the offer. It would mean more money for his research than he had ever imagined and enough trained people under him to explore ideas that he had been thinking about for years, but which he had neither the time, money nor technical assistance to pursue. Yet he was hesitant to accept the offer. There were drawbacks. He enjoyed the actual experience of working at the lab bench, but if he took the Jefferson University offer he would be so busy with paperwork and administration that there would be little chance to do experiments with his own hands. For years he had been preaching the evils of big labs to whoever would listen. A single individual like Potts could control enough resources to support dozens of small research labs. Science thrived on diversity, but large labs not only controlled a disproportionate share of resources, they naturally tended to work on the same "hot" topics because that was where the money was.

"Would you like to take a day to think it over?" Henry said in response to Keaton's silence.

"Yes, I would." Jack hung up. While he was on the phone, his mother had busied herself clearing off the remnants of the lunch she had brought him. She would not allow him to eat the hospital food that was delivered to the patients, which she accurately described as inedible. The hospital cafeteria made food that was at somewhat better, and three times a day Daisy would go to the cafeteria to get meals for the two of them. Daisy was an old hand at hospital life and she had learned that certain cafeteria items, such as eggs, French fries and salads, were usually safe. Jack understood that the trips for food were therapeutic for his mother, and he made no effort to dissuade her.

"What was that about?" she asked. Jack explained the offer to her. "Are you going to take it?"

"I don't know. I am not sure I want to become an administrator. And after all these years of criticizing large labs it seems hypocritical of me to take over one." His mother started wiping his bed stand with a sponge that she had appropriated from the nurse's storeroom. It irritated him to see his mother, barely recovered from her brain surgery, cleaning up after him. "You know you may be depriving a poor minimum wage hospital employee of his job by doing that," he scolded.

"No I'm not," she said firmly. "I am giving him an opportunity to do something more useful with his energy. Maybe now he'll have some time to actually help patients." Jack watched his mother finish cleaning his bed stand. She had a point, and Jack saw immediately that she had also pointed toward a solution to his dilemma. There was nothing intrinsically wrong with large labs; it was just that they tended to misuse their resources. It was like a hospital using MDs to clean bedpans. He remembered Liu's unhappiness with her job and how Potts had crushed her creativity. A well-run lab would unleash the imagination and energy of people like Liu. Jack suddenly knew what his answer would be to the Jefferson University offer. He called Henry back and gave him the conditions under which he would take the job. Henry resisted at first, but Jack was insistent, and he soon gave in.

Jack was released from the hospital the next day. Although he was still too weak to do much productive work, it was important to begin the process of reorganizing what had been George Potts' laboratory. He began by calling all of Potts' staff together for a meeting. They assembled in a paneled room lined with portraits of notables from Jefferson's past, and filled by a polished wood table that probably cost more than Jack's annual salary. The members of Potts' laboratory entered the room one at a time, took their seats and waited silently. Jack was familiar with a few of them from meetings and conferences, but none of them acknowledged Jack's existence with as much as a nod.

He had hoped that Liu would come to the meeting, but was hardly surprised at her absence. The few words he had for Potts' staff seemed barely adequate. It was easy to make promises, and his offer of more openness and research freedom were met with quiet indifference. Actions, he hoped, would ultimately win them over. After adjourning the meeting he sat at the table for several minutes, idly running his fingers over the glossy surface. Eventually he gathered the courage for his next task.

He found Liu in the cubical that served as her office. A large trash can, filled with notebook paper and shredded computer printouts sat next to her desk. She was going through a desk drawer, placing some objects in a small cardboard box, and others into the trash can.

"How are you Liu?" Jack asked. Liu turned to face him. She looked terrible. The red, swollen eyes told of tears that had flowed copiously and for too long. Her complexion, pale at best, had turned ashen. She was clearly surprised to see Jack. The ballpoint pen that she held in her hand dropped to the floor, breaking the tense silence.

"I will be out of here in just a few minutes, Dr. Keaton. All of my data is in a box in the laboratory and I will leave my keys on the desk when I go."

Keaton stepped toward Liu, his hands reaching for hers. He felt the urge to hold her tight and tell her that everything was all right. But he didn't. Instead he stopped short and spoke to her in the formal voice of professor to student. "As you probably heard," he said, "I have been asked to take over Potts's lab. I have talked to the chairman of the department and he has agreed that you can stay. That is if you want to."

Liu sat quietly for a while, staring down at her hands. Slowly she raised her head to look at him, and spoke in a voice that was barely audible. "What do you want? Do you want me to stay?"

"Yes." Again Jack felt himself at the edge of a precipice. The words "I forgive you," came to him, but his tongue was strangely paralyzed. What came out was "I need . . . your help." He found himself explaining how he wanted to reorganize the lab, to give more autonomy to the staff and to release their creativity. He needed somebody, he explained, who knew the lab and its personnel.

"I have made arrangements to return to China." Liu's voice was cold and flat.

"If you could stay for even a few weeks, it would be a tremendous help."

"I suppose I could do that, until my flight back to China. What do you want me do first?"

Jack had made plans to go to Winston's house later that day to begin the process of reorganizing and sorting the data on the restored hard drive. This was going to be a complex task. Each file would have to be opened, identified and renamed. Winston had promised to help, but he was no biologist and most of the information would be meaningless to him. "I need to begin work on recovering my computer files. I could use some assistance."

"I'll be glad to help, Dr. Keaton."

48

Now that he was out of the hospital Jack found that he had become the center of a media storm. Potts had implicated Hopkins in the death of the homeless men in St. Louis, as well as Goodman and Cooke, in return for a lighter sentence, but Hopkins had fled the country at the first news reports and before the police could arrest him. Airline records suggested that he had gone, via Mexico, to Cuba, where he would be protected from extradition. With the shootings and the arrest of a respected scientist there was no hope of maintaining secrecy and news of the immortality virus spread around the world in hours. The National Institutes of Health responded by establishing a team of high level scientists to examine the data and make recommendations for future action. They were, of course, severely limited by the fact that all samples of the virus had disappeared. It would be up to Keaton to reassemble his restored computer data and make a report.

Winston had copied the data files to the hard drive of a second computer to allow Liu and Jack to work simultaneously. They worked in nearly complete silence, interrupted only by occasional questions from Liu about how to rename certain files. After two uninterrupted hours of sitting in front of the computer Jack's gunshot wound, not to mention his eyes, began to hurt and he suggested a break. Liu used the opportunity to go to the bathroom.

When Liu was safely out of the room, Winston spoke. "What the hell is going on with you two? I could cut the tension between you and her with a rusty spoon."

"I cannot forget what she did."

"Let me show you something." Winston set down at the computer with the restored hard drive and made a few mouse clicks. "You're software stores a record of all file transfers." A dialog box appeared that said "Restore Deleted File? Yes No"

"What is your point?"

"Look at the name of the file, and the drive designation. The last deletion was on a USB device, and at a time when Liu was in your lab. She may have copied your files, Jack, but she subsequently deleted it. Now why do you think she did that?"

Jack shook his head. "I don't know, but I guess that explains why Potts wanted the data from your computer."

"I think she cares about you."

"She spied on me."

"And then she didn't," Winston said. "She swiped your precious data, and then she threw it away. So you tell me, which act is more telling?"

"I don't know," Keaton said. "And I don't see what difference it makes."

"Because I see how much you like her."

"I don't love Liu." The words echoed strangely in his ears.

"I didn't say anything about love. How about compatibility and mutual respect. Contrary to what you learned at the movies, love is not a causative agent, it is a consequence. Even the uneducated masses know that earthquakes are not caused by buildings falling down, and that wet streets don't cause rain. But they seem to think that love is what brings people together." Winston paused and wiped something from his eyes. "Enough about you, let's talk about me for a while. Did you ever wonder why I live alone?"

"Not really. I assume you made a lifestyle decision, just as I did."

Winston let out a satirical laugh. "You never made a lifestyle decision, any more than I did. It may surprise you to know that I was in love once. When I got out of college I took a job with a small software company. I worked with a young woman called Molly. We were both dedicated to our work and our careers, but we found time when not writing code to have some fun."

Winston sighed and wiped his eyes again. "You know what killed our relationship – we were too perfect together. Being together was so natural and so easy that we never gave it much thought. Perhaps if we had fought or found fault in each other, like so many lovers do, we would have appreciated more what we had." Winston paused again.

"What happened to her?"

"She got a good job offer in California. Only when she was gone did I realize what I had lost. But I did nothing other than send a few pointless e-mail messages. You know, stuff like 'Hope you're enjoying the good life in California — but please don't become a Republican.' Over time the messages became fewer and fewer. Then one day . . . "

Winston stopped, unable to say the words. After a few deep breaths he continued, his voice tight. "One day I discovered that I was lonely. Work had been my only companion for years and then one day, for no reason that I have ever been able to determine, I was sitting in front of my computer . . . " He paused to point to an obsolete IBM shoved into a corner. "That computer, to be exact. I was sitting there attempting to solve a nested loop problem and out of nowhere I began to cry. Months of holding back my loneliness fell away like a busted dam. When I stopped crying I picked up the phone and called Molly in California. A man answered. Her new husband of course." Winston had to stop again.

"Maybe it just wasn't meant to be, Molly and you."

"That's just it. It *was* meant to be, it most certainly was meant to be. I chose to let it not be."

"Why do you think you did that?"

"Fear. Ignorance. Stupidity. Arrogance . . . Take your pick. One from column A and one from column B. People, unlike computers, are complex and rarely act for a single reason. If I were a computer program, I could have located a software error, re-booted myself, and perhaps my life would have been different." The sound of a toilet flushing came from the hallway. "Remember what I said to you when you first came to me with the redwood idea."

"Not exactly."

"Follow your instincts."

Liu came back and she and Jack returned to sorting out his computer files. During the five years of his experiments he had regularly taken photographs of the animals using a digital camera.

He was cross checking the JPG image files against the restored computer records. There were hundreds of photographs and each one had to be matched with the appropriate entry in his computerized notes. Liu pulled up a chair next to him.

"Can I ask you a question, Dr. Keaton?" He nodded. "When I was in your lab that first time I observed that the date when each mouse was born and its experimental treatment group was written on the cage label."

"You mean when you were spying for Potts." Keaton said, hating himself immediately for his cruelty.

"Yes," Liu sighed. "When I was spying. You may not believe this, but I greatly respect you as a scientist."

"Thank you. I respect you too, but I have to wonder whatever made you get involved with Potts. Why did you ever agree to spy for him?"

Liu was silent for a while. "I don't know." She sighed. "It's a question I have thought a lot about recently, but the truth is I don't really know why I did it."

"Did Potts threaten you?"

"It wouldn't matter if he did."

"But you had to know that what he wanted you to do was wrong."

"Of course. I know that." Liu paused and stared at her hands for a moment. "What people do sometimes cannot be explained, and even good people can do bad things."

Keaton remembered that Liu had very possibly saved his life. "And even bad people can do good."

"Yes, that too."

It was time to change the subject. "You had a question for me?" Jack said.

"What bothered me was that the mouse labels were not encrypted. Shouldn't you have used a blind protocol in your experiments?"

"In a way I did. When I started the experiment, I assigned random numbers to each animal. The traditional protocol. Then I realized that I could not avoid remembering which mouse was born on which date or which one had the virus. In retrospect, I should have had someone else give the animals a code number, but at the time I wanted to keep my work as secret as possible. As an alternative I came up with a system that would actually confuse me so I would never be totally sure of the status of any animal."

Jack opened the computer's graphics program and wrote the word YELLOW which he colored red and the word BLUE, which he colored green. "Read to me the colors you see, not the words but the actual colors." Liu quickly discovered that it was almost impossible to avoid calling the red-colored word "yellow" or the green-colored one "blue."

Jack explained what was happening. "Your brain sees the written word and that data takes precedence over the information that you know is actually correct. I realized that if I gave each animal a label with a fictitious birth date and a fictitious treatment record my memory would get so confused that I would never be sure what was correct. So if I saw a mouse labeled as having the virus treatment, I would tend to think that it did, even if I knew that it didn't. By the end of the experiment I was so confused, only the computer knew for sure which animal was which."

"So the animal that I saw which had the code number 317C and was labeled as having the virus treatment and being five years old was not what the label said."

"Probably not." Keaton made a few key strokes on the computer. "Mouse 317C was barely a year old when you saw it, and never had a virus treatment."

Liu smiled and shook her head in amusement. "So if I had seen a cage with an old, untreated mouse but with a label that said it had been given the virus, I would have assumed that your experiments had failed and all of this misery could have been avoided."

"Probably," Jack admitted. It was nice, he thought, to see Liu smile. Jack made a few more key strokes. "Here is an animal that was labeled as being young and untreated, but is actually the oldest animal in the treated group."

"That is a strange looking mouse," she said.

"It's not surprising. Would you believe that mouse is almost five years old?"

"It looks good for such an old mouse, but that's not what bothers me. Show me a photo of one of the control animals." Jack made a few mouse clicks and brought up another image. "Can you place this image and the last one side by side?" Jack could not see what had sparked Liu's interest. He had spent years with these animals. If there was any difference he would have picked it up. But there was no harm in humoring Liu and with a few more clicks he had the two mouse images side by side on the monitor.

"Oh my god." Jack moaned. "How could I have missed that?" The differences, though subtle, were obvious when the animals were viewed next to one another. The changes in the animals had been so slow that he had not seen it as it happened. He quickly scanned the other images. Every experimental animal showed the same changes.

"Check your quantitative data," Liu suggested. "Something might show up there." Jack had taken weekly measurements of body weight and size for each animal. There was considerable variation in the data but a spreadsheet program quickly combined all of the data into a pair of graphs. The graphs confirmed the interpretation of the photographs.

49

Once Hopkins had settled in Cuba, he began the task of establishing a new life. He was disgusted to find that most of the money he had sent to maintain the estate had, apparently, been siphoned off to various corrupt government officials. As a result, the grounds and the main house were filthy and decrepit, like much of Cuba, but it would not be long before it would be restored to its former glory. Hopkins felt better than he had in years. The brief attack of flu-like symptoms had quickly passed. It may have been a case of wishful thinking but he was convinced that he was feeling younger and more vigorous. Certainly his appetite had improved. He seemed to be always hungry and started to put on weight. One morning, a few months after arriving in Cuba, Hopkins split a jacket that had inexplicably become too small for him. All his clothes were becoming snug, but when he examined his body it was as lean and fat free as it ever was. As months passed he had to replace his wardrobe several times. The only things in his closet that still fit were his hats.

Back in the United States Potts had begun his ten-year sentence. Potts, of course, had not given all of Keaton's immortality virus to Hopkins. That would have been foolish, and Potts had kept plenty for himself. It was fortunate that Keaton and Winston had lived and that the police had never tied Misha's death to him, or he might have been given a life sentence, which could have lasted for a very long time indeed. As it was, he could look forward to a good life even after his sentence was completed. It was too bad that Hopkins's had escaped. The prosecutor was upset, but a deal was a deal, and it wasn't Potts' fault that they had taken so long to work out the details.

They put him in the minimum security prison at Allenwood. It was no country club, but it wasn't hell either. They kept him fed and clothed. Speaking of clothes, he would need to see the Warden about getting another prison outfit. The one they gave him on admission must have shrunk in the wash. He needed a larger size.

50

Jack analyzed the data over and over. The facts, he knew, were not going to change, but he needed to reassure himself of the conclusions. Growth of the fetus and the ensuing transformation of the child into an adult were the events usually associated with human development. But aging was also a stage of development. The satellite DNA sequences appeared to control the timing of many developmental stages. Each step of development was closely interconnected to all of the others. Disturbing one stage would undoubtedly alter some other part of the developmental program.

The differences that Liu had noticed between the control mice and the ones treated with the virus were real. To even attempt human trials would clearly be unethical. He picked up the phone and dialed the number of the Aging Institute at NIH. He asked for Albert Westfield, the newly appointed director of the Ageing Institute and was connected to his secretary.

"He is in a meeting right now. I will have him call you back as soon as he is done."

Jack responded as forcefully as he could. "No, you will go and get him right now. Tell him that this is urgent." Moments later Albert was on the phone.

"Albert, have you ever heard of the term paedomorphosis?"

"It sounds familiar, the term means 'child-shaped' if I remember my Latin."

Jack took a deep breath and explained what he had discovered. "My colleague, Meiling Liu, and I were analyzing the data from the mice that had been injected with the anti-aging virus. We noticed – actually she noticed – that the treated mice had grown larger than normal."

"That doesn't seem so strange." Albert said. "After all they were significantly older."

"Yes, that's true. But they weren't larger in general, only their bodies were larger."

"So they got fat?" Albert sounded annoyed that he had been called out of a meeting for what seemed trivial information.

Jack got to the point. "No, they were not fat. Their bodies, bones, muscle even internal organs had grown larger. But their heads had stayed the same size."

"Why is this important?"

"Because of Paedomorphosis," Jack said. "Paedomorphosis is the theory that human evolution was based, in part, on the premature arrest of embryonic development. The head of mammalian embryos develops faster than does the body. At early stages a human fetus looks pretty much like every other mammalian fetus, a large head attached to a tiny body. But at birth a newborn human still looks, in terms of head to body proportions, like a mammalian fetus. Humans, as compared to other mammals, are all premature births."

"But eventually we grow up," Albert interjected.

"That's just it," Jack said. "We don't grow up. Not in terms of head to body proportions.

As people grow their bodies began to catch up with the head, but never quite make it. As a result, an adult human has a head to body ratio similar to that of an infant chimpanzee. The relatively large brain of humans, and the enhanced intellectual abilities that come with it, reflect the fact that, developmentally speaking, humans are overgrown babies."

"And what does this have to do with the action of your virus?" Albert said. "I thought the satellite DNA was only supposed to control the rate of aging."

"Apparently it does more than that. The mouse data suggests that the satellite DNA also controls the onset of developmental maturity. It determines, among other things, when the body stops growing. Fooling with the satellite DNA starts it growing again."

Albert seemed incredulous. "Explain this to me again, but this time in terms that I could use when I have to explain to a congressman why we should drop this project."

"Tell him that if he takes the anti-aging virus he may live for many, many years, but he will probably do so as a very large chimpanzee."

51

Hopkins could no longer find clothes that fit him. This did not bother him though. He rarely thought about it, or about anything else these days. In his brain neurons that enabled higher levels of thought were being pushed aside and replaced by the growing needs of his ever larger body. Planning beyond the next minute had become an impossible chore. His mind was filled with thoughts of food and sex, but little else. Most of the people he had hired when he came to Cuba had long since left. Occasionally he tried to talk with his nurse, who had stayed on to look after him, but all that seemed to come out were meaningless hoots. He scratched under his armpit and wondered vaguely when his food would be coming. Finally the door of his room was opened and his nurse came in. She tossed a bunch of bananas at his feet and left again without a word.

Potts had been removed from the Allenwood minimum security prison. They were not equipped to care for him there and eventually, after much discussion by the authorities, he was transferred to the Yerkes Regional Primate Center in Georgia. As a scientist Potts would have been impressed with the army of researchers and range of expensive equipment that was being devoted to the study of his body. He was, however, no longer capable of such human thoughts. All that he knew was that his body was being poked, prodded, stabbed and abused on an almost daily basis. He tried to object, but his research team had long since learned to ignore his hoots and hollers, which were no worse than those of any of the other apes in their experimental program.

52

Jack picked Liu up at her apartment. "Where are we going?" she asked. He had not given her a reason for picking her up today, other than that it was important.

"You will see soon." Shortly he pulled the car up in front of a large, grey industrial looking building. Liu guessed where she was from the animal smells and the sound of barking that wafted from behind a low brick wall.

"It's an animal shelter." She noted. "What are we doing here?"

"Be patient," he said and led her inside. Muffled barking came from behind a closed door. Jack spoke to an elderly black woman sitting at an old wooden desk that was piled with papers. "I am Jack Keaton. I was here the other day."

"Oh yes Mr. Keaton. Your paperwork is ready." Jack signed a couple of forms and the woman opened the door behind her, setting the dogs into a renewed round of barking. She yelled at the top of her voice to carry over the noise. "Corey! Bring out the two for Keaton."

"Two of what?" Liu wondered. The question was soon answered as a worker emerged through the door. In front of him, prancing excitedly, was a puppy on a leash. He looked like a mix between a poodle and a terrier. Liu knelt down to greet him and he responded by leaping into her arms and licking her face furiously. "I think he likes me!" Liu laughed. "He is about the cutest puppy I have ever seen."

"I am glad you like him."

"The woman said 'two for Keaton.' I assume more is on the way." The worker left the dog in Liu's arms and returned to the kennel. He returned with a cage. Inside the cage a kitten, unhappy to have been disturbed during her afternoon nap, meowed plaintively.

"What possessed you to adopt a dog and a cat?"

“It's not for me. It's for us.”

“For us ....” Liu repeated dumbly.

“If you will have the three of us.”

Liu blushed and threw her arms around Jack, nearly crushing the dog between them. Oblivious to the shelter workers, who looked on in amusement, they kissed deeply while the puppy, suddenly finding two human faces in reach, went into a frenzy of licking.

THE END

If you enjoyed this book, you might also like my soon to be released psychological thriller Bird In The Window. Here is Chapter 1:

The shrill beep of the alarm clock woke C.R. at six a.m. Next to him on the bed Tawana mumbled something unintelligible, and rolled over onto her side. His wife had learned to ignore the alarm, and would sleep for another hour or more. C.R. envied her. There would be no extended sleep for him, unless he wanted to be late for his job at the post office, and that could have bad consequences. Just yesterday he had blown up at his supervisor, who had complained about his "productivity."

While being reprimanded C.R. had felt as if a black cloud was floating through his brain. Briefly, he had thought about smashing a fist into the smirking face of the supervisor. Even better, would be to put a bullet between his flapping lips. It was a good thing that the supervisor was on the other side of the desk, and that C.R. was unarmed. After a few moments the dark cloud had passed, but he had been shaken by the experience. It was as if another person had taken over his mind. C.R. had never hit anyone in his life. Yes he had a gun, but it was in the bedside chest, and it was for protection – not murder. Fortunately, the real C.R. had returned before any real harm had been done. But another black mark on his record could cost him the best job he ever had, or could imagine.

Truth was, he was not moving the mail as fast as he used to. At one time he took pride in his ranking as one of the fastest sorters in the office. But lately he had begun to view his job as meaningless scut work, which was a common view of his coworkers but a new one for him. It was difficult to take pride in a job that was rapidly becoming the task of microchips and scanners. Yet they still needed people like him to interpret the scribbles on the envelopes that the machines spit out into as unreadable. At first he had viewed each letter that he handled as a personal duty to its unknown sender and recipient. A child's letter properly delivered would not change the world, but it could bring joy to an elderly grandmother – and make C.R. proud.

Now he really didn't give a damn.

He sat on the edge of the bed for a moment to let his sleepiness dissipate. The aspirin he had taken last night had long since worn off, and the dull pain in his head had returned. Tawana had already gone back to sleep. She looked peaceful curled up in the bed next to him. Her skin, normally chocolate brown, gleamed like polished ebony in the morning light. Even after ten years of marriage, waking up next to this beautiful woman made the start of each day special.

Tawana gave grunt and began to snore.

"Damn," C.R. muttered, and stood up. He sped through his morning routine, and was dressed and ready for work in half an hour. Before leaving he poked his head into his daughter's bedroom. She was still asleep. C.R. rapped on the door. "Time to get up sweetheart."

"In a minute, daddy."

He played this game nearly every weekday with Serena. Typically he would go to the bed and tickle her feet or rap her on the head with a pillow. He was in no mood for such games today. "Get your butt out of bed, and get ready for school." he shouted. "And go get your lazy mother up."

His day, and his mood, did not improve at work. The problems began with a single letter. For each piece of unreadable mail that came to his work station C.R. would type in the correct zip, which would be attached to the envelope as a bar code strip. The automatic sorter would then send the envelop to the correct outgoing bin. In this case, the sorter had immediately spit out the bar-coded envelope. This was not that unusual. Only about half of the 100,000 possible zip codes were in actual use, and senders were often careless. His super had picked up the envelope, made a grunting noise and walked over to C.R.'s station.

"What the hell's wrong with you," he shouted, as he tossed the envelope on C.R.'s desk. "You know there are no zero zero codes."

C.R. glanced at the address. The first two numbers of the zip sure looked like a pair of zero's. He looked closer, and realized that the first zero had a small tail, and was no doubt a nine. Which made sense, as the letter was addressed to a California destination. However, he was not about to give the supervisor the satisfaction. "Hey, my job is to read what people write."

"Your job is to see that people get their mail in a timely fashion."

"And your job, apparently, is to be an asshole." The supervisor stared at C.R. for a moment, as if he couldn't believe what he was hearing. For that matter, C.R. could hardly believe what he had just said. "What the hell is wrong with me," he thought. The supervisor said nothing, but took a pad from his shirt pocket, made some notations, then turned on his heels and stomped away.

That evening, C.R. watched a Phillies game (Another blowout loss. When the hell were they going to a fifth starter who could throw strikes?) and went to bed around midnight. A couple of aspirins and half a six pack had taken the edge off of his headache and he looked forward to a good night's sleep. Tomorrow was Sunday, and a blessed day off. He slipped into bed quietly, so as not to wake Tawana, and was soon sound asleep. . .

"Tap . . tap . . . .tap . .tap . .tap . . . .tap . .tap . . ." C.R. awoke with a start, and opened his eyes. The dim reddish light of the bedroom told of a sun that was just rising. He glanced at the clock, blinking several times to clear his blurry eyes. It was six-fifteen.

His wife stirred. "What is that noise?" Tawana asked, her voice thick with sleep.

"Tap . . . tap . tap . tap . . . tap . .tap . . .tap"

C.R. sat up and looked out the window behind his pillow. "Crazy Charley's back," he said. Crazy Charley was the name they had given the bird who had first appeared at that same window last summer. The bird, an undistinguished grey creature, had awakened them one morning by pecking at the glass. Apparently, at least this was his theory, the bird was responding to a reflection of himself in the window. Determined to expel the intruder from his territory the bird had attacked it unmercifully. This crazy behavior had continued for over a week, ending as mysteriously as it had begun. Now, a year later, Crazy Charlie was back.

C.R. groaned and shook his head. The beers from the previous night had taken their toll, and a splitting headache now filled the void left by the alcohol. Tawana had already closed her eyes and gone back to sleep.

"Tap ..tap.. tap......tap..tap.............tap..tap..tap..tap..tap."

C.R. waved his hand at the window and the bird flew away. "And don't come back," he said, and fell back into the bed. He had to get some sleep. He thought about going to the bathroom to get an aspirin, but the headaches seemed be getting impervious to over-the-counter pills. A couple of Percocet's remained from an old prescription (for wrist pain that had come from years of sorting letters), but he would save those for a major headache, when only a powerful pain-killer would let sleep come.

"Tap ..tap..tap.........tap........tap...tap ..tap..tap..."

C.R. bolted upright. "That's it!" he shouted. He opened the drawer of the bed-side chest and pulled out the loaded pistol that he kept there "just in case." In this part of town crime was a constant threat and he had a family to protect. The bird was perched on the window sill, and just the upper part of his body was visible. C. R. raised the gun. The bird cocked his head and gave C.R. a puzzled look.

The gun exploded, and the face of the bird was replaced by a perfectly round hole in the glass. A network of lacy cracks surrounded the hole, but the window was otherwise intact. C.R. was surprised that the window hadn't shattered into a thousand pieces.

"Cleophus! What are you doing!" Tawana screamed.

"Getting rid of that crazy bird."

"You're the crazy one, Cleophus. You just blew a hole in the window. Where you going to get the money to fix it?"

C. R.'s head was pounding. He did not like to be called by his full name. He had told his wife to call him C.R. His name, he had told her a thousand times, is C.R. Phelts. Cleophus was a joke that his parents had played on him.

"Don't be calling me Cleophus," he said.

"What you talking about." Tawanda's voice was like fingernails on a blackboard. "You just blew a hole in the window, and now I shouldn't use your name." Tawanda took a deep breath and began to shout at the top of her voice. "Cleophus ...Cleophus...Cleophus..."

"Man, I need some sleep," C.R. muttered. His head was pounding. The gun exploded again and the room became quiet. Tawana had fallen back on her pillow and appeared to be sleeping peacefully. Blood, impossibly red in the morning light, poured like syrup from a hole that had appeared in the center of her forehead. It flowed down her face and began to spread across the sheets. "Damn," he muttered. If the bed got wet, he would never be able to get back to sleep. He pushed at her, but she was a dead weight, and barely moved.

"Get up," he said.

The door opened. "Mommy, what was that noise?" Serena said.

"Go back to bed, sweetheart," C. R. answered, and pushed again at Tawana's unmoving hulk. Serena's mouth flew open and she gave out a piercing scream ...

ENDORSEMENTS

An intriguing and captivating read that's scary and hopeful in the same time. Scary of the thought of what could happen if we don't wake up and become more proactive participants on our life on Earth ... and hopeful about the impact this book can have on people around the world, increasing our awareness about the consequences of ignoring the water's power. It was here long before us, and it will still be here after humanity vanished from Earth... if we allow it this to happen. We still have a choice... but not for long!

—Gabriela Casineanu, Thoughts Designer, Coach, Catalyst
http://GabrielaCasineanu.com

Claudiu Murgan's 'Water Entanglement' provides a unique and compelling view of how water is connected to all life. What we do to water, we do to ourselves."

—Nina Munteanu, author of *Water Is...The Meaning of Water*

"Claudiu Murgan's book, Water Entanglement, takes readers on a fascinating journey into a barren, water-rationed Earth several decades in the future, revealing the uncomfortable and shocking reality of where the Earth is headed if humanity continues to behave unconsciously and ignorantly towards water. Water Entanglement serves as a wake-up call to humanity, challenging all of us to seek a better understanding of and greater respect for water, so that we may one day know that water is intelligent, conscious, and divinely coded. This heightened awareness will facilitate greater communication with the species of water, a future development that may be the fastest and most direct path

out of the world's current water crisis and into a brighter Earth
reality saturated with respect, love, cooperation, and compassion."

—Rainey Highley, author of *The Water Code—*
Unlocking the Truth Within

Claudiu Murgan's Water Entanglement is a gripping story of the
disorder that is caused by the Earth's inhabitants disrespect for
water. Intriguing plot takes us through futuristic events. Water
needs to be rationed leading to catastrophic worldwide phenomenon. Water Entanglement leaves us with an awakening message
for us all about our relationship with water.

It pulls us in to rethink about our connection with water and the
power of water.

—Susan Ksiezopolski, President/Founder of WriteWell and
author of *"The Writer's Workbook, Free the Writer Within –*
Tap into the Power of Creativity", www.mywordsnow.com